# If She Only Knew

## Eva Mackenzie

Published by Craven Ink Press

PO Box 3081 Warrenton, VA 20188

ISBN: 978-1-7333939-6-6

ISBN: 978-1-7333939-7-3

Editors: Alyssa Matesic

Lillian Schneider (Murphy Rae)

Cover design: Stu Bache (Bookscovered)

 Created with Vellum

*This is dedicated to Guardian ad Litem's. Thank you for your dedication to all the children.*

*We don't see things as they are. We see them as we are.*
  *--Anonymous.*

# Chapter 1

Eden

She staggered down the pet food aisle toward the back of the supermarket; her hand dragged over the corrugated shelves for support. The wet smack of her bare feet and her ragged breath echoed in her head. The air was chilled, and it shocked her overtired brain awake as it blew over her bare belly and naked thighs. An awareness, though faint and ignored, decerned she was nearly naked. A rhythmic shriek of cart wheels receded as she lurched forward. The mouth of an older man dropped open as a can fell from his hand, creating a hollow crack against the floor as she scrambled past him.

*Can someone please help me?* But the words clung to her lungs, and her lips pressed shut. The mild smell of spoiled milk flooded her nose. Thoughts, jumbled and disjointed, bounced around her brain: *How did I get here? Why did I come? Whose blood is this?*

The pads of her feet burned over the cool tile floor as she

reached the end of the aisle, eyes darting left then right. The sight of the baby carrier caused her to stop.

"Please, please, please," she muttered to herself.

It was just like the one Eden's friend Emily had given her at her baby shower two months earlier—the same one, she was sure. And it dawned on her why she was here as she shook off her recent confusion. She stumbled forward, arms outstretched toward the cart and what she would find inside. A woman's hand stretched lazily over the cart's handle; her face turned away as Eden approached.

"What are you doing with my son?" Eden snarled at the woman dressed in yoga pants and a t-shirt. The woman's smile dropped from her face as she turned to see Eden next to the cart. Confusion etched in wavy lines on the woman's forehead.

"No—" The woman began to speak, but her words stuttered to a stop as her fingers brushed over her gaping mouth.

Standing only inches from the carrier, Eden reached for the cream-colored blanket wrapped over its arching handle. It felt like velvet against her blood-stained fingers. Soft as her son's cheek.

"What are you doing?" The woman splayed her hands over the carrier, possessing it. "Don't touch my daughter."

Eden pulled back as if the blanket had combusted into flames that now licked up her naked arms. Sweat streaked down Eden's thighs and over her knees.

"My son—" Eden said.

The woman's lips trembled under wide blue eyes. Retreating, she pulled her cart to safety, away from Eden.

*I'm not a monster. Someone, please help me—*

"Are you okay?" the woman asked as her eyes darted around the aisle, giving Eden the impression that she didn't want to ask but felt obligated.

Eden reached up to touch her face, and the metallic scent of blood flooded her nose.

"I'm not sure." She caught a glimpse of a hand reaching out from the reflection of the nearby frozen-food case. She pulled it away, its blood-covered skin retracting back to her side. Pressure flared in her chest as she caught sight of her engorged breasts, reminding her why she was here. "I need help."

A rush of voices came from nearby, but Eden's mind flashed to a memory. Images of blood pooling on the hardwood floor of her home like droplets of summer rain. Bloody footprints leading to her bed. *What have I done?*

The woman's eyes shifted as a man stepped in front of her. He had one hand braced in the air, palm out toward Eden; the other rested on a gun at his hip. Panic shot through her when she saw the weapon.

"Ma'am. I'm Drew. I'm a police officer." And for a split second, she thinks, *Yes, yes. Kill me. Pull your gun out and put me out of my misery.* Her mind sank into the relief death might bring. It had to be better than living with what she had done.

"Are you hurt?" he asked instead, as he hedged toward her.

"No—I don't think so." Eden looked down at her blood-covered skin, too shocked to be ashamed of the blood trailing down her legs or the breast milk leaking down onto her stomach. Her brain couldn't gather the requisite information to understand how this had happened. Whose blood was all over her?

Suddenly, she remembered. "I need to find my baby. He's gone. Someone took him." Eden's voice rose as she looked back at the woman with the child, but she had disappeared. What if the woman had lied about it being her daughter? Eden had let her get away.

"I can help. Can you tell me when and where you last saw him?"

She shook her head. "No—I don't know. I don't remember anything." Tears blurred her vision as more police, these in uniform, moved into her line of sight. Noise sparked to life around her—the squelch of boots on tile, shouts echoing beyond shelves as something crashed to the floor.

"There's an ambulance outside. I'd like you to come with me and get checked out." His hand was poised in the air as if she might launch herself at him. She didn't want to get checked out; she wanted to find Finn. She shook her head; the abrupt motion caused her vision to wobble.

"I can't go with you—I have to find Finn." She stepped back from him, but before she could turn away, someone anchored her arms behind her.

"Shhhhh. It's okay." A woman's voice.

Eden tried to pull away from the female officer behind her, but she had no place to go, and her effort was quickly eclipsed by fatigue.

The officer talked to Eden while she secured her arms, but Eden didn't understand what she was saying; didn't understand what was happening as they slowly marched past all the strange faces, shaking heads, and whispers. A short walk brought them to a waiting ambulance, its red lights flashing bright as the sun crested the mountain. Once she'd settled onto the stretcher, the officer removed her cuffs, laid her back gently, and then reattached the cuff to one of the stretcher handles. The metal clapped as she tried to pull her hand back.

"Can you tell me your name?"

There was a long beat of silence as Eden tried to focus on the officer's brown eyes.

"Eden."

The officer nodded. "Where did you come from this morning, Eden?"

A sharp memory hit her; it tumbled over her like hail

beating down on a long, lonely road to nowhere. A gasp escaped her lips, and she squeezed her eyes shut at the image of his dead body. The blood pooled in the foyer, his vacant stare as she tried to help him. Her carving knife jutting out of his back. Its sleek black handle smeared with blood. She loved that knife. The same blade had carved their Thanksgiving turkey.

"What is it?" the officer asked.

"I think I killed him."

# Chapter 2

Eden

38 days until review hearing

The fog-covered glass reflected her muted, pale face. From her third-story window, the landscape fell before her in orderly clusters of buildings, old and shuttered, littering the flat grounds of Middle State Psychiatric Hospital in Virginia. Forty-five buildings in total, most shut up with shadows and creeping things, sat atop twenty acres of state-owned land. Once an army base in the fifties, it was now the grounds for a hospital housing the criminally insane. The cracked and sagging buildings crouched under a bright blue, late April sky. Blooms sagged on tree limbs as spring awoke the dreary landscape. It was hard to reconcile the beauty she saw with the misery festering inside of her.

She had survived her first week here—her temporary home. After an initial stay in a different hospital to stabilize her after her psychotic break, Eden had spent the last nine months in jail before becoming a ward of the state's behavioral health system.

The Commonwealth of Virginia charged her with murder, and the judge found her not guilty by reason of insanity. A ruling her longtime attorney Lauren Ross had fought for, claiming the system left new mothers behind when addressing post-delivery mood disorders. Eden still wasn't sure what all of that meant, only that she wouldn't be spending the rest of her life in prison.

She focused on her breath, expanding and contracting her lungs. Screams crawled through the wall behind her, accompanied by a steady thump, thump, thump. She forced herself to focus on the soundless beat of her heart as she covered her ears with her palms. The plain white walls of her room surrounded a single bed and nightstand, the only furnishings in the small space she occupied alone. Confined to her room by a wide metal door that locked from the outside.

She preferred to spend her time looking out the single window next to her bed. The glass was unbreakable, they said. She didn't bother to test its strength but imagined falling from the sill in a graceful movement. She would rush past windows filled with haunted faces as the ground snatched her up.

"Snap out of it, hun." A voice echoed from the doorway. Eden turned to see Marsha lumbering into the room. "You got that look in your eye," the nurse added as she delivered two white paper cups. Eden tossed the pills back and swallowed, graciously opening her mouth for Marsha's inspection. A nod and Eden pressed her lips closed.

"What look is that?" Eden asked after a moment.

"The look of something you ought not to be thinking, that's what. You know better than that. Do you need me to talk to the good doctor about upping your meds?" The tangy scent of oranges rose off the nurse's fingers, her hands stained from its peel. A slim gold band seemed embedded on her finger under chipped nails.

"I won't do anything stupid. Don't worry." Eden thought of

her son and knew it was true, but she still found herself turning away from the nurse's knowing gaze. She assumed Marsha had seen a lot in her years working here. All forms of manipulation, lies, and paranoia.

Eden was determined to root herself in truth.

*I am a mother.*

*I am a survivor.*

*I am a killer.*

"You do look a bit better." Marsha took the empty cups and openly appraised Eden.

Eden snorted. "Better than what?" Her reflection in the window displayed pale, thin arms aglow against the rising sun, her greasy hair hanging down around her face. A lonely, vacant stare looked back at her. All the while she was trying to piece together what was happening to her. She didn't feel crazy. She didn't want to hurt herself or others. An evil force had wormed its way inside her after she'd given birth to her son, and had culminated in a murder, then slowly drained from her in the months following her psychotic break, after she was found in a local grocery store covered in blood. "I need to take care of my son. I don't care what I look like."

"Hun, you can worry about that later. I'm talking about in here." She pointed to the tuft of gray hair at her temple. "Get your mind right."

Annoyance flooded Eden for an unguarded moment. They regularly treated her like a child, though she was thirty-two years old.

"You get to meet Doc Jones today." Marsha sent her a knowing wink as she turned to leave. "Why don't you take a shower."

It was a polite suggestion. Eden hadn't left her room since she'd arrived six days ago. Each time she was asked to go to group meetings or the cafeteria, she had declined. But if she had any hope of getting out of here, she would need to put in the effort.

"What's she like?" Eden asked before Marsha closed the door.

"Who, Jones? She's nice enough, but more importantly she'll be the one who fills out your evaluation." Marsha smiled and locked the door behind her.

A prick of fear opened inside of her. She would soon meet the woman who would let her out of this place. Somehow, she would have to make sure their meeting went well.

Eden stood and shuffled toward the bathroom, not realizing she had set her mind to it until she felt the cool tile on her naked feet. The bathroom was small, its walls, shower, and tile all a blinding white. She flicked the light off to allow the natural light from a nearby window to guide her way.

She turned the shower knob, and with a gurgling hiccup, water sprang from the showerhead and rained onto the floor. Like blood—dripping down her legs. Her memory wasn't clear, but smells, tastes, and sounds triggered short memories, none of which were welcomed.

She shed her jumper onto the floor and huddled under the warm water. Her hands found her flat stomach and rubbed at the former resting place of her son. She pictured his pouting pink lips pulled into a cupid's bow under the tiniest nose she had ever seen. He was perfect in every way. With his soft whips of black hair and brown eyes, or were they gray?

It was a long time before she realized she was still rubbing her belly, missing its fullness, missing the tender nudges against her hands. She was missing her son.

\* \* \*

"How are you feeling today, Eden?" Doc Gwen Jones peered over her tortoiseshell-rimmed glasses from an oversized wing-back chair facing the sofa where Eden now sat. After an orderly dropped her off, she had gone right to the couch, determined to win Doctor Jones over, but she was struggling to move past her awkwardness and secure some footing in this, their first meeting.

The air smelled of vanilla, and the temperature was comfortable at first, but as her eyes began to take in all the certifications, awards, and honors, it began to feel too warm. The doctor's prestige shouted from every available surface. She shrank back into the sofa.

"I'm doing okay."

Doc Jones's smile looked contrived as Eden's eyes shifted to a silver frame of the doctor shaking hands with a former President, her greedy hand reaching for yet another accolade.

"As this is our first meeting, I want to give you an idea of what's going to happen and how I'm a part of your treatment here at the hospital." Doc Jones shifted back in her seat, nearly slouching now. "Do you understand why you're here?"

Eden nodded.

"Good. Do you understand what's going to happen now?"

"No."

"The trial court's acquittal leads to a temporary evaluation to be done by one of my colleagues here at Middle State and me." Doc Jones looked down at her papers and back up at her for a moment. "Taking in all the particulars of your case and how well you do with the treatment, you could receive an unconditional or conditional release or stay here for more treatment."

Eden's hands clutched together as she struggled with what she could possibly say to assure Doctor Jones's support. "Thanks so much for giving me a chance to prove myself."

Doc Jones shook her head; a look of disappointment transformed her features. Eden had done it again: said the wrong thing.

"This is treatment. It's not about proving anything," Doc Jones chided. "This evaluation phase will take forty-five days, and then we'll make our recommendation to the court."

"I'm feeling much better."

Doc Jones nodded. "Postpartum psychosis is a genuine threat that can have lingering effects. I noticed that you've had a total of—" Her voice seemed to suspend in the air. "Eleven hospital admissions." Silence swelled in the room, and Eden ignored the feeling of shame growing in her. It wasn't her fault. "It looks like over the last thirteen years."

Eden's voice was flat when she finally spoke. "That sounds right."

"Do you want to talk about any of those visits? I see the last one was—two years ago. A hospital in Florida."

Eden shook her head. She didn't have the emotional strength to discuss that. Not yet.

"I miss my son." Her voice cracked with the weight of her situation, and tears pressed against her eyes. She was trying to hide her emotions for fear of judgment, but maybe showing no emotion was worse. Then she was just a cold-hearted woman who'd killed her husband.

"I understand," Doc Jones said.

"Do you?" Her tone was sharp, but Doc Jones didn't even flinch. As if she'd been expecting the outburst, the doctor observed it with a nod and moved on. Eden searched the space for pictures of a family, children, or a lover, but there was nothing. How could someone who hadn't loved or lost as much as Eden had empathize with her situation? There was no obvious way to tell.

"I'm sorry," Eden said.

"Don't apologize." Somehow, in Doc Jones's sympathetic response, Eden found rejection rather than comfort. Eden considered whether Doc Jones was able to detect her reluctance to trust her and how that would affect her evaluation. Did she think Eden was just a paranoid lost cause? Perhaps the doctor was looking for Eden to be open with her in a good faith effort to move forward.

"I've been thinking about him a lot. Sometimes I think I've forgotten what he looks like. If it weren't for the pictures Layla sends me, I might have." The two precious weeks she'd had with her son were a hazy dream at best. She'd probably filled in most of her memory with what she thought had happened. She wanted nothing more than to hold him, press her ear to his chest and listen to life beating through him, to feel the pressure of his fingers squeezing hers. The birth of her son seemed years ago—though it had only been eleven months.

"Have you been hearing any more voices?" Doc Jones asked.

She was happy not to lie. "No."

"I think your medication is working nicely." The doctor pursed her lips. "How long before your pregnancy had you stopped taking your lithium?"

Eden's heart tripped for a moment. She knew she should have kept taking her medication and seeing her therapist after moving to Virginia.

"After Ben and I moved to Virginia from Florida, and we were actively trying to have a baby. I stopped taking the medication because I couldn't conceive."

"And you didn't find a new therapist?"

Why was she asking a question she must certainly know the answer to?

"No."

She watched as Doc Jones took down a note. Eden's pulse

began to rise—it felt like things were moving in the wrong direction, but like someone in a strong current, she was powerless to change the course of things. Several times during her treatment she'd refused the medication, not liking how it had made her feel. Now she knew her actions had prolonged her initial recovery by months.

"We're going to get you better. Women who have postpartum psychosis do recover, but it's a long and scary process." She said this with such confidence that the trapped air in Eden's lungs began to leak out. "You didn't know what you were doing that night, and possibly for some time leading up to what happened." Doctor Jones smiled. "Your son's in good hands, right? With your friend?"

Eden noticed a tightening around the doctor's mouth, a narrowing of her eyes.

"Yes, that's right." Eden stumbled. "Thank God for Layla. She saved him—she saved me."

Doc Jones nodded solemnly. "How did the two of you meet?"

"Layla and me? We met at a support group for women who couldn't conceive. I always thought I needed a child to feel whole, complete." She said the words as though she no longer believed them, but she did. After all her hospital stays and the agony she'd endured, she had thought she had gotten better, that she could bring a child into the world and stop hurting the people she loved. She was wrong.

# Chapter 3

Layla
Before

There were four familiar faces and one new woman in the group tonight. The new face, a pretty woman with raven-black hair and hazel eyes, looked around suspiciously. She introduced herself as Eden but quickly fell silent, listening to the other women in the group. Layla watched as Eden's discomfort became more evident: she shifted in her seat while twisting her bracelets in her hand. Welcome to the dark side, Layla thought grimly—the end of the line. The place where Layla's hope of becoming a mother had died.

Layla felt the usual awkwardness as the women shared with the group. It always began with small talk—"How was your week?" "How's work?"—and would slowly shift to the joyless discussion of infertility. Layla knew each of the women by name, but they shared little in the way of interests, and she considered none of them her friends. But she was still coming to the meetings, more out of habit than any genuine fulfillment.

The truth was, she wanted to get out of the house; it was too depressing to sit around there every night of the week.

Minka, the group's leader, cleared her throat. "Layla, tell us about your week."

"I've been busy, and that's good for me. I don't like to be idle." She cringed at her tone. She sounded like her mother, Janet Hughs, God rest her soul, who'd appeared perpetually exhausted from breakfast until sundown. Often Layla would picture her picking up her burdens in the morning like Santa's sack, strapping them over her thin shoulders until hiking them to the floor at night, only to pick them back up the following day. Oh, no. She was turning into Janet.

"Any news on the adoption?"

Who was Minka kidding—Layla wasn't going to adopt. It was just something she had said one day because something needed to be said. The truth was that single women in their forties rarely got to adopt babies. And Layla had come to terms with that right from the start. At age forty-five, she was over the prospect of becoming a mother and almost welcomed the relief of that certainty. She killed the hope she had been harboring for years, freeing herself. She was too old to chase a child around. There was no more wishing or wanting, just a comfortable surrender to the universe and its ideas.

She shook her head and, for some unknown reason, couldn't make eye contact with any of the other women. She felt like she was a fraud, pretending she still wanted to be a mother around these desperate dreamers.

"Well." Minka curled her fingers around her knees and sat forward. "There's hope."

Layla cringed inwardly. Minka's delivery sounded more akin to "I hope it doesn't rain today" than "I hope your dreams come true, and you don't die alone."

Her eyes drifted to the chessboard on a nearby table, its

pieces standing ready for the next players. How many times had she looked over this room, and all its items? Too many. Perhaps it was time to move on from here.

Layla wondered what Eden's story was. She was young and fit. Beautiful in a way that caused people to stare. But she didn't seem to notice, with her quiet reserve—not the awkward quiet that Layla seemed to experience around others.

"Eden, welcome," Minka said for the second time since the meeting began, mercifully moving on from Layla. "Why don't you tell us a little something about yourself?" Her voice was a little too cheery, and Layla found herself biting the inside of her cheek, muffling a groan. Minka acted as if she was happy their sad little group was growing.

"Hi." Eden lifted a hand, creating a delicate chime of bracelets. "I just moved here from Miami with my husband Ben about three months ago." She seemed to hesitate at the mention of her husband.

"We've been trying to conceive for two years now." Her voice rang like a beautiful bell, hollowed out by some unknown emotion. "It took me several years to convince him to have a child to begin with, and I thought it was going to be easy." She laughed then; her mouth closed tight, muffling the sound.

"I had an unplanned pregnancy my freshman year at college that ended in a miscarriage." Eden paused. "I don't talk to my husband about any of this stuff. He's swamped, and I think he's just worn out on the disappointment. I decided I needed some support." A murmur of agreement grew from the women. Layla wondered if her statement was a confession or her husband's excuse. It sounded so much like Layla and Todd. Until he left her, that was. He had had enough disappointment too. He might have even used that very same word—she couldn't remember. She impulsively picked at her sweater.

"We're on a baby break right now. Ya know. Get back to the

simple life. I saw the group advertised on a board at my gym," Eden said. Layla doubted anything about this woman was simple.

"Well, we're so glad you're here," Minka said as others in the group nodded. Layla's eyes flickered toward the ceiling in an attempt to stop the eyeroll she felt was imminent. "Looks like our hour is up."

Smiles grew from all the women as if they got something out of their time together. As if it filled the empty cribs in their homes or their dormant maternal instinct. Her motherly love was morphing into an onslaught of aggressive behavior, even as she claimed not to be bitter about her situation. Nothing too noticeable, more like cutting off an aggressive driver or catching up to someone who littered and saying, "Hey, I think you dropped this," in the sweetest voice she could manage. At least she could live inside their shocked and sometimes angry expressions for a while—so there was that.

The community center rested on the edge of Cedar Lake, a small town in south central Virginia. When Layla walked out into the hot summer night air, she felt gooseflesh rise over her arms as the lake breeze brushed against her. The steady drum of a basketball echoed as a group of teens jumped and dribbled, shouting at each other under the lit basketball court.

"What'd you think?" Layla asked while standing under the glow of a lamppost as Eden approached. Her new model Toyota sat quietly next to Eden's Lexus SUV, a fitting comparison of the two women.

"I'm sorry?" Eden asked with a hint of a smile on her face.

"What did you think of the group?" Layla wanted to know what Eden's real story was. It couldn't be what it appeared, a bored housewife who couldn't conceive—or could it? Layla found that her own story could be deceiving.

"Can I be honest?" Eden moved closer in the semi-dark,

and her eyes caught the light. "It didn't do much for me." There was a beat of silence as they surveyed each other.

"I'm in a bad way," Eden managed to say, and under the light she appeared to blush at her confession.

"I don't get anything out of it either," Layla said, trying to rush away Eden's embarrassment.

"Why come then?" Eden asked, wrinkling her nose.

Layla shook her head, and the breeze caught her hair. "I don't know." She unlocked her car door. "Beats eating alone every Tuesday night." She wasn't sure if she had said it because it was true or to make Eden feel better. "You wanna grab a drink?" Layla asked. She never had any interest in spending more time with any of the other women in their group, so she was surprised that she'd offered.

"Yes," Eden blurted.

* * *

McMahan's was loud. The buzz of the music, coupled with the raucous Tuesday night crowd, filled the place; it crackled with energy. Layla found a small table in the back, and they sat.

"Do you come here often?" Eden asked, scanning the room. Heavy oak trim lined the bar, and a dartboard and pool table crouched in the back near them.

Layla shook her head. "I don't get out much."

Eden's fingers rested on the rim of her glass and traced along the top. A silk camisole flattered the feminine curves of her body. Layla tried not to notice or, at least, not to be too obvious about noticing.

"What do you do for work?" Layla asked.

"I used to teach—little ones in an elementary school when we lived in Florida." Her eyes shifted away from Layla's. "I had to quit. I couldn't take being around the children after—you know. So much time—"

Layla found herself nodding. "I think that's why I fell into computer work. I don't have to be around people much."

The music faded as a song ended, and the relative quiet was quickly filled with excited voices and shouts from the bar as the TV replayed some sporting event.

"Have you had any tests done yet?" Layla cut right to it, using her history as her guide. She sensed Eden needed to vent. Layla didn't think anyone's story was as painful as her own, and she was objective enough to assume everyone felt the same way.

"Yes, we both went. They said we were both able to conceive, and everything looked fine. Ben's resistant to fertility treatment at this point. I think it's an ego thing." Eden's chin lowered into her chest. Her voice didn't ring with bitterness or anger, which surprised Layla. During her marriage to Todd, any resistance was met with outrage from her—sometimes lasting a week. He didn't want fertility treatment either, but it didn't much matter; Layla's body didn't produce viable eggs. When she decided that it didn't bother her to carry some other woman's child, her body had rejected all the eggs before they could implant. It wasn't meant to be. Now, after divorcing Layla three years ago, Todd lived in Tennessee with his new wife and their daughter. Layla let the cold, bitter beer rush down her throat. One day, when the pain and disappointment weren't so fresh, she would forgive him. It was a wonder how resentment could move into one's life and take the place of pain. She never even noticed it was happening until she felt the first angry burst in her life. Felt the jealousy of what others had that she would never experience.

"My ex has a family now," Layla said. "I don't know why it bothers me—shouldn't one of us be happy?" But she didn't mean it, and sometimes she would imagine Stacy, his new wife, having an affair with someone she worked with, or a brutal car accident that would leave him disfigured, and Stacy leaving him as he had left Layla. She tried not to indulge in the fantasies too often.

Eden's golden eyes blinked back at her. "What about this adoption thing?"

"Maybe." Layla's voice sounded disconnected. "All the adoption agencies are probably looking for two-parent homes and someone younger than me. Someone more like you." Layla waved a hand toward Eden. When Eden didn't jump in to refute Layla's assumption, she found it refreshing. Not like everyone else who always wanted to assure Layla that her time was coming. A look of bald honesty was what she needed now.

"No, Ben said no adoption."

A small group of men began playing darts near their table, and Layla caught their gestures toward the two of them, eyeing Eden. She couldn't help but wonder what it would be like to have everyone fawn over you. Layla was a wallflower, or at least that's what she'd overheard two coworkers say about her when she was in a stall in the restroom as they gossiped by the full-length mirrors. Her best feature had always been her long blond hair, but at forty-five, she had stopped caring about that too. Stands of gray now weaved in made it more silver than blond. She was also holding onto those last twelve pounds she had gained during the divorce as she struggled through life without makeup. But not Eden; she wore just enough to exploit her assets and no more.

"So, what's the end game?" Layla asked.

Eden pulled her eyes away from surveying the crowd. "Do you think it's just because I'm so stressed out? Because I want it so bad?" She pulled toward Layla, but before she could answer Eden swerved to the next topic. "Ben and I used to be so different before all of this. Late-night chess games, last-minute trips overseas for work. Now it's all snarky comments and sex twice a month." There was a distinctly desperate tone in her voice as she spoke, and Layla was left speechless for a moment.

"Well, any guy in this bar would take you home." And as the words dropped, Layla wondered why she had said that. Was that supposed to make Eden feel better?

"I don't even like to get all dressed up—it's for Ben. He likes me to look a certain way, and I want to make him happy. Sometimes, I say to hell with him, but deep down, I love him."

Layla wondered what was at the root of all Eden's marital problems. Was it like her own failed marriage? Maybe Ben couldn't understand what infertility was doing to his wife; how hard it was. It wasn't an easy struggle, and if you were in it with someone who didn't want it as badly as you did, there were bound to be problems.

"What does Ben do for work?"

"He owns a consulting firm, a civil attorney."

"Bet those are some long nights." Layla felt pity for her; it was the last emotion she'd expected to have for this woman. It would appear Eden might have it all from the outside, but once Layla took a look at the inside, she found a desperate person just trying to hold it all together.

Eden nodded. "The thing is, I don't care. I want to find out what I want now. Does that make sense?" Eden's head tipped gently to the side. "I didn't want to leave Florida to come here, but I gave in. Now I have no friends, no child, and my mother is a thousand miles away."

"Yeah, it does," Layla said, and she meant it. "Sometimes you just have to recognize you're not happy, and then once you're there, you make the hard choices."

Eden's eyes seemed to brighten. "Yeah—maybe I just need to stop asking myself what everyone else wants and see where that leaves me. But I know I want children. I'm sure of that," she added.

Layla found herself loosening as she finished off her first beer. "Want another?" she asked Eden, who nodded.

After waiting a moment to flag down their waitress, she abandoned the pursuit and walked to the bar, gently shouldering her way through the crowd of people, and asked them to bring two beers to their table. When she returned, she noticed a man standing next to Eden, his body swaying slightly, his speech slurred. "Don't I know you?" he said. The man didn't even notice as Layla retook her seat.

"No." Eden's features suddenly darkened. The rapid change confused Layla as the man raised his hands in surrender under Eden's frosty glare.

"I can take a hint." He continued to the bathroom without another word.

Eden turned back to her, and Layla wondered if the crack in her sweet facade had been a figment of her imagination. As quickly as the look had come, it melted away.

"Cheers," Eden said, and they tapped the rims of their glasses together.

# Chapter 4

Eden

37 days until review hearing

After her first meeting with Doc Jones yesterday, Eden was encouraged to try group therapy. The doctor had been adamant about how vital the treatment would be and signaled that her release might be held up by her resistance to go. Now, as Eden walked down the scuffed, wide hallway, she focused on the sound of her steps rather than the peals of agony around her. Frenzied cries called out beyond darkened windows. In the short silences between outbursts, she resisted the desire to run down the hallway, away from its swallowing dread. The air turned sour in her mouth as if she could taste the agony. She wanted to remember the fresh smell of the lake air after a spring rain, but she couldn't summon the memory. The orderly, Gilmore, a thin short man in his thirties, kept glancing over at her, beads of sweat clinging to his shaggy brown hair. He'd showed up at her door, informing her he was taking her to group therapy. She had seen him before —hadn't she?

"How you feeling?" His voice was high-pitched, and his tongue jutted out over his dry lips in a quick swipe as he glanced at her. Her head swiveled in hopes of spotting other people in the hall, but they were alone.

"I'm okay." Her perfunctory response to anyone who asked, because she didn't know the answer. If she allowed herself to reflect honestly on that question, she feared a downward spiral of sadness and regret—but she was determined to make it through the next thirty-seven days, according to her count.

A boom erupted behind one of the closed doors, and Eden jumped to the other side of the hall. Gilmore let out a short, abrupt laugh and walked to the closed door, raised a hand, tapped on the dirty glass square, and said something in a low voice. The response from whoever was on the other side was to kick the door so hard that the big painted hinges shifted. Gilmore laughed again and moved along. "C'mon—he ain't that friendly."

She rushed to catch up to his quick stride. Her nerves vibrated as they passed each new door. Some of the square windows were empty; some showed men and women standing behind them, staring out as they passed. Some shouted or kicked the door; some, she imagined, were capable of doing horrible things to her if they escaped from those tiny rooms.

The hallway opened into a large area with a wall of windows facing the back property line and its tall fence crowned with swirls of barbed wire. "This is the day room." Gilmore waved a hand toward a space filled with card tables, worn couches, and a television.

They continued past several more doors until he stopped. "This is group therapy. You can head on in." He hiked his chin toward the door. Was it her imagination, or had she felt his light touch on her shoulder? Was he allowed to touch her? She shifted away from him, but when she looked back, he was already walking down the hall.

She didn't want to be left alone with a bunch of—she didn't allow her insensitive thought to germinate. They were people in need of help, just like her, but that didn't make her any less reluctant to make friends. After all, she'd been through this before during her numerous hospitalizations, and was beginning to understand the need for allies.

Inside the room, a dozen chairs were arranged in a circle, a few of them occupied. Eden was determined to find a secluded spot—away from the others. A woman with coppery red hair and pale, freckled skin smiled over at her.

"You must be the new girl." The woman tipped her head, evaluating Eden. "Come, sit next to me." Her hand slapped the empty seat to her right. A rail-thin man with glasses perched on the end of a swollen, bruised nose sat in the chair to her left. His hand absently rubbed his ear, his eyes cast to the ground. Eden considered making an excuse and thanking the woman for the offer, but there was nowhere to be alone in the small room.

"I'm Nina, but everyone calls me Jinx."

"Hi." She fumbled as she took the offered seat. "I'm Eden."

"Eden. That's a pretty name. This over here is Chaz." She poked a thumb toward the quiet man, and Eden smiled at him, though he continually avoided her eyes.

"Wait till you get a load of Doc McDreamy," Jinx said as she elbowed Eden gently in the ribs. "You're in for a real treat, my friend."

Jinx shifted her brown eyes back toward the door, but it wasn't a doctor who came in. A big man in a jumpsuit a size too small lumbered to the window, ignoring the chairs. The cuffs of his pants hovered inches over his white sneakers.

"That's Arnie," Jinx said. "You don't wanna talk to him too much." She circled a finger around her ear. Eden felt her stomach drop as she looked at Arnie's hunched shoulders and bearded face.

"He really went bananas on Chaz here," Jinx added, frowning.

"What do you mean?" Eden asked, looking over at Chaz.

"Isn't it obvious?" Jinx asked, waving her hand next to Chaz's face. "He punched him right in the nose. He isn't always this ugly."

"Shut up, Jinx." Chaz finally spoke. "If you hadn't—"

Jinx sent a stern look at Chaz, who abruptly stopped talking. His eyes shifted away from Arnie's direction, and he made himself just a bit smaller in the plastic chair.

"All right, everyone. Let's get to our seats." A man strode through the door as three other people followed. Eden watched as Jinx sat up straighter and smiled wide.

"I'm Doctor Lucas," he said, looking at Eden. His sandy blond hair was a bit too long, and his white coat fell open, revealing a Nirvana t-shirt and blue jeans. Not at all like Doc Jones's stiff, unwelcoming manner. Doc Lucas's smile touched his eyes, and his movements were easy and unscripted. Giving warm encouragement to all those in the circle, he took his seat.

"Arnie, get over here, man," Doc Lucas said in a firm but friendly voice. Arnie turned from the window and shuffled to a seat, his eye cutting across the room as he pulled a chair back out of the circle before sitting.

"Okay, everyone. We have a new resident. Everyone say hello to Eden." He clapped, and a murmur of hellos came from around the circle. Glassy, empty eyes hovering over cracked smiles aimed at her. Did they see her how she saw them? A shiver rippled through her. *I can't belong here—*

"We left off with you, Chaz," Doc Lucas said, finding him in the group. "You wanna finish up?"

Chaz's lips worked as if a wave was building underneath them, but no sound broke free for a long moment. Finally, his voice sputtered to life. "Do you see what he did?" His rigid finger pointed to his damaged nose. "He attacked me."

Doc Lucas frowned.

"I'm sorry that happened to you, Chaz," Jinx said as she tapped Chaz's leg.

"No touching. I don't like anyone touching me." He shifted away from her, sending her a sharp look. "I don't wanna go again today. Skip me. I didn't even wanna come, but the orderly said I had to." The last of his words tumbled out like a tedious whine. Eden looked away from his face, unable to witness his discomfort.

"That's okay, Chaz," Doc Lucas said. "If you wanna pass, I think it's a good time for us to learn something about our newest member." Eden's thoughts caught on the term "member"—like she was part of a club. Her heart sped up as all eyes fell on her. Arnie's grim expression deepened, and Jinx squeezed Eden's arm gently.

"Okay," she began, her fingers twisted in her lap. "My name is Eden." What was she supposed to say about herself? Why she was here? She didn't want to talk about that. She felt her cheeks grow warm.

"Tell us something about yourself. Something simple," Doc Lucas encouraged.

"Um. I have a son. I had him just before I came here." The memory tugged at her. "I think about him all the time. He was a miracle baby. I always wanted a child, and I just knew my life would be complete once he was here." As she said the words, an odd detachment spread inside of her. She felt as though she was talking about someone else. She should be feeling a wholly different emotion, living in a better situation than the one in which she found herself. She was a mother now—something she had dreamed of for years. It should be the best time of her life. But she was locked away from Finn, surrounded by these strangers. "I just knew he would make me so happy."

The room was too silent, and she didn't want to talk anymore. Talking wasn't helping her at all; it made her feel uncomfortable. But she pressed on, wanting to beat back the silence. "Anyway. I had Finn, and he was—is—so beautiful. But he's with his godmother now." Eden said this like "Aunt Layla" was babysitting for a weekend. Eden had taken to calling her that even though they weren't related.

"How'd you kill him?" Arnie asked abruptly. His posture suddenly rigid. "Did you cut him up?" He drew a finger under his thick neck, and she thought his fingers were too small for such a big man. His tongue clicked loudly, and his wormy lips broke into a proud smile.

"Arnie, you know better," Doc Lucas scolded. Arnie shook his head in apparent frustration but turned his gaze back out the window.

"I love your story," Jinx said in a jittery voice as her foot bounced lightly off the floor, creating a soft tap, tap, tap. Eden wanted to tell her to stop moving—the thought screamed in her head.

"Thank you, Nina," Doc Lucas said.

Jinx beamed at his praise and began telling a story while Eden's thoughts returned to Finn. Ten perfect fingers and ten perfect toes. She missed him so much, and she would do whatever it took to get back to him.

\* \* \*

"Leave it alone or it won't heal," Jinx snapped from her seat, a mountain of untouched lasagna on her plate. She rolled her eyes dramatically. "You're a wimp."

Chaz sat to her left while Eden sat across from them both. The cafeteria smelled of marinara sauce and garlic, and she could hear the soft scuff of shoes as two patients paced the floor near their table.

"They just twist it back into place." Chaz motioned with his hand, a jerk over his nose.

"You know I was a nurse, right? Before all this." Jinx scowled at him. "Before all that stupid stuff happened."

Eden couldn't help but wonder what that stupid stuff was, but she didn't want to ask. When she'd arrived, Jinx had waved her over to sit with them. Jinx took a forkful of food as she looked over at Eden. Their group therapy session felt like days ago rather than a few hours.

"What's your story? Is it what they say, you killed your husband?" Jinx asked after she swallowed.

Eden knew the question would come. She'd rehearsed what she would say when asked, but now that the question was posed, her answer caught in her throat, and she could only nod.

"Why'd you do it?" Jinx leaned toward her, eyebrow cocked.

"Leave her alone. She doesn't want to talk about it," Chaz said.

"How do you know?"

"Just look at her." It was the one thing Chaz hadn't done since she had taken her seat with them: look at her. His eyes constantly darted around the room. But it was clear she had missed how perceptive he was.

"She doesn't have to talk about it. But I wanna hear it from her," Jinx said.

"He's right," Eden said.

"Keep saying things like that, and he's gonna get a giant ego to go with his busted nose," Jinx teased.

Eden looked around the room, her eyes settling on nothing. People moved around her, and sudden noises and quick movements caused her to jolt. It was overloading her senses. With longing, she considered how quiet and peaceful her room must be right now. It had taken no time at all for her to get used to the silence of her jail cell and then her room here. Nothing like the chaos that surrounded her now.

"How about old Arnie over there? I think he likes you," Jinx said to Eden. Chaz's eyes skipped over to watch Arnie's lumbering gait cross the cafeteria, his tray small in his grip.

Eden shook her head, uncertain what Jinx could mean. Was it meant to be a joke?

"I'm serious. It's a little bit like how Doc Lucas looks at me during our sessions. I know it's completely inappropriate, but he hasn't ever tried to touch me or anything."

Eden felt her brow furrow as she looked back at Jinx. Eden knew she wasn't functioning at her standard capacity with all the drugs and the lingering effects of the psychosis, but she had difficulty understanding what Jinx meant by her comments. Was she implying that Doc Lucas was inappropriate with his patients?

"How do they choose who will be our doctor? Do they rotate them? Or do they keep us with the same one?" Eden asked. Dread followed the thought of having to work with Doc Jones for another month.

Jinx cocked her head to the side. "They generally keep you with the same one. I've been with Doc Lucas for the last six months. He likes me. How about you, do you like me?" Jinx asked Chaz.

Chaz shrugged, visibly uncomfortable with the question.

"Whatever." Jinx took another bite of her food. "Idiot."

The sun was bright outside, and Eden tried to remember summer, fall, and winter passing since she'd had her freedom. She was going to miss Finn's first birthday three weeks from now. The thought caused an ache in her chest. She tried to focus on Jinx and not Finn.

Jinx explained how Middle State kept its residents on a status scale. Patients were allowed certain privileges based on their behavior. She bragged that she could walk to her therapy and group sessions with only one orderly now, and after only three years of being here.

"Why did you have two orderlies?" Eden asked and watched Chaz's eye muscle begin to twitch.

"I didn't play well with others," Jinx joked with a wink. Eden pictured the redhead wrestling with the white-coated doctors, a group of orderlies swarming her like ants sieging on a hill. How dangerous was Jinx?

"When do we not have to have an orderly with us?" Eden asked.

"The orderlies walk us anywhere we have to go. Appointments and different group settings," Chaz explained. "It will be until you leave this place." Yesterday Gilmore had, all too excitedly, told Eden that she was assigned to him.

"Do you think they would give me a new doctor if I asked to switch?" Eden blurted. Both Chaz and Jinx looked at her. Was it because of the desperate edge in her voice? Even after only one session, Eden couldn't seem to connect with Doc Jones, and if she was honest, she felt like Doc Jones wanted to slow her treatment down, while Eden needed her to speed things up.

Chaz shrugged over his bowl of soup. "Why? You don't like either of your doctors?"

"What do you mean, 'either of my doctors?'"

"Doctor Jones is an evaluator and eventually the one who

puts her stamp of approval on patients for release. Then there's clinical psychologists—the ones that are supposed to help you 'get better.'" Jinx put air quotes around the words "get better" as if the concept were a myth. "You might have Doc Jones for that too."

Eden felt a heaviness. Doc Jones didn't like her; she knew it. "I don't think I'm a good fit with Doc Jones."

"I like her," Jinx said. "What's wrong with her?"

Eden took a moment to think. There was nothing wrong with her, but she didn't want to mention that she felt the doctor was out to get her. It was impossible to explain because she didn't know what she was trying to say.

A loud clatter came from across the room as Arnie dropped his half-filled tray to the shiny floor. Red sauce splattered around his feet as he growled at the mess and stomped out of the room—two orderlies struggling to keep up.

"That's your boy," Jinx said with a giggle. Eden wasn't sure who Jinx was teasing this time, her or Chaz, who was gently palpating his nose again.

Jinx turned to Eden. "I miss my daughter too."

"I didn't know you had a child." Eden leaned toward her. "How old is she?"

Jinx's eyes grew wet, the flecks of gold shimmering in them. "I had her when I first came here three years ago."

"What's her name?"

Jinx shook her head and wiped a tear from her cheek. "I don't want to talk about it." Her tone was almost angry. Silence swelled around them while they contemplated their losses together.

# Chapter 5

Eden

36 days until review hearing

She felt a bubble of excitement balloon in her chest. Today was the day Layla and Finn would visit her. She pictured Layla strapping him into his car seat, ready to set off; the thought preoccupied her.

When Marsha finally brought her medication, Eden couldn't help but ask, "Will I get to hold him—will they let me?" The words sprung out like a leak in a boat, her excitement too great to contain.

"Now, don't get your hopes up. I would hate to see you disappointed," Marsha insisted as she handed two paper cups to her.

"What does that mean?" she asked, too sharp, too crazed-sounding, and Eden recoiled. She wasn't that person anymore; she'd changed.

"I'm sorry. I'm just nervous, is all. I'm sure they'll let me know what the rules are."

Marsha didn't say another word as she left the room.

The last time she remembered seeing Finn was just after his birth, and even then, the memories were disjointed. Part of the psychosis, she was assured, and warned that she might never remember what happened during those first few weeks of Finn's life. Layla sent her pictures and wrote several letters while Eden was in jail, awaiting her sanity trial's conclusion; if not for that, she wouldn't know what he looked like at all.

Though she recognized her excitement, she couldn't help feeling sadness and trepidation at having missed the first year of his life. What if he cried when she held him for the first time in months? It might be too much to handle.

"Are you ready?" Gilmore stood in the doorway. The question sent shoots of nervous energy through her body.

Her voice was a wilting sound. "Yes."

Eden left space between them as he held the front door of the ward open for her. "Where are we going?"

"Visitors center's just inside the front gates."

The expansive sky was crowded with dark clumps of clouds hiding the mid-morning sun. They followed the cracked, sun-bleached pathway as it slithered past boarded-up buildings. She looked away from the darkened windows, her brain expecting pale faces to pop into view at any moment. Crows' wings flapped, and their caws shattered the quiet morning's soft breeze. She pulled her jumper up around her neck as she shivered. They passed by one last building, and a newer facility came into view; just beyond it, the tall wrought iron gate to the outside world. The sight of the gate caused her breath to catch in her throat. A desire so heavy and out of reach sank through her; she couldn't imagine a scenario where they let her pass through to the outside world again. If and when that happened, she would feel like she was getting away with murder.

She knew little about Middle State or its history, but the

dread she felt was growing each day she stayed here. This wasn't a good place. Jinx and Chaz had discussed who Eden should watch out for, which caused her to question everyone around her. She wanted to ask Gilmore about this place, but she sensed her curiosity might be taken the wrong way—giving him the idea she wanted to get to know him better.

"We're here," he said, stepping back from the door he held open. Eden walked into a wide open room not unlike the day room in her ward. About a dozen tables scattered over the old tile floor, fresh white paint, and pictures adorning the walls gave her the impression she was anywhere but an institution for the insane. Maybe that was the idea—to provide visitors with the appearance of a nice place. Several patients occupied the room with their visitors. The excited squeal of children reached her before her eyes fell on a pair of toddlers nearby. She walked past a bank of windows facing the pond, a tan rim of dirt riding its edges where the water dipped low due to lack of rain. The sun shimmered off its surface, reminding her of Cedar Lake and her other life.

"Hi." The voice behind her pried open loving memories, something long buried. Eden took in a breath and turned to see Layla standing before her. Her blond hair was longer than Eden remembered it being and bright with strands of gray. She had lost weight, and her cheeks glowed. Her flat brown eyes filled with tears as she looked over at Eden.

Eden's eyes traveled the room before her panic-filled voice asked, "Where is he?"

A look of confusion passed over Layla's lined face. "I told them I was coming alone. Your doctor suggested it was best not to bring Finn." Layla spoke as if she were telling Eden a secret.

Doctor Jones said to keep her son away from her? Anger slashed through her, and she had to bite her lip to smother a growl. "When did you talk to her?" Eden couldn't help but feel betrayed. She imagined Doc Jones pulling Layla into her tidy, pretentious office, or calling her on the phone asking about Eden—digging up dirt. This must be a breach in her patient confidentiality.

"I don't remember when she told me." Layla frowned, anchoring a hand to Eden's arm. "I'm sorry. Does it bother you that she reached out to me? I would never say anything bad."

The shrill cry of the children cut through her, and she squeezed her eyes shut and took a deep breath. She focused on her breathing and took a moment to regroup. When she finally opened her eyes again, Layla was looking at her with pity and stepped forward to hug her. Eden was the first to pull away.

"Sit, please. I hope you brought pictures," Eden said as she tried to recover from the letdown. She couldn't spiral in front of Layla; she would do that later, when she was alone, with no witnesses. Her consciousness was like an overfull closet. If she didn't slam the door shut, everything would begin to pour out, and then there would be no stopping her inevitable over-reaction.

"Yes, lots. All on my phone. You can look through as much as you like."

On her phone—more disappointment.

"So, what's the food like in this joint?" Layla smirked, and just like that, they were back in her house at Cedar Lake talking about life problems and joking about the horny old neighbor.

"As good as you might expect at a state-run hospital for the criminally insane."

Layla laughed softly. "I missed you. You look better."

Better than what, Eden wondered?

"I feel better." That was true today, but tomorrow might be a different story. Doc Jones had warned her she could spiral out of control with little to no warning. "I'm a totally different person."

"Have they told you what's going to happen now?" Layla asked as she set her purse on the seat and retrieved her phone. She passed it across the table, and Eden snatched it up greedily. "He needs his mama back," Layla added.

Her eyes moved over the images, the most beautiful sight she had ever seen. Finn's lips pulled into a wistful smile under his closed eyes and button nose. He looked like his father in the carefully taken shots. Black wisps of hair poking out from under a light gray blanket.

"Did you get everything from the house that you needed?" Eden asked as if the need was imminent and not eleven months overdue. She didn't recognize the blanket Finn was wrapped in and wondered if Layla had made the purchase.

"I have the crib and his nursery furniture, but babies don't need much."

Why buy the blanket then? Eden chased the sour thought away. Layla was helping her.

There were twenty pictures in total, and Eden silently looked through them a second time. Her son. It had taken so much to create this perfect human, but now he was just as far away as when they'd been struggling to conceive. Unreachable.

"I don't know how to process what's going on—what's happening to me." They lapsed into silence. The clock ticked loudly nearby, and a hushed murmur rose. "But they say I'm doing better—that I could get out soon." That wasn't entirely true. Doctor Jones had mentioned forty-five days, when her evaluation was due. At times, Eden felt like her old self again, so they would have to let her go. The frenzy she had emerged from lingered now only as a shadow in the recess of her mind which she had programmed herself to ignore.

"That's great!" Layla said. "Did I see Doc Jones here?" She

twisted in her seat to scan the room as if Eden might point her out.

"Has she told you things about me?" Eden asked with a grimace, unsure how superficial their relationship was. "I don't think she likes me."

"Is that what she told you?" Layla's features looked surprised.

Had Eden said something wrong? She backpedaled. "No. She didn't mention anything to me." There was an awkward pause as Layla slid her phone back into her bag.

"Do you miss the lake?" Layla asked, casting a glance at the stagnant pond.

The thought of Cedar Lake caused a bitter feeling to grow in her. She wished she'd never agreed to move there with Ben. When she got out of this place, she was going back to Miami. She missed the sun and heat. She missed her family and old friends. She'd experienced nothing but problems since moving here; everything but meeting Layla was a regret.

Eden's voice was nearly a whisper: "I miss being free."

"Tell me about life on the outside," Eden said. "Do you have a caretaker for Finn? Has my attorney been sending you the money?" In her mental haze and with the help of her long-time lawyer, she'd been able to make Layla Finn's temporary custodian. Since then, they'd had two status updates on Finn's situation, and the lawyers all seemed to support Layla's continued guardianship.

"Yes. We have more than enough. I have a girl; she's great. Her name is Scarlett, and I've known her for years."

"Good. Good. Oh, I can't wait to get out of here. My medication is working great. I'm having group therapy. I'm making great strides," she said. She heard the soft echo of a need for approval in her words.

"You'll be out in no time then, it seems."

"I never said thank you." Eden stared at her. "You saved Finn's life, and that means you saved mine."

"Stop it! You know I love you, and I love him too. I'll take care of him until you get out of here, and then we can all be together—just like we planned."

Eden wasn't prepared to tell Layla of her plans to leave Virginia once she was released. They'd discussed moving in together before Finn was born. Eden couldn't remember when the idea had first emerged, but clearly Layla still felt that was the plan.

"Can you tell me what I did after I had Finn? How was I acting?" Her throat was closing, and she swallowed to chase the feeling away. She didn't want to ask but couldn't help herself. She needed to know. After all the blurry days and nights, she had to hear the truth. All the doctors she'd spoken to since the event were vague with her, as if it was a secret they were keeping from her.

Layla's lips pursed into a thin line, her eyes dancing away from Eden's.

"They tell me I had a psychotic break," she said quietly as a group of visitors settled near them. "That I won't ever remember what I did." A blessing, she was now sure.

"After you gave birth, you were different. I was so worried about you."

"How?" She bit back on her impatience.

"You were spending all your time in your room. You were saying things about the neighbor—odd things."

Eden recalled what Doc Jones had said about delusions and a break from reality, and she nodded somberly. She felt her brow wrinkle. So, it was true.

"I was worried because you would just let—" Layla sat back, her mouth caved into a frown, and Eden felt goosebumps rise over her skin.

A loud laugh erupted from across the room, and her head jerked involuntarily.

Layla's voice drew her back. "You were just forgetful, that's all."

But Eden knew she wasn't telling the truth. She wasn't telling her the ugly parts, and Eden needed to face the harsh reality.

"What did I do?"

"You missed some of his feedings. You would—stay in your room most of the time with the blinds drawn. You mentioned hearing voices."

"Oh, no." Her hand sprang to her lips. She shook her head, and the familiar feeling of a downward spiral began. She remembered the voices, and only very recently had they retreated entirely.

"How could I do that to him? He could have—" She choked on the words. "I don't understand—I wanted to be a mother, and Finn's...a miracle."

Her heart ached as she pictured Finn in his room, crying out for her. What kind of mother did that? Ignored their baby?

"Stop it right now. I see what you're doing. Don't do that to yourself. You were sick. But now you're getting the help you need so you can be the best mother," Layla encouraged. "You're going to get through this. I promise." She reached out and touched Eden's fingers. "And when you're out, we can stay together—until you're better."

"I'm so lucky to have you. You saved us. Both of us."

"I need to tell you—" Layla frowned. "That Olivia stopped by."

Olivia Wyatt, Ben's older sister, and pure evil, was in Virginia? Spit dried up in her mouth as she thought of her sister-in-law.

"I think she might be trying to get information on your situation." Layla's eyes traveled around the room. "She was asking about Finn."

Eden's heart began pumping harder.

Olivia was here in Virginia—not in her two-bedroom apartment in Hollywood. This new information simmered in her mind. A month after Eden's arrest, Olivia had come sniffing around to find out who was getting Ben's money—or at least that was what Lauren, her attorney, had told her.

"I think she has a new tactic." Layla wore her disapproval openly. "She told me she's thinking of filing for custody of Finn."

"What!" The noise of the room fell away, and she was swallowed by a roar in her ears. Her hands were shaking as her heart thrashed against her ribcage. Layla's warm hand pressed against her arm. The sounds around her pierced through the roar.

One of the residents nearby began yelling. The squeal of the children transformed into horrible shrieks as images around her slowed to a crawl. She closed her eyes and took several deep breaths.

"She can't be serious. She has no right to Finn." Her breathing accelerated, and her lungs felt like they were shrinking. She needed a minute. Had meant to say those words out loud, but from the worried expression on Layla's face, she assumed the words hadn't come out.

"Help," Layla said loudly enough for the rest of the residents to look over at them—if Eden's outburst hadn't been enough to garner their attention. Layla reached for Eden, but she kept pulling lose from her grasp.

"I'm okay—" she sputtered, but she wasn't. The walls were moving in. Panic pressed on all sides, nowhere to escape, pulling her under with no hope of recovery. She had been on the edge of this wave too often not to recognize its approach.

"She wants to take my son..." she whispered as Gilmore moved to stand over her.

"What's wrong with her?" Layla asked as Eden hinged forward over her knees.

"Panic attack," Gilmore said in a matter-of-fact tone. "I think it's time you go, Miss," he said to Layla. The tunnel grew darker around the room, like clouds covering all the light.

# Chapter 6

Layla
Before

"Can you believe it?" Eden's voice was thick with drink, and a giggle followed. "I watched him stand on his porch for twenty minutes, nuts in his hands as she threw all his clothes out the second-story window." Eden's fingers fluttered through the air as they both laughed. The sun sank beyond the mountains as the women shared drinks on Eden's patio in the warm breeze. The crickets chirped from the shadowy recess of her yard that opened to the lip of Cedar Lake. Layla had always wanted a place right on the water, but after Todd left and there was no child in her future, she'd thought, what was the point, there was no one to share it with her. Two hours and ten beers later, they were still consoling themselves in the fading light.

"I mean, I didn't want to watch, but it was like a car accident—I couldn't look away. It was a good thing it was nighttime, but his ass was so pale—" Eden trailed off in a fit of giggles, hinging forward at the waist, soft snorts escaping her. It was nice to hear her laugh. Tuesday night support groups had turned into happy hour at Eden's house. Now they were talking daily and met often. Eden's initial reserved manner grew into a goofy, freewheeling soul that had surprised Layla. Eden was brimming with energy: a substance Layla had only recently acknowledged was absent from her own life.

"I would have snapped some pictures." Layla's laugh echoed into her glass, and she realized she was laughing more at Eden's amused expression than at the tragically funny retelling of her neighbor's affair.

"Yeah," Eden agreed, but her expression turned severe; her features transformed into sadness.

"What?" Layla asked, leaning toward the table that sat between them.

"Nothing." Eden took a long drink of her beer. She was stewing over something when Layla arrived, when she had opened the door with a beer already in hand. The conversation quickly turned light and fun, and that's when Layla had realized Eden was already on her way to being drunk.

"I know something's bothering you," Layla said. Water sloshed against the dock in the abrupt silence. The outline of a new pontoon boat hung above the water in the boathouse.

Eden finally spoke. "It's Ben."

Ben was absent from most of their conversations. Outside of his business success, Eden seemed almost detached from him. After eleven years of marriage, that could happen. Especially given their fertility battle. Something like that could drive a wedge between the strongest of couples. But Layla got the impression that they weren't that strong from the beginning. Layla and Todd had not been strong enough either. She thought of the last call she ever got from him. In the most reserved manner possible, he had shared the news.

"I'm—Stacy's pregnant," he had said and let out a long breath. "I just didn't want you to look on Facebook someday and see." She had imagined hearing his thoughts: *There, I said it, now I can move on from this crazy woman.* And then she had felt he had the overwhelming urge to hang up on her, put her securely in his past.

"Wow." That was all she had managed to say. What a dumb response. He could have cold-cocked her and it would have hurt less than those few little words. It had taken weeks until it wasn't the first thing she thought about each morning and the last thought that put her to bed. Over and over, an echo in her somber mind. "Stacy's pregnant," like a horrible jingle from a commercial or a catchy chorus to a song she hated. Then she had done something awful, something she would never forgive herself for. The reason she had—

"He's cheating on me." Eden's words broke Layla's concentration. No longer loud, alcohol-stained laugher, but a tone breaking with the weight of the words.

"What?"

"Yes. I mean, I'm pretty sure." But she didn't look sure; she looked lost.

"How do you know?" After everything Layla and Todd had gone through, at least he had left her before finding someone else.

"This is going to sound silly." Eden's cheeks flushed deeper in the semi-dark. "It's the way he smells—like a peach tree."

Layla had only met Ben twice since coming over to Eden's house, and he was everything she thought Eden's husband would be: attractive, charming to the point of being magnetic, pulling you into a conversation and making you feel like he heard you, that he cared. But as they sat in the semi-dark, Layla wondered how she'd never considered that Ben might be cheating. He was never around, and Eden acted as though he didn't exist. A man like Ben seemed to thrive on attention.

"It's a lot of things, but it's not silly. Have you confronted him?" She imagined how the conversation would go with a silver-tongued devil like Ben, but Eden was no pushover. Layla had only seen it once when they were out at the bar together and that random stranger had hit on her: Eden's dark side.

"I want to follow him, catch him in the act." Her voice was suddenly sharp and determined.

"Let's do it!" Layla smacked the table in front of her. "Yes. I'll follow him after work one day. Is that where he is right now?"

Eden ignored her question. "Really? You don't think I'm being paranoid?" she asked.

Layla watched as a flicker of hope died in Eden as she now understood what she wanted Layla to say: that it was all in her head.

Layla reached out and covered Eden's hand with hers. "Let's nail the bastard."

Darkness cloaked the house as moonlight shaved through the trees, dancing on the edge of the yard. Hot air spilled into her driver's side window; the engine of the Toyota was silent as she sat alone. The high whine of a mosquito drew near, and she swatted blindly at it in the dark interior.

Ben's truck rested at the curb, in full view. Wasn't he even concerned about getting caught?

Layla looked up at the second-story window of the single-family home a mile from Eden's house. A woman's shadow flickered off the back wall of the upstairs bedroom. The mirror hanging over her dresser caught her reflection as she unclasped her black lace bra, exposing tanned skin in the lamp's glow. She wasn't alone. Ben scooped up a breast in his palm as her mouth fell open and her head lolled back onto his shoulder. Layla could imagine the moan escaping the woman's lips and ricocheting off the walls.

Heat flashed across Layla's cheeks as she pinched her eyes shut. Poor Eden. The woman in the room was a titan of sexuality, from what Layla could observe. Her curves demanded to be touched, kissed, explored.

She expected a flare of anger, but when nothing came, she lifted the binoculars to her eyes and looked back into the room. She had to do this for Eden. The tall blond woman pushed back into him as his hand twisted in her lengthy hair, tugging her back onto the bed, falling out of view.

The digital clock read 10:30; Layla's hand fell into her lap.

The scuff of sneakers echoed off the pavement just before a dark figure emerged and ran past her car. Instinctively, her head ducked low, concealing herself from sight. The figure quickly receded into the night as her heart continued to pound in her chest.

After a moment, she picked up her phone and dialed Eden, the words she should say at the ready as she listened to it ring, but when Eden finally answered, she found herself saying, "I don't know where he is. I lost him at a traffic light."

Eden let out a deep breath. She had been expecting the worst; that was obvious. But why lie? She pictured Eden's beautiful face covered in tears, her heart hurting as she waited for Layla's call. She would tell Eden what her lousy husband was doing, but she would wait for the right time.

# Chapter 7

Eden

35 days until review hearing

E den's tongue jabbed the inside of her cheek as she inhaled a slow breath, pulled her journal onto her lap, and focused on the three short statements she'd written a week ago.

*I am a mother.*

*I am a survivor.*

*I am a killer.*

A feeling, dark and unyielding, filled her as she realized that only one of these facts felt real: she was a killer. She didn't feel like a mother; her time with Finn had been too short. And this couldn't be surviving.

She was still recovering from Layla's visit yesterday, refusing to eat lunch or dinner. Now she would have to make a great effort to appear fine, when she so clearly wasn't fine.

A sharp rattle of a key in the lock preceded Gilmore's raspy voice. "You gotta go see Jones."

She watched his keen eyes graze over her body, and she had to suppress the desire to cover herself with her arms and give away her discomfort.

She didn't like how he always found a reason to touch her, even in the most subtle ways, as though he was helping her out and she should feel grateful to him. What were this man's qualifications?

Eden decided she wouldn't make it easy for Gilmore this morning. "What's this about?"

"Gotta go see her, sweetheart."

She openly flinched when the word "sweetheart" dribbled from his lips. As if his creepy attention wasn't enough, now he was being more direct. It was often on the tip of her tongue to confide in Marsha about how uncomfortable he made her feel, but she feared appearing unreasonable. And after what happened yesterday during Layla's visit, she would need to be on her best behavior. Though she hadn't found a rhythm to her new situation, she was sure it wasn't her usual time to see Doctor Jones, nor had Marsha mentioned it, which she had always done before.

This was going to be about yesterday; she had thrown away all her progress. She'd talked herself into the idea that Finn would be with Layla yesterday, and he wasn't, and that was all Doc Jones's fault.

Her son. That was what she needed to focus on. She had to make them think she was okay, to get out of here and back to him.

They both entered the hallway, and she followed him, making sure to keep half a step behind him as he pulled out his phone to stare down at it.

"You're looking better," Gilmore said without looking up. For a moment, she thought he was talking to someone on his phone until his eyes flickered over at her.

"Umm." Eden's eyes shifted to the floor as she continued to follow, not knowing what to say to him. She wondered if asking for a new orderly was even possible. She liked Jenkins—but he only worked on Gilmore's days off.

Doctor Jones's office door came into view, and she watched as Gilmore's arm reached up to guide her to the door, but she rushed past him to wait next to it, her back to the wall. Her heartbeat was coming too fast, and the air was cold against the sweat breaking out across her neck in anticipation of this unexpected office visit and under Gilmore's groping eyes.

Gilmore knocked on the door while peering up from his phone to wink at her. The hallway was empty and silent; no rescue was in sight as he shifted his weight toward her. The stale scent of cigarettes wafted off his faded navy uniform.

"You're real pretty," Gilmore rasped. Horrified, Eden thought he was going to reach out and touch her, but Doc Jones's voice called through the thin door.

"Come in."

Gilmore opened the door and reached out to nudge her inside. *Don't touch me,* her mind screamed, but instead she mumbled, "Thank you."

"Oh, good, Eden. Have a seat." Doc Jones stood up from her desk and moved around to the front only to turn to retrieve her glasses and take her usual seat.

"Hello," Eden said as she sat, fingers twisting in her lap.

"How are you feeling after yesterday's incident?"

She knew it! All the pressure Eden placed on herself made it hard to act normal. She would have to work extra hard to come back from this slip-up.

"I'm much better. It was just—" She paused, not knowing what to say, before she decided on the truth. "Layla told me some unpleasant news yesterday, and I'm afraid I didn't use my recently discovered coping skills when they would have helped." She winced; her statement sounded like it was out of a medical journal. She wanted to say she wasn't crazy, and that some woman was trying to take her son while she was locked in here, but her lips only sputtered. The truth would make her sound more unhinged.

"Well, is there anything you want to talk about?" Doc Jones asked, looking down her nose at Eden.

"I just told you." Was Doc Jones trying to bait her into saying something she shouldn't? They couldn't seem to click, she and Doc Jones, and now it was a game about who could outplay the other. Eden just needed to prove to some board of highly educated psychologists that she was no longer a danger to herself or her son, and they would have to let her go, no matter how long Doc Jones wanted to keep her locked up here. Even though Eden was feeling better than she had in a long time, it wasn't translating in her useless sessions with Doc Jones. She seemed even more concerned about Eden's behavior and Eden was sure the doctor's ego had something to do with her trying to handicap Eden's progress. What Eden didn't understand was why. What had she done to her? They had never met before Eden's arrival at the hospital, had they?

"I wanted to move things up a bit in light of what happened yesterday."

What did that mean—take her off the meds? Her heart lifted. "Like fast-track me?"

"No—no. I mean, I didn't want to wait for our usual appointment time because you were very distressed." Doc Jones's lip twitched into a smile that could have been a smirk.

Eden scooted forward on the couch, an action the doctor didn't fail to notice. Eden forced herself to stop wringing her hands.

"Why don't you tell me about this bad news." It wasn't a request.

"Layla told me that my sister-in-law might file custody paperwork to take my son." The words poured quickly out of her. Surely Doc Jones would understand her outburst after knowing what Olivia was doing to her. "See, she wants Ben's money. She probably thinks there'll be child support because I'm paying Layla. It's always about money with that woman." Her voice was saturated with bitterness. She pictured Olivia's smug satisfaction at winning this battle, though the prize meant nothing to her. She pushed herself back in the seat as the harsh sunlight cut through the open slats in the blinds and glared off Doc Jones's glory pictures. Eden heard the scratch of a pen on paper as the doctor made notes.

"I see. Will Finn be in danger if he's in Olivia's custody?" How did Doctor Jones know her name? Had Eden mentioned it at their last meeting? She didn't think so.

"I—" She thought. "It would be better for Finn to stay with Layla. Olivia lives in Hollywood, for goodness' sake. She shares a two-bedroom apartment with a fifty-year-old man. Is she going to take him across the whole country away from me?" Her voice was raised too high, and her fingers were twisting the hem of her shirt. She had to hold it together. "But I'm feeling so much better; I'm sure I'm not going to be here much longer."

Eden recalled Olivia's behavior at the rehearsal dinner the night before Eden married Ben. The occasion had been marked with red roses and heartwarming toasts. Weeks before, Ben had begun his campaign for Olivia to be Eden's Maid of Honor, suggesting she had never had the opportunity. Eden had given in, only to regret her decision soon after. Olivia used the title like a rite of passage or high honor that she'd earned rather than been gifted. She assumed veto power over the bridesmaids' dresses Eden chose and demanded seating changes because she didn't want a particular guest seated near her. She had gone so far as to suggest Eden should rescind several invitations based on her ideological differences with Eden's friends that she'd found on their social media accounts.

Once, when she went to the bathroom, she had heard Olivia's loud voice echo down the hall, promising someone she had one of the better suites in the hotel because her brother insisted on it.

"He gives me whatever I want." Olivia bragged. "And I hope Eden's on the same page."

Eden had spent the rest of the day trying to remember a time Ben had told his sister no—she couldn't think of one. Eden understood from Ben that he felt bad about his sister's situation. Her lack of a high paying job even after attaining a four-year degree from a well-known university. The fact that both Ben and she had come from the same opportunities was lost on him.

Doctor Jones nodded. "I see."

Eden felt her heart trip when she realized she was relating the story aloud. Why did she get the sense that Doc Jones thought she was the problem and not her overbearing sister-in-law?

Eden pictured it. Doc Jones would strut to the stand with her fancy suit and perfectly styled hair at the custody trial. When she finally spoke, she would declare what a good guardian Olivia Wyatt would be if given a fair chance. She seemed like just the sort of person who felt her words were important enough to change the whole outcome. Eden would lose Finn.

She felt the overwhelming desire to scream.

"But this is only temporary. I'm feeling so much better, and once I'm cleared, then I'll get out of here and care for him. No need for her to step in and take him to California." She was rambling now. The steady lub dub, lub dub of her heart shook her chest. She needed to stop talking.

Doc Jones's head tilted to the side, her brow pulled low and her eyes broadcasting her skepticism.

"We need to take this one day at a time. It might be prudent for you to start thinking about what's best for him. I know how badly you want to be with him, but he needs stability."

Eden's mouth opened to speak, but the words evaporated against her tongue. Appalled, her thoughts froze. Doc Jones must have sensed her struggle to respond and continued. "Layla seems like a wonderful guardian, but I've spoken with her, and...well, we can wait on that, but I think having something more permanent would take some of the stress off you. That way, you can focus on getting better. Postpartum psychosis doesn't just go away. Some women suffer with it for years, and then there's aftercare to think about."

"What?" Eden's voice was tiny, defeated.

"You need to focus on your care now, Eden," Doc Jones said in all her smugness.

Years? "But you said forty-five days?"

Doctor Jones shook her head slowly. "I said your evaluation is due in forty-five days. That's according to the state statute. It doesn't mean you will leave then. I'm sorry if I gave you that impression."

"I need to take care of him; he's my son. And if you're suggesting that just because I'm in here that somehow, he isn't my responsibility anymore—I reject that. I'd never give him to Olivia—money-grubbing bitch." Eden's hand punched her thigh before she could stop herself. A loud silence proceeded for several moments until she coughed, realizing her mistake and wanting Doc Jones to overlook it. Doc Jones's carefully manicured eyebrow raised a fraction.

"I'm sorry." Her gaze shifted to the floor.

"I see. So, Olivia is unfit to care for your son because she needs money?" Those words made Eden sound like she was withholding something Olivia deserved.

"No." She shook her head. "No, that's not what I meant to say. She won't take care of him. That's all I meant."

She nodded at Eden and jotted down more notes, and when she looked up again, there was condemnation in her eyes. Eden had failed another test, and somehow, she knew this was different—this time, she would pay the price.

# Chapter 8

Layla
Before

She found herself drifting through the baby aisle again, forgetting why she was at the store to begin with; each tiny outfit calling to her. Little shoes resting in her hands, onesies, and pajamas wrapped in blue and pink ribbon soft to her tender touch.

She pushed the cart past, fighting the urge to grab a pack of diapers or a hygiene kit. No one would know. She could put it with the other things she purchased that she would never use. She thought of the inconspicuous blue tote sandwiched between the Christmas and spring decorations she kept in the guestroom closet. Recalled Todd's expression when he discovered it there. Something akin to sadness mixed with horror, as if the innocent tote contained a rotting body. It hadn't been long after, when she refused to see a therapist, that he decided to leave her. He treated her like it was criminal behavior rather than trying to fill the void—and yes, maybe pretending a little. She wasn't hurting anyone.

Later, after she was forced to see a doctor because of her little brother Richard's demand, she remembered thinking how pointless the visits had been. The doctor hadn't helped her urge to become a mother or change the way she'd thought. Only time wore away the raw edges of her obsession. All the fuss had made her believe society wanted to change her instinct to be a mother—that there was something wrong with her.

Tears pulled at her eyes as she rounded the corner to the paper goods section, her cart protesting; one bent wheel shrieked and dragged against the force of her effort. It was always her luck. Get the barren womb, doomed to live alone and the damned bent wheel. The universe hated her. Layla was busy with her pity party when she almost ran into her: the tall blonde she'd spied on last night, the other woman in Ben's life. Her mouth went dry as she watched the woman pull a pack of toilet paper into her cart. It was an odd contrast to see her pick up something so unsexy—so ordinary. She was too beautiful, too delicate and feminine for this stuff. Where were the lace panties and siren-red nail polish? It was hard to watch her hips sway and not recall her perfect breast in the dim light.

The woman was alone, and when she looked in Layla's direction, Layla looked away quickly. Some women just had it all: stunning good looks, a child of their own, a great sex life. This last thought sank in her gut like a rock with a bitter splash. How could she think that? There was nothing great about Eden's husband having fantastic sex with Malinda. Even her name dripped with sex appeal. Layla was still trying to work up the courage to tell Eden the truth. She didn't want to be the one to devastate her friend; no matter how hard Eden tried, she would always associate Ben's behavior with Layla after such a declaration. It had happened to Layla once before, and the relationship had never recovered.

Eden had no clue that Layla was following Ben, probably assumed Layla had stopped after her initial claim that she had lost him in traffic. Malinda walked past, leaving peach-scented air in her wake.

Layla kept moving away down the aisle and resisted the urge to look back over her shoulder, sensing that maybe Malinda was keen on her now. She had seen her earlier at the coffee shop in town; the encounter had been accidental, unlike the current one.

Why should this woman have what Eden so desperately wanted? Malinda should keep Ben—Eden could do better—but why should she have a perfect four-year-old daughter named Sophie? Layla had first seen Sophie on her third visit to the house, and it was by far the most emotionally gutting time she had spied on them.

Layla's phone chimed from her back pocket.

"Hello," she said.

There was a soft gasp on the other end of the line, and Layla pulled the phone back to see Eden's name on the screen. "Eden, are you okay?"

"Where are you? I need to talk to you." Eden's usual level tone was raw and uneven.

"I'm at the store. Where are you?" Layla turned her cart toward the exit with her two items and wondered why she had even grabbed a cart at all.

"Can you meet me at the park over off North Street?" Was she crying? A series of sniffles chased her distant voice.

"I'm on my way." Layla abandoned her cart near the closest rack and rushed out the exit.

* * *

People lingered at the park, enjoying the late afternoon warmth. A pair of women on their lunch break talked and ate salads at a nearby table, and several joggers rushed past her toward the loop around the green space. When Layla caught sight of Eden's wild eyes and blotchy red cheeks, she knew she had been right; Eden was crying. She stood as Layla approached.

"Let's get out of here," Layla suggested, and Eden nodded. She sniffled several times on the walk to Layla's car but said nothing as Layla's hand clasped hers, trying to offer some immediate comfort.

As soon as they settled into Layla's car, she turned to Eden. "What the hell is going on?" Immediately she considered a list of the worst-case scenarios; there were many, but she was at least confident it had to do with Ben. She brushed the hair out of Eden's eyes and watched as fresh tears began to press past her thick lashes. She wore no makeup, which made her look more youthful; vulnerable.

"Ben," she managed to get out before a hiccup of sobs. A feral growl came out of her lips as she pressed them together with what looked like some effort. But it wasn't sadness painting her features or revealed in her movement; only the tears signaled that emotion. No, underneath, Layla detected rage—like the throes of a wave or an empty moment before an explosion.

"Shhhh. Take a minute, and slow down. Just let it go."

Eden did. She cried for a long while as both women sat. Layla rubbed Eden's shoulder, as she might soothe a baby, resisting the urge to rock her back and forth. Questions popped into her mind, but she had to give Eden time to process her emotions—time to recover.

Finally, Eden looked over at her. "She's his—" Her voice

broke off into sputtering sobs. Eden must have found out about Malinda.

"What are you saying?"

"Ben has a daughter." Eden's breath fired off in a short burst, culminating in a sort of hyperventilation until her lips pinched shut. "Sophie is Ben's daughter."

"What—" Layla said, confused. "I mean, I know how, but how?"

Eden's slim fingers wrapped around a worn tissue clutched in her right hand. "He's been seeing this woman named Malinda for five years. Five years!" Eden's voice squeaked. "He got her pregnant five years ago."

"Son of a bitch," Layla spat, slapping the steering wheel. "How did you find out?"

"I hired a private investigator," Eden admitted as if she was the one who'd gotten caught. "The PI got ahold of some of his emails, and I was looking through our bank statements. He's been paying her child support since Sophie was born." Eden's voice wobbled on the little girl's name.

"Oh, sweetie. I'm so sorry," Layla said, grabbing her hand. She was grasping for any way to comfort this broken woman but found it difficult as her shock left her incapable of much thought.

"That means it's me," Eden said.

"What's you? Don't you dare blame yourself. He's the one who's messed up here." She'd seen it once too many times: the spouse who was stepped out on making excuses for the cheating prick.

"No. Not that." Eden stopped speaking and put a finger to her lips, catching herself. "I guess I'm the reason we can't have a baby. It's me."

Layla wanted to argue with her, to make her feel better, but the truth was she was probably right. Just like Layla's fragile situation. Todd probably knocked his wife up on the first try. It wasn't fair.

She put herself in Eden's shoes. It was bad enough that Todd had divorced her and now had his own child with Stacy, but how would Layla feel if they were still married and she made this discovery? Hell, it didn't even look like Ben was planning on going anywhere.

"Why do you think he's staying?" Layla asked.

Eden looked over at her, wide hazel eyes blinking. Her ordinarily flawless skin discolored, the whites of her eyes stained pink. "Money, I'm sure. It has to be. We didn't have a prenup. Ben had no money when we were married. He's worth millions now." Eden said it so flatly Layla wondered if she would even go after any of that pot of gold. Ben was a greedy son of a bitch. He had come from meager means, and now that he was rich, he wouldn't want to give up half to his wife.

"So—take him to the cleaners," Layla said.

Eden let out a humorless laugh. "I don't care about the money."

She wouldn't either. Through conversations with Eden, Layla learned that the woman who'd adopted Eden was well off and in her late seventies now. Eden didn't need his money.

"It's not about wanting the money. It's about what it would do to him to lose it. He shouldn't get everything he wants," Layla said. She'd never thought of herself as a vengeful person, but the thought of Ben's smug satisfaction after rolling off his mistress and washing up to go home to his wife for the night made her want to see him suffer. But Eden wasn't like her; she was kind, and a little weak, if Layla was honest.

Eden sat back in her seat with a loud sigh. "I don't know. I'm going to take a while to think about this," she said. As Layla looked over at Eden, she didn't look like a woman in thought; her mouth was pinched shut in anger, and her shoulders were rigid with wrath.

# Chapter 9

Eden

35 days until review hearing

S unlight streamed through the windows in the day room and splintered into light rainbow refractions against the dirty wall. Eden curled her legs underneath her at one of the small tables in the corner. Jinx and Chaz sat side by side across from her, arguing over an article in *Psychology Today*. Four orderlies swarmed the room, more than average, and it made her feel uneasy. Their eyes shifted around at the ten or so patients lingering, pacing, and lounging. Some gargled random cries as they stalked around the room. She would never get used to this place.

"I think you're that way because of trauma," Jinx said with an air of authority on the subject, which Eden recognized as her general tone for all things. What did Jinx do to wind up in this place? Did she kill her patients like the nurse from *Misery*? Eden pictured Jinx standing at the end of her bed, sledge-hammer clamped in her hands, a crazed look on her face.

"Whatever." Chaz tugged on his right ear and turned away from her to scan the room again.

"What do you think, Eden?" Jinx turned to her in hopes of winning the argument by getting Eden on board.

"I don't have an opinion." This much was true; she was only half-listening to them talk, her thoughts unable to focus for very long. It was easier to bow out, but Jinx scrunched her nose in obvious annoyance.

Before leaving her earlier visit, Doc Jones had recommended a new medication until the stress of her current legal battle was finished. Eden wanted to argue that she had no intention of being in this place in July, but she needed Doc Jones to believe that Eden trusted her. Now she was having a harder time than usual trying to focus with all the noise and Jinx's loud chatter.

She tugged the collar of her jumper up to her chin as she attempted to make herself smaller. The medication swallowed up all her recent memories and left a fog of confusion behind. The faces of the other residents were blurry; letters in her journal seemed to dance out of focus. She couldn't remember the names of those around her, including some of the staff, and she found herself smiling her greeting rather than speaking, in case something random were to come out of her mouth instead of an informed thought.

It reminded her of her first hospitalization when she was nineteen. It had been hot that day as she sat in the back of the police cruiser. The manager of a high-end clothing store had called the police when Eden tried to purchase nearly twenty thousand dollars' worth of clothes with a debit card from her mother. When those moods hit, it was as if she couldn't help herself. Shopping, spontaneous road trips hundreds of miles from home, and sleeping with Shawn, her neighbor, whom she'd never really liked. Buying all those beautiful things was her way of letting out the energy that had been growing in her throughout the prior month. Like she was on top of the world.

The clerk had eyed her suspiciously as she continued to pile slinky dresses and five-hundred-dollar shoes and bags onto the sparkling glass counter.

"I'm sorry, your card was declined." The store clerk had looked pleased.

Eden began to pace and mutter to herself, and someone had called the police when she became increasingly agitated. Once the police arrived, she was asked questions, many of which she didn't seem to know the answers to. She didn't understand what was going on.

"What are you doing with me? I didn't steal anything," Eden pleaded.

"Yes, ma'am. We're aware. We're trying to reach your mother now." But he never explained why they detained her. She might have been upset, but this natural high she rode for days wouldn't allow her to sleep or eat much, and it was making it hard for her brain to connect the dots. She was under arrest.

"My mom?" Eden felt the first sort of sinking feeling. "She's gonna kill me."

But Ruby hadn't. Her adoptive mother did quite the opposite. Eden was taken in for an evaluation—no arrest—after which she was committed to a hospital for treatment.

"They just want to make sure everything's okay," Ruby had explained, hugging her.

"What does that mean?" She had become anxious since arriving at New Hope Hospital, but that feeling of euphoria was still just under the surface.

It would be weeks later that she was officially diagnosed with bipolar I disorder, and told she was experiencing mania. Her mother stuck with her through it all.

"What's wrong with her?" Chaz asked. "She looks like she

bit into a lemon." He giggled, and his neck shrunk between two bony shoulders.

"Eden. What is it? Thinking about Finn again?" Jinx asked.

"No."

"What is it then?" Jinx stood and rounded to the seat next to Eden and sat. "Tell me."

Eden shook her head. "I don't want to talk about it." Her tone was scolding, and Jinx shifted back in her seat like she'd been slapped.

"Is this about your little friend, Layla?"

Eden shook her head.

The way Jinx said "little friend" kept playing in Eden's mind for a moment as Jinx fell silent.

Eden had noticed that Jinx became jealous at times with no warning. Would Jinx suddenly melt down into a seething, violent woman if she felt betrayed by Eden? The doctors wouldn't let dangerous patients walk among the docile—would they? Her eyes shifted to Arnie, who was only a few feet away, hunched at the next table. Where did they put the patients who were too violent to be around others? Were they in the rooms she shuffled past each morning?

"What is it then? What did Doc Jones say?"

"Ace. Ace. Ace," Willie, a longtime resident of Middle State, chanted from a nearby table, clapping his big hand down and rocking the table legs with the tremor.

"Shut up!" Arnie roared. He pushed up from his chair across from Willie and threw the cards down onto the scuffed table. "You dirty cheat."

"Ace of heart. Ace of hearts. You have no heart." Willie tapped his fingertips together in a sort of dance as he kept his gaze on his cards, showing no apparent fear of Arnie's outburst. Perhaps the poor man couldn't understand how violent Arnie could be.

"Arnie, come with me," Gilmore said, grabbing Arnie's arm. Even at a foot shorter than Arnie, Gilmore led him effortlessly from the room like the rudder of a great ship.

"It won't be long before that psycho goes back to the fifth floor." Chaz palpated his split nose as if touching the memory. "And I hope he never comes back."

"Now, Chaz. Be nice. Arnie likes me," Jinx said in a singsong voice.

"Everyone likes you," he shot back.

Eden tried to track all the activity around her, but it strained her eyes, and she looked back at Jinx.

"That's true. Especially him." Her eyes floated around the room to insinuate that *him* was someone present. She winked. "My little friend."

"Nah, not him," he said. Did Chaz know who this mystery man was?

"Whatever. We aren't talking about me; we're talking about Eden," Jinx said. "Layla?"

"What about her?" Eden said.

"Is that why you're in such a mood? Did she do something to you?"

Eden shook her head. Fact: Layla had saved Finn's life that night. Eden owed her everything, but she wasn't about to share that with Jinx.

"It's nothing. It's just family stuff."

"Uhhh, juicy. Is it your money-grubbing sister?" Jinx rubbed her hands together and leaned forward, waiting to feast on the gossip or the misery. Eden's recent mention of her sister-in-law to Jinx had been a mistake.

"Sister-in-law. She isn't my sister." She wanted to say she didn't have a sister but only added, "Ben's sister."

Eden had been thinking about Olivia's tiny two-bedroom Hollywood apartment, with Finn sleeping in a small corner, crying out for love and attention. Olivia counting Ben's money at her kitchen table. Cramming Finn into her used Jetta, which she drove because she insisted only hot chicks drove Jettas.

Her superficiality was only beat out by her lack of basic understanding of how to treat other human beings. Or maybe it was because of that shallowness—

"I bet she hates you. You know, because you killed her brother," Chaz said. The harshness as much as the truth of Chaz's statement caused her to recoil. It wasn't an angle of her situation she thought of that much. Did Olivia want to hurt her for killing Ben? Probably.

"I know that face. She's going to be following Arnie back to the fifth floor," Chaz said.

"What are you talking about?" Eden asked, turning her gaze on him. "What's on the fifth floor?"

Jinx nodded while looking at Chaz. "Violent nuts up there." Her finger poked toward the ceiling and Eden's eyes followed it. "People who become too unstable to be around us," Jinx said in a whisper, her eyes on Eden's face, taking in her expression.

Eden swallowed. "Have you guys been up there? How do you know?"

A look passed between Jinx and Chaz, but neither added anything.

All of them dropped the subject, but Eden was still troubled by the idea of the fifth floor. She tried to remember if any staff had mentioned it before. Nothing came to mind, but that didn't mean a conversation hadn't happened. Ever since stumbling into that grocery store, she couldn't trust her mind.

Jinx gave a conspiratorial look around the room and turned back to Eden. "I think your friend's out to get you."

Eden's eyes narrowed. Jinx brushed her red hair behind one ear and leaned in. "She's been saying bad things about you to Doc Jones. Sabotage," Jinx proclaimed as she made her fingers explode like a small bomb had detonated in her fist. "Boom!" she yelled.

Eden took a deep breath and sat back from the sudden display.

"What bad things? Like what?" Chaz's fingers rubbed more frantically against his ear in his growing excitement.

"Things, so our little miss pretty has to stay here forever. I'm sure she's feeding her lies." Jinx turned to Eden with a pitying glance. "You know she hates you, don't you? Doctor Jones does too. She's just looking for a reason to put you back on the fifth floor to hide you away from me because we're such good friends. And my man thinks you're pretty, but he loves me more." Jinx surveyed her nails. "We all know when I get out of here, we're going to be together, him and me. I don't belong in this loony bin."

Listening to Jinx, Eden was stunned into silence. How would she know what Layla was telling Doc Jones? It was just as plausible that she was making the whole thing up, trying to manipulate her. And Eden had never been to the fifth floor—

"He doesn't like you," Chaz said.

Jinx jumped up from her seat, sending the chair back to the floor with a loud clatter. Half the residents in the room didn't even bother to look up; the other half came alive like a beehive, voices buzzing, frantic movements. As though Jinx had just stepped on an anthill, everything began teeming with life. Jinx turned to Chaz and snapped her teeth at him. "You don't know anything—you're crazy. I'm not crazy; you're crazy," she yelled. "I'm not crazy; you're crazy, and you, and you." Jinx went around the room, pointing her finger as if it were a wand blessing the chaotic masses. "And you. And you."

Jinx didn't scream or protest when Gilmore grabbed her wrist and led her out. The echoes of her decree continued to fade down the hall as she moved farther and farther away. The room settled back into a wave of low murmurs, and Willie's chanting a moment later was almost relaxing to Eden's energized nerves.

"What's gotten into her?" Eden turned to Chaz. "Who's the mystery man?"

"Doctor Mystery," Chaz said in a low laugh. Could he mean Doc Lucas? Eden couldn't see him being interested in Jinx.

"You know what happened to her friend?" Chaz's eyes darted around the room.

"No. I have no idea." Eden looked back to the doorway where Jinx had disappeared.

"There was a girl here named Jaybird. Well, that's the name Jinx gave her anyways. I don't remember what her real name was. Anyways, Jinx fell hard for her."

"Like in love with her?"

"No—not romantic, they were good friends." Chaz looked up from his fingers into Eden's eyes and quickly looked away. "They found her at the bottom of the stairs one day," Chaz whispered. "And Jinx told me it was an accident, but I don't believe her. I think she killed her, and she didn't want to go back to the fifth floor, so she lied to everyone about it."

"And they believed her?"

Chaz looked down at the ground as if to admire his white Crocs. "She asked me to say I saw it and that she slipped."

"And you did?" Eden felt her stomach tighten. Just what was going on behind these walls?

"Yeah—Jinx, she isn't well sometimes, and it starts with catching someone's eye, and it ends badly if she thinks someone wants what she thinks is hers." Chaz jumped up from his seat and hustled toward the door where an orderly met him, and they disappeared down the hallway.

Eden shook her head slowly at the odd display and his abrupt departure. Sitting alone now, she turned to survey the room and its occupants. Some were propped in chairs, unresponsive, while others talked to themselves or paced the floor, and for the first time since coming to this place, she was scared.

# Chapter 10

Layla

Before

"Hey, you," Layla said, hiding her bitterness over Eden's long absence; she felt cut out. She had to remind herself that Eden was going through a tough time, so she lifted her voice when she saw Eden's name in the caller ID box. Eden had been gone for three months without hardly a word after her revelation, ignoring most of Layla's outreach. When Eden finally answered one of her calls, she'd told Layla she was visiting her mother for a while until she got her head right.

"I'm back!" Eden's tone was musical, not at all what Layla expected. "Come over and see me. I miss you."

And that was all it had taken to bury her sour feelings. Layla would forgive her for anything, she was sure, and if the last three months had taught her anything, it was how much she needed Eden; she was family. Being alone had nearly sent Layla into a spiraling depression. Eden was a breath of fresh air

in Layla's life when she needed it the most, and since her revelation she thought they could be there for each other. Instead,
Eden had abandoned her.

Eden's SUV was the only car in the driveway as Layla
parked on the tree-lined street. This was an established corner
of Cedar Lake, where the wealthy kept their summer homes.
Eden's house was new compared to the well-kept aging homes
around it, but no less opulent.

As Layla waited after knocking on the wide double front
door, she prepared herself for the worst. But when Eden
answered, her skin was flush with a Florida tan, and her smile
was wide and catching.

Eden embraced her, and Layla hugged her back, taking in
her friend's familiar scent of warm vanilla.

"I've missed you," Layla whispered.

Layla swallowed the guilt for having gone by Malinda's
house after their last talk. She had to go see Sophie again for
herself, and now that she knew the child was Ben's, she was
starting to notice the similarities in their features, the same chin
and dimpled cheeks.

"Come in. I have food out back." She grabbed Layla by the
arm and tugged her inside. Layla's awkwardness melted away
as she followed her through the house to the patio. With each
new step, she realized that Eden was eager—happy. The back
doors were swung open, and the lake was restless as the breeze
licked over its surface.

"What have you been up to all this time? You look fabulous," Layla said when they'd both taken their seats. For a
moment, Eden's color faded, and Layla thought she would
burst into tears, but it returned quickly.

"Florida was amazing. Seeing my mother and spending
some time away from Ben was exactly what I needed." Eden
lifted a glass of orange juice to her lips and sipped. Layla

waited for the big reveal, the "I'm not going to be with this son of a bitch any longer" moment, but the silence dragged. The air was thick with moisture, and the sun climbed the mountain toward the ridge. The silence tilted toward awkward, but when Layla finally looked back, Eden was smiling out at the water.

"How's Ben?" Layla asked, feeling that Eden would avoid the subject if she didn't ask.

"He's good." A blush lit Eden's skin, and Layla felt her brow pinch. What was going on? Had three months away erased the last eleven years of their rocky marriage? The sharp glint of Eden's diamond ring cut across Layla's vision. Did she know where Ben had spent the last three months?

"What did you do while you were in Florida?" A more pertinent question would have been what was in the water there, because Layla needed some of that.

"Went to the beach, hung out with old friends." There it was again, that glow. Maybe she needed to find time to go down to the beach. Let her hair down—it'd been years since she'd traveled beyond work obligations for her IT office.

A loud hum sounded from inside the house.

"What's that?" Layla asked, looking through the open doorway.

"Garage door. Ben must have forgotten something."

She stood, her petite frame filling out her shorts and tank top. Layla tried not to watch as she walked away but couldn't help herself, Eden's hourglass figure demanding attention.

"Let me see what he needs." Eden disappeared through the doorway, and a moment later, Layla heard Ben's voice, and she couldn't stop herself from sneaking to a nearby window and looking inside. The kitchen lights were blazing, and she watched as Ben stood next to Eden at the counter. His frame, a foot taller than hers, was pushing against Eden's. Was he hurting her? Layla's first instinct was to run in there and protect her, but then she watched as Ben lifted her onto the counter and his hand pulled her head to his for a long kiss, his hands trailing down her back, pulling Eden into him. Confusion bloomed in Layla's mind. She watched in horrified silence as Eden sunk to the floor and unzipped Ben's pants, lowering herself onto him.

He shook his head toward the patio, and they both laughed softly. He pulled her toward the powder bathroom and pushed her against the wall, his fingers tangled in her black hair, only finally kicking the door shut with his foot.

Layla's hand smothered a gasp, and she resisted the urge to walk to the water's edge. Instead, she took her seat at the table and ignored whatever was going on feet away from her. Should she leave? Should she stay and face Eden when this was all over? She was sure she wouldn't be able to hide her embarrassment once Eden reemerged.

Layla's mind was so confused she settled on watching the workings of the natural surroundings. A squirrel hopped across the yard, and the wind shivered its way through the leaves. A neighbor walked the length of the white fence surrounding Eden's yard and waved a greeting. Layla absently waved back, feeling like she was in a daze.

When Eden finally returned, her skin was so flushed it was nearly red, and Layla assumed it was from Ben's stubble scratching against her cheeks.

"Sorry about that. Ben forgot his work computer." Eden didn't look at her, as if she knew Layla had seen them just moments ago. Why would you have sex with your husband while your friend was a hundred feet away—supposedly unaware?

"Guess he has his mind on other things." Like spontaneous sex with his wife and his mistress, and he must think he's the luckiest man in the world, Layla thought bitterly.

"I just wanted to let you know Ben and I are working through things," Eden began. "And I don't know if you are or not, but please don't follow him anymore." Her tone was stern, and she turned her eyes to Layla's. "I know who he is, and we're going to figure this out. He's just looking for a way to end things with her without it getting messy."

Layla felt heat flush through her body with the anger. How could Eden be so naive? Would she always be making excuses for him? But at this point, it was critical for Layla to keep the peace. No matter what happened in Eden's marriage, Layla would always be there for her. That was all Layla needed to focus on now.

"I'm here if you need me," Layla said as she reached out a hand to cover Eden's.

"And..." Eden smiled again. "He's agreed to look into adoption."

And there it was: Eden's sacrifice. What she was giving up for a life she wanted. She would live with a cheating husband.

# Chapter 11

Eden

34 days until review hearing

"All rise—"

Eden shifted in her seat and rotated her wrist where the handcuffs had been, rubbing the memory of hard steel away from her skin. She was sweating in her suit as she always did when she had to be in court; her life, and Finn's fate, so precariously hanging in the balance. She felt Lauren's hand on her arm, helping her to her feet, as the bailiff swept the judge into the room. The judge was an older man with white hair and large glasses on a bulbous nose. She recognized him from her previous hearings, not for his kindness but his abrupt contempt for her attorney.

"Be seated and come to order," the bailiff commanded, and everyone around her sat. Jacob, Finn's guardian from the court, was the only person in the gallery, and she felt disappointed at the absence of Layla and Finn. Layla had been present for all the other status hearings, but today she must be running late.

"Let's see. We have the Wyatt case." The judge looked down his nose at a sheet of paper in front of him. "What are we doing with this counsel?" The judge eyed Lauren, who stood.

"Your honor, Lauren Ross for the petitioner. This action is on behalf of my client to ensure that continued temporary custody of her son remains with a family friend, Ms. Layla Hughs," Lauren began in a steady voice. Eden recalled the two prior hearings where she verbally agreed to give Layla temporary custody of Finn. Eden was adamant with Lauren that she wouldn't sign custody of Finn over to anyone, including Layla. This was all just temporary; she had to remind herself of that.

Eden looked around the unfamiliar courtroom with its ornate oak paneling and aged red carpet. This wasn't the same courtroom where her criminal trial concluded, though she only vaguely remembered it due to being highly medicated.

"Is there no family for the child?" the judge asked, and Eden's heart shuddered. She was not expecting him to ask the question.

"Your honor, none that my client would feel comfortable caring for the child at this time. As the court may be aware, my client suffered a psychotic break after the birth of her son, and her recovery is expected to be short. Ms. Hughs is a wonderful caregiver and trusted friend of Ms. Wyatt."

Eden nodded her head vigorously in the direction of the judge, who barely glanced at her. The judge continued looking over his paperwork and began to shake his head.

"I'm showing someone filed a petition for full custody and child support in the amount of—" He humped from the bench and turned to his clerk. "Is this a typo?" The clerk took the paper from him, read it, and shook her head.

"In the amount of seven thousand dollars a month," he finished. Eden felt a scream building in her lungs. She was willing him not to say it, not to say her name.

"How dare her. Greedy bitch," Eden snarled. She looked between Lauren and the judge, pleading for her lawyer to say something, do something, make this right. "You have to do something. Fix this."

"You'll advise your client not to have outbursts in court," the judge warned her attorney while throwing a withering glance at Eden.

Lauren turned to her and moved close. "Let me handle this."

Eden took in a large breath as she nodded but felt her body move to the edge of her seat.

"My client is unaware of this petition. In fact, I just checked yesterday, and there was nothing filed."

"The clerk got the paperwork this morning. It didn't find its way into the file until just before court started. I believe opposing counsel is present." Eden took another glance around the courtroom. Beyond Jacob, a heavyset man in a dark gray suit stood.

"May I address the court?" the man asked in a humble tone.

*No—no, you may not,* Eden's mind thrashed. *You can go to hell if you're helping that greedy woman.*

The judge nodded and sat back in his chair, fingers steepled under his chin.

"Robert Foster for the plaintiff, Ms. Olivia Wyatt. We filed our petition and intended to seek full custody of the child. She is his aunt and—"

"She's a gold-digger." Eden shot up from her seat.

"Order!" the judge shouted from the bench. "Ms. Wyatt, one more outburst, and this hearing will be over." He continued to talk, but she didn't hear him; she saw only red as Lauren anchored both of her hands on her shoulders, forcing Eden's eyes to hers.

"Calm down," Lauren hissed and turned to the judge. "We

need a moment. If the court please, a short recess, my client's in a fragile state."

When Eden looked back toward the judge, she noticed the deputy had moved from his post near the beach to just beside her, ready to pounce. She only shook her head at him; she wasn't violent. His eyes narrowed, but he nodded as though they had made a silent agreement.

"Well, clearly, we can't keep the status quo with this new petition," the judge said, waving the papers. He looked at Lauren with an exaggerated frown. "We have to continue this out for a trial date. If you have any motions make sure to file them in a timely manner so we can move this forward." He was already turning to the clerk as she typed.

"What does this mean?" Eden whispered to Lauren. The oak-covered walls seemed closer than when she had first taken her seat, collapsing her world into a tiny box with no escape.

"It means we have to go to trial." Lauren began leafing through her folder as they both took their seats. "He isn't going to give her custody today; we have to wait for that."

Eden wanted to think Lauren sounded confident, but she detected uncertainty. Would the court favor family over a friend? Perhaps Layla would forfeit Finn to avoid an ugly court battle. She felt her eyelid begin to twitch over a growing pain emanating from the same eye.

"Layla will have to co-petition," Lauren said to her. "Will she do that?" But before Eden could answer, the clerk spoke.

"We have July 17 and 18."

"Does that work for council?" the judge asked.

"Do you have anything sooner than that, judge? My client is very anxious to reunite with her nephew," Robert said while moving to the bar—not even sparing a glance at the pocket calendar in his hand. Eden wedged her index finger into her mouth and bit down hard enough to feel the pain. How dare she do this! The thought of that horrible woman taking Finn back to Hollywood to what, live in a shared two-bedroom apartment with who knows who. She wanted to argue, stand up and tell this judge off, but she had to stay silent for Finn.

"Your honor, Finn's in excellent care; I have the GAL here if the court has any questions for him." Lauren indicated to Jacob in a desperate attempt to sway the judge.

The judge shook his head. "I'm not hearing evidence today," his voice thundered, his patience clearly waning.

"Yes, your honor. July dates work for me," she said, looking over at Eden with a confident nod.

"Mr. Foster, can you make July work?" the judge asked with one raised brow. "The court's docket is heavy."

"If it please the court, you are aware that Ms. Wyatt is a ward of the state after she killed her husband. My client and I intend to introduce evidence that suggests, might I say proves, that the murder wasn't due to her mental state, but was premeditated."

For a moment, all the air was sucked from the room, and Lauren's head jerked to look at Robert, who smiled back at her, clearly enjoying the ambush.

"Can they do this?" Eden whispered to Lauren as she shook her head. How could Olivia know about—

"No—your trial is over. That's not why Mr. Foster brought it up. He's desperate. Trying to make you look bad." But Lauren looked troubled.

When Eden looked back at the bench, she felt the eyes of judgment on her. Maybe it wasn't enough to put her in prison for life at this point, but it might be the edge Olivia needed to gain custody of Finn.

# Chapter 12

Layla
Before

As Layla placed the last dish on the drying rack, the chain lock on her front door jumped from frantic pounding. Her heart squeezed in her chest as she squinted at the microwave: it was only 7:30 am. She dried her hands and crept to the door, aware that her movements might alert a possible psycho to her presence. Maybe they would go away if they thought the place was empty. But it was Eden's face on the other side of the fisheye lens.

"Let me in," she teased, moving closer to the peephole as if she were the one spying on Layla.

She unlocked the deadbolt and removed the chain lock.

As soon as the door cracked open, Eden shot past her toward the bathroom saying "I gotta pee," leaving Layla opened mouthed staring after her. They had fallen back into their routine now that Eden had been back from Florida for nearly a month. They spent most nights here at Layla's tiny apartment, binge-watching TV while they perused adoption sites, but the last week or so, Eden was different. Taken over by a thoughtful spirit, she would sometimes stare off and not hear Layla when she spoke.

"Have you heard from an agent yet?" Layla called as she heard the commotion in the bathroom fade out. She listened to hear what Eden might be doing in there after she didn't respond to the question. She could hear movement, something crinkling. It was five minutes before Eden emerged from the restroom; her fingers twisted together as she grinned.

"I guess you really had to go." Layla held up a mug. "Coffee?"

"No thanks." Eden placed her purse on the small table and promptly began to pace the cracked linoleum of the small kitchen.

"What's going on?"

Nervous energy poured out of Eden's movements as she checked her watch a second time and continued to pace. Eden's thumbnail wedged between bright white teeth as she absently chewed at it, a recently adopted habit.

"Sit," Layla ordered, pointing a finger to a mismatched wooden chair. She had picked out the three-piece set at a few different antique markets back when she and Todd went on the weekends. It always bothered him to have things that didn't match, but to her, it added character.

Eden sank into the wicker-thatched chair and looked up at Layla. Her black hair was glossy, and her skin luminous with a tinge of pink. She looked—frenzied. Layla took the seat next to her and resisted the urge to reach out for Eden's hand.

"Tell me what's going on." Layla tried to keep her voice even and casual.

"I think..." Eden's cheeks flushed, and her hand reached up to cup her mouth, her eyes brimming over with tears, her black hair aglow with the early morning light through the window. "I think I'm pregnant."

Layla's mouth hinged open.

"I just took the test—it's in your bathroom."

"Oh, sweetie. I don't want you to get your hopes up." Layla shook her head. She had been there a hundred times before, and so had Eden. What Eden was doing to herself would no doubt end in a negative pregnancy test and an ugly cry. But Layla thought back to the lustful encounter she had seen between Eden and Ben not so long ago and which had continued the handful of times she had seen them together. They were like newlyweds, unable to keep their hands off each other. She'd never gained the nerve to ask Eden what had changed, but it was clear they had rekindled their sex life.

"It's not like all the other times. This is different—I feel different. My breasts are heavy, I've been crampy, and I missed my period." Eden's hand fluttered to her chest, and tears slipped over the edge of her dark lashes down her cheeks. "It's two weeks late."

"Two weeks." Layla was shocked it had taken Eden this long to tell her. "What does Ben say about all this?"

"I haven't mentioned anything to him yet. I wanted to make sure first."

Layla felt her heart swell at the thought of Eden choosing her to be the first to share the news with. She'd rushed over here to take the test, wanting to be with Layla when she learned the results. Eden's hand absently rubbed at her belly, and Layla knew this would end badly. She had never seen this much hope in Eden, and raw hope could be a scary thing sometimes—Layla herself had missed periods but still wasn't pregnant. The body did odd things, like trick women under stress to conceive.

Eden's eyes drifted to the bathroom door. "I don't know why I closed it."

"If you don't go in there and look, I'll do it for you." Layla stood. "It's been long enough."

Most of those tests could tell in a minute or two.

"No—wait. I'm going." Eden reached up and pulled at her arm. Layla nodded her encouragement, but for Eden's happiness, she would swallow down her bitterness. Besides, the test would be negative, and Eden would need her support. And she could only hope that with this disappointment, Eden would wake up and kick Ben to the curb. Find a child through the adoption agency and live her life.

The door screeched as Eden pushed it open and walked inside. The test rested on a small pile of toilet paper on the white counter. Eden closed her eyes and took in a deep breath as she clutched the test to her chest.

"All or nothing," Eden whispered, and Layla ached for her, for the devastation she would soon feel.

When Eden opened her eyes, a gasp escaped her lips. Two quick breaths and she sank to the floor as Layla reached out for her. "Oh, honey. I'm so sorry." Layla gathered her into a hug. "We'll get through this together."

Layla felt Eden's hot breath mumble words against her shoulder, and pulled away to understand what she was saying. "What?"

"I'm pregnant."

Layla felt the air drain from her lungs as she shifted back onto her butt, the tiles cool against her jean-clad skin. "What?" she stammered.

"I'm pregnant." Eden turned the test for Layla to view. Two dark pink lines lay in the display box. How many times had Layla scrutinized a similar little window that never changed color? She had peered closely and imagined a faint line when none was there. So much hurt. She wasn't sure now what emotion was stirring inside of her. A mixture of love and regret in a chorus tore at her.

"How?" Layla asked, unable to stop the words.

Eden shrugged as if she'd never even considered that the test wouldn't be positive. Her glow seemed to pale in a moment, and her eyes widened. "Ben," she whispered, her fingers sliding over her lips.

"What about him?"

"I'm not sure how he's going to take this," she said, as her eyes stared at the source of her joy.

"He's going to be excited, I'm sure."

Eden was going to have a baby, and it was terrific, and they were friends, and she would support Eden in any way she needed. Who cared about what Ben thought.

"Well, we talked about it before I left. He said he changed his mind and doesn't want children now."

"Well, isn't that rich, considering he has Sophie." She said her name as if the child was a murderer, and she watched Eden flinch away.

"It's not Sophie's fault," Eden said gravely.

"Okay, fine. It's not her fault. That anger should have been directed at your husband," Layla added, standing up from the floor. She reached a hand out to Eden, who took it and stood, still clutching the test to her chest. They embraced for a moment, and Layla could feel Eden's body gently trembling. Though Layla would never know what Eden was feeling, she thought she was wise enough to understand, and she guided Eden to the couch in her cramped living room.

"Everything's going to be great," Layla said, though she had a lot of reasons to believe that wasn't true, but what would a messy divorce matter if Eden had what she wanted all along—a child?

"I have no idea how I'm going to tell Ben."

"How about an elaborate dinner at his favorite restaurant with family and friends so I can see the look on his face when you tell him. It would give me great joy," Layla teased.

"Hmmm." Eden's eyes shifted around the room. "I like that idea. He's going to have a heart attack; might as well do it in a public place, so no one can say I killed him." Then her eyes took on a faraway look. "You know, we used to be so happy. He was so serious about his success, so focused, but when he was around me—he was different." Eden rested her chin in her hand, propped on bent elbows. "He loved me so much, and if he was still the same man, I think I might be okay not having this baby." She rubbed her stomach. "I think I could have made it work, but I don't even know who he is anymore. And the parts I do know aren't parts I love. He's never home, and when he is, he's distracted by his phone or work obligations. I feel like I'm going through this life alone."

"Then why stay with him?"

When Eden turned, Layla didn't recognize the woman looking back at her. Her eyes were too fixed, her cheeks tight with anger. "Because he owes me."

# Chapter 13

Eden

33 days until review hearing

She ripped the blue-lined paper between her fingers and watched it rain into the toilet bowl like confetti on New Year's Eve in Times Square. With a shaking hand, she flushed, watching the evidence disappear in a rush of water.

It was early, not even 6:30, when she found herself rising for the day, unable to hold onto sleep. When she looked across her dark bedroom, she caught sight of her journal. The need to capture her thoughts on paper overwhelmed her. A fear, constant and growing in strength, occupied her thoughts. She had to deal with Olivia.

When she reached for the journal, one of the few possessions in the small room, she felt better. Yes, these were the coping skills they were teaching her, what she needed. Maybe it was working after all, and she was getting better, not just pretending.

But when she opened the pages to the last entry, she felt her mouth fall open. She looked it over in disbelief.

*I hope you die. You've ruined everything. I won't let you take my son from me, and if you try, I will kill you. Kill you. Kill you. Kill you.*

"No—no, no, no," she chanted. She tore at the page, not satisfied with the rip of the paper until she destroyed each ink-stained corner.

She stumbled to the bathroom without deliberating, grasping the evidence in one shaking hand. It never existed, she told herself, but the knowledge of it wouldn't go away. She closed the door and collapsed at the base of the toilet. Maybe she wasn't getting better after all?

She turned her fist toward the water in the toilet bowl and opened her hand to let the paper fall lazily inside before pulling the handle to flush twice before the bowl could fill again.

"You in there, Eden?" Marsha's voice carried through the thin wood door, and Eden jumped.

"Yeah. Be right out." She flushed the toilet a third time and rushed to the sink. Cool water poured out, and she splashed it over her face and scrubbed at the beads of sweat that had gathered at her hairline. She looked frantic—guilty. She took one last glance into the toilet bowl to be sure nothing had come back up before she exited the bathroom, as composed as she could make herself.

Marsha waited near her bed, two cups in one hand, the other resting on her hip.

"How are you feeling today?" Marsha asked, her eyes collecting her own opinion, looking inside her to the gruesome parts. Eden felt her arms cross over her chest, pulling everything back in, her mind racing as her eyes darted around the room. The blinds were closed but the morning light pressed against the slats.

"I think you have a visitor at ten-thirty, according to my notes. You up for it?"

Eden flushed, knowing Marsha was onto her—knew something was wrong. Her eyes moved unwittingly to the bathroom and back to Marsha.

"Visitor?"

"It's your lawyer; that's all I know, hun." Marsha held the cups out to her. "You okay?"

"Yeah. I didn't sleep well last night." Eden rubbed her cheeks with her hand. It was partly true, and someone like Marsha could detect an outright lie.

"Maybe we should talk to Doc Jones about your medication?" Marsha's head tilted to the side as her eyes scrutinized Eden.

"No, please," Eden begged. Before she could stop herself, she was reaching out to grab Marsha's arm. The nurse didn't pull away or try to stop her; instead, she took a breath.

"You know, Eden." Her tone was even and low. "You ain't fooling anyone here. They see your BS a mile away. So instead of trying to game the system, why don't you buckle down and work on getting better—for real."

Tears of frustration and hopelessness spilled out of her eyes, and she nodded. Marsha was right, of course. The best way to protect her son would be to focus on her treatment here at the hospital. But how could she stand by and allow Olivia to take Finn? Even though she was physically absent from his life, it was her job to be sure he was taken care of. Eden swiped at her tears with the rough cuff of her sleeve.

"You're right. I can't be with my son until I'm better." She meant it. Finn needed to be protected, even from Eden if necessary. But she needed a plan to fix Olivia. She wasn't about to trust a broken system with the one thing that meant more to her than living.

Marsha nodded. "You rest now. I'll tell them to cancel your visit."

"No. I'm fine. I'll rest until then." Eden pointed to her mattress. "Promise."

After a moment's pause, Marsha added, "Gilmore's off today, so if you're intent on going, Jenkins will be here to get you." The nurse turned and left.

Eden's eyes caught the edge of her journal, abandoned to the floor, where she'd thrown it. Had Marsha seen something? Did she know Eden had found something sinister in the pages? No—she was paranoid. No one knew what she'd found because she'd destroyed the evidence.

When Eden joined Lauren and Jacob in the conference room, both gave Eden polite smiles. Surprised by Jacob's presence, she immediately thought of what had happened in court yesterday. Was she losing Jacob's support after that windbag's accusation?

Lauren stood and walked to her, reaching a hand to touch her arm. After her outburst, Eden had been removed from the courtroom and whisked back to the ward. Lauren must have made the appointment to visit today as Eden was being driven back here.

"How are you, Eden?" Lauren's eyes moved over her like a doctor's eyes searching for injuries.

"Fine." They moved around the table to where Jacob, Finn's attorney, sat. It was silly to think of a child less than one year old having a lawyer. Well, technically, he was a guardian at litem. The state had assigned him to address Finn's best interests while he had no parent in the picture, like a court-appointed parent. Eden had limited interaction with him, making her uneasy about the amount of sway he would have with Finn's future.

"Hello again, Eden." Jacob smiled from his seat, where stacks of papers rested before him.

She reached out, and he looked amused but shook her hand. Wasn't that the normal thing to do? As Lauren took her seat next to Eden, she felt better; Lauren would fix this. She was one of the best family lawyers in the state; Eden had made sure of that.

"I'm doing better. Much better," she said as her eyes skipped between the two. "Let's just figure out how to fix this before it gets any worse."

Jacob frowned, and it made him look like a fish. "I want to give you some updates on Finn if you like," Jacob said.

"I'm doing much better," she repeated, and her mouth snapped shut when she realized she'd misspoken.

Eden leaned back in her chair and ran a thumbnail over the smooth edge of the table, only looking up when she felt Lauren rest a comforting hand on her shoulder. "It's okay. We understand."

If there was one thing she was sure of, it was that they didn't understand, but now wasn't the time to be combative; she desperately needed them on her side.

Jacob spoke again: "Today, I wanted to talk about Finn's situation, and Ms. Hughs gave me some pictures to give to you."

Eden's heart leapt. Pictures. "Can I keep them?" she asked as he pushed several matte photos toward her waiting hands. She gave a smile of apology after she snatched them up.

"Yes, you may."

"How's he doing? Layla's great, isn't she?" The pictures looked very similar to the ones Layla had showed her on her phone the other day. His cheeks were so plump and begged to be kissed. His eyes were open as he looked into the camera, right at her. "Oh, he's so perfect," she whispered, and had to acknowledge how much he looked like his father. That fact would haunt her all the days of her life—and what she had done.

"Yes, he is. He's a delightful baby."

Lauren spoke. "Layla is doing great. We've been able to set up her bank account and help her retrieve all his items from your home."

Relief flooded her. "I want her to have whatever she needs. It's not her burden," Eden said, finally setting the pictures aside but keeping them in her line of sight. "Whatever it is."

"I'm so happy to see you're coming around the bend," Lauren said.

"Yes. I'm happy with my treatment, and I think I'll be out of here really soon."

Lauren's smile collapsed just a touch. "Well, I wish it was all well-wishing, but we have some business to discuss. You up for it?"

"I understand." She wasn't sure she did.

"We need to think about what's best for Finn right now," Jacob said as if Eden had never considered this before. As if every endeavor she was undertaking was for selfish reasons and not to help Finn.

"Yes, of course. It's always about what's best for him," she agreed, quickly smothering a glare at Jacob.

He pulled out some papers. "It's been over eleven months now. Why have you chosen Layla as a caregiver for Finn and not Olivia?"

Eden felt her face transform into a scowl.

"Have you been talking to Doc Jones?" The words shot out of Eden's mouth unchecked, angry. Doc Jones was talking behind her back to everyone, making all kinds of plans to get Layla out of the picture so Olivia could move in and gain custody. Eden racked her brain over why the doctor might be doing this and there was only one explanation. She was working with Olivia.

Lauren and Jacob exchanged a look, and both shook their heads.

"I trust Layla more than anyone in the world, outside of my mother, and she's too old to take care of such a young child." Eden rested her elbows on the table. "She loves Finn as much as I do."

"Well, those are good reasons," Jacob said, but in a condescending tone, as if she were a child. Did he think she was crazy? "You see, Layla is an excellent candidate if she were the only one. Now that Olivia is asking the court for custody, we need to revisit everything," Jacob added gently.

"No—I don't consent." She looked at Lauren. "Isn't there something you can do about this? She's a horrible person."

"Let me finish, Ms. Wyatt." Jacob's tone was stern now. "She's asked for visitation with the child while the court works its way to the case."

"Visitation?" Eden's eyes searched around her. "She doesn't even live in Virginia." She was going to add that she didn't even like children, but that wouldn't help either.

"I believe she's been staying at your residence." Jacob's mouth set in a tense frown. Eden pulled back in her chair, her hand raised to her chest. Was Olivia sleeping in her bed, going through her things? Eden's mind raced so fast she couldn't form the words to say. Now Olivia's lawyer's accusations made more sense...Olivia was snooping.

"I can help with that—" Lauren began, but Eden's hands shot up.

"You both don't get it. Olivia isn't a nice person. She's

trying to get my son for money." The last word hissed past her teeth.

She would need to get ahold of Kendrick and have him meet her. With Olivia at her home, it might be tough, but not impossible, to get inside and get what she needed out of that house, assuming Olivia hadn't already found it. She jerked up and walked to the door, unable to hold it together another second. It would become a pattern and not a fluke if she had another meltdown. If she was honest, she knew the following question from Lauren might be what evidence Olivia's attorney had that would indicate she planned to kill her husband. She wasn't able to pretend she didn't know just what that evidence might be—she had a pretty good idea.

# Chapter 14

Layla
Before

A week after Eden learned she was pregnant, Olivia flew in. Eden was planning to tell Ben and Olivia the news at dinner, along with both their parents and a few friends. Olivia's response to the invitation had been quick, and Layla wondered if she was really as bad as Eden suggested.

Layla watched as Eden tediously reviewed her meal plans for the next few days as Layla tossed grapes into her mouth. Olivia had many food allergies, or some such fake nonsense, Eden had joked.

"It's an excuse for her to complain about my cooking—I've never seen her have any type of reaction."

"I can't believe you put up with that." Layla frowned. "What did the doctor say?" She smoothly shifted topics.

"Huh? Oh, yeah. That everything looks great, and the baby just reached twelve weeks." Eden smiled down at her belly, and Layla reached out and squeezed her hand. Eden never explained how they were working through Ben's infidelity, but

Layla assumed Eden had confronted him about it. Out of curiosity or maybe habit at this point, Layla continued driving past Malinda's house sometimes, and Ben had been there only two nights ago. It was true he was there less than he used to be, but he hadn't ended things like he'd probably told Eden he had. Layla wanted to tell her this, but then Eden would know that Layla was following him, and she'd promised she would stop. She wanted to stop driving by, she really did, but she knew Ben was lying to Eden—not that it would change anything. She would have to let him get caught without her own direct involvement.

Now that the big reveal was going to happen tomorrow night, she was more anxious than ever to find out what was happening in this house.

"How are things with Ben now?" she asked, eyeing Eden closely.

Eden smiled a wide genuine smile. "Things are good."

"Did he come clean about Sophie?"

"Not really—no. I didn't—" Eden slammed the cookbook closed, startling Layla. "I didn't mention that part of it to him when he visited me in Miami."

"He visited you?" This was the first Layla was hearing of this.

"Yes."

"Why didn't you ask him about her?" Layla wasn't sure who she meant, the mistress or the lovechild, and it didn't matter.

"I don't know. I guess I decided it won't change anything now."

"Did he agree to stop seeing her at least?" Layla wanted to stop questioning her, but the words kept pushing and shoving their way out of her mouth. She had the grace to be embarrassed as she cornered her friend.

Eden's eyes danced around the kitchen, its gleaming subway tiles sitting over polished granite countertops. Several vases of flowers littered the surfaces, sending off perfectly placed pops of color around the space. Eden had outdone herself for the weekend, making it clear to Layla just how nervous she was about the announcement.

"I don't want to talk about them anymore. Please drop it. I have to handle this my way." Eden's words rang with finality.

Layla bit her tongue. Hadn't she been a supportive friend to Eden? She knew she could come on a bit intense sometimes, but she was just trying to help. It was more evident than ever that Eden had a secret, maybe more than one.

"I—um," Layla stammered.

The front door opened, and Eden looked almost relieved by the interruption.

"We're here," Ben's voice boomed from the foyer.

"This looks amazing. You're doing well for yourself, little bro." A woman's voice.

Layla turned to see Eden squeeze her eyes shut, probably mentally preparing for her sister-in-law's presence.

The sound of heels clicked across the hardwood as they made their way to the kitchen. Ben's smiling face rounded the corner, white teeth gleaming against his tan skin, and his dark hair a little longer than he usually wore it—this was relaxed Ben. Layla always forgot how disarming he was until she saw him again. It wasn't often, given how much she saw Eden these days. Dropping two bags to the floor, he crossed the room to gather Eden in his arms and hugged her. She beamed, and they looked, for a moment, like the perfect couple. She could almost see it, the false reality before her. An ideal wife preparing to give her perfect husband the best news. But the image shattered at the sound of his voice.

"Let me introduce my sister, Olivia. All the way from

Hollywood, California," Ben said proudly. Olivia moved further into the room and removed oversized sunglasses. She was curvy and wore tight jeans; her large breasts crested her snug top, making it clear what she assumed to be her best asset; expensive shoes coupled with a cheap bag.

"Hello, Eden, and..." Olivia looked at Layla with a hand draped in the air, fingers dangling.

"Layla." She waved.

As if she had forgotten her name already, Olivia smiled and said, "Hi, friend."

"Can I get you a drink, Olivia?" Eden moved toward the refrigerator anticipating her response.

"Yeah. Wine—bet you guys have the good stuff here," she said as she began walking into the two-story living room, touching vases and looking at pictures. Layla turned to Eden and gave her a conspiratorial wink as if to say, If this turns into a street fight, I got your back.

"Remember this, Ben?" Olivia held up a picture of his graduation. Next to a capped Ben, Olivia stood beaming, ten pounds lighter and smothered in youth. Of course he remembers his graduation, Layla thought, fighting the urge to roll her eyes. "I haven't seen this picture in years," Olivia added, setting it down on the table rather than the mantle where she'd found it.

"That was fun," Ben said absently, looking down at his phone.

Eden walked gracefully across the room and set the glass of wine on the kitchen table. Olivia's forehead caved in confusion.

"We don't drink in the living room, sorry," Eden clarified, as if to excuse her rudeness for not personally delivering her wine.

"Whatever." Olivia waved her off. "What's this dinner all about?" Her question was directed to Ben, who was still on his phone. Layla caught sight of his slim fingers and recalled them caressing Malinda's perfect breasts, and tousling her hair. At that moment, he looked up and smiled at Layla, and she looked away. It was as if he knew what she had been thinking.

"I don't know; you'll have to ask my secretive wife." Ben winked at Eden.

"It's a surprise." She smiled, but her eyes shifted away from Ben back down to the counter and she reopened the cookbook.

Olivia swiveled on the stool and looked over the room again. "That's a cute purse." She pointed to Eden's bag hanging by the door. "What's something like that go for?"

Layla felt her mouth drop open and quickly snapped it shut. Eden had warned Layla about Olivia, but she'd felt maybe Eden was exaggerating. Nope, it was all true, worse perhaps—high maintenance on a low budget, she'd said.

"I've gotta run to the office for about an hour." Ben pouted to Eden. "I'm sorry, hun." He kissed the top of her head and turned toward the front door without any room for discussion.

"I heard there's a pool now?" Olivia eyed the patio.

Eden nodded toward the back doors. Olivia popped out of her seat with her wine in hand, red liquid spilling over the side and onto the wood floor, unnoticed by her as she let herself into the backyard.

"I'll get it," Eden called out as if Olivia were concerned. Resignation took over Eden's features as she moved to clean up the mess. It was a good thing Layla was here.

"Are you sure this is what you wanna do?" Layla hitched her chin toward the backyard.

Eden looked to be holding back tears. "I'm just worried about how Ben's going to take the news."

"And this horrible *friend*," Layla mocked and both women laughed.

"She's going to ask me if she can keep my purse now."

Eden's eyes drifted to her purse. "Ben's probably out there trying to find the exact one so we won't have to listen to her."

"How does she afford to live in Hollywood?" Layla watched as Olivia perched poolside on a lounge, her back to the sun, talking on her phone.

"I think Ben gives her money."

*Ben sure has a lot of secrets...*

"Eden, dear. A refill." Olivia held her empty glass above her head, no attempt to move.

"Wow. You know I'm not good at this kind of thing. I'm gonna tell her off; I just know it," Layla said, getting another laugh from Eden.

"Why do you think I invited you?"

"Mission accepted." Layla grabbed the bottle from her. "Let me get this; check on the oven."

Olivia still had her phone to her ear as Layla walked across the stone patio.

"Yeah, you should see this freaking place, friend." She laughed. "I'm gonna ask him before I go—he never says no."

There was a pause before Olivia added. "He's going to leave her, but there's no prenup—that's why he's dragging his feet." She set her glass down. "I can't stand her, but it won't be long now." Layla nearly lost her grip on the neck of the wine bottle. Had she heard her right—Ben was going to divorce Eden?

"She's crazy, you have no idea. Real psycho stuff." Layla's shadow fell over her and she turned, a discreet smile on her face as she held up her wineglass for a refill. Layla felt sick.

# Chapter 15

E den was sluggish—more than usual after taking her medication. She suspected Marsha had slipped a sleeping aid in last night. She refused to leave her room for dinner and her stomach ached, waking her early. Everything was going so well—well, as good as could be expected given the situation she found herself in, and given what she was up against. There was no doubt in her mind that Doctor Jones would make a big deal of her behavior following that court hearing and walking out on her lawyer yesterday, if she found out. She didn't think Lauren and Jacob believed that Olivia's intentions were pure evil and somehow it hurt that at the very least Lauren wasn't going to side with her. Wasn't she allowed a moment to take a breath? To slow things down and figure out what she needed to do next? Finn was with Layla, safe and sound, and now all that was being threatened.

Try as she might, she was unable to stop thinking about

Olivia. It was only 3:00 am, and she was staring up at the cracked ceiling, recalling the time she had spent with her. All the snide comments and the abusive tone that Eden had ignored. She had only put up with it because, at one time, she loved her husband. As much as Eden didn't understand it, Ben had doted on his older sister, inviting her on pricey trips and sending her expensive gifts. She wasn't sure if Ben knew Olivia was always about material things or if he genuinely wanted her in Turks with them. Lucky for Eden, Olivia always managed to break off from them and find her own crowd.

After she had worn herself out thinking of her sister-in-law, those tiny last words from her attorney niggled at her—the murder wasn't due to her mental state but was premeditated. It wasn't true.

*They're just lying to get what they want. How was it possible Olivia knew about Miami?*

After hours of lying in bed, she shuffled to the bathroom as light broke over the sky. She couldn't lie there any longer thinking those terrible thoughts, with nothing to do about them, battering her nerves and making her nauseous.

She turned the water on hot and stepped under the stream. She was going to have to come up with a plan. She wouldn't let Olivia take her son so the greedy woman could get child support from her. Money was the key to Olivia's heart and her compliance.

When she shut off the water, she reached for the towel draped over the toilet, but her hand only caught empty air. She pulled the curtain back and looked around the bathroom. She shivered as the cool water slid down her naked skin, and she wrapped her arms around her breasts. Had she only imagined putting the towel on the toilet? It was what she always did before a shower.

She stepped onto the smooth tile and moved to the door. It

was ajar. She pushed it with her toe as light pierced the empty darkness. Gingerly she stepped into her room and, out of the corner of her eye, caught sight of a moving figure. Short with scruffy hair. Gilmore's rough fingers groped her breast and she stumbled back against the doorframe, crying out in pain as his grasp twisted away from her tender flesh.

"Careful," Gilmore said as he reached for her again. "You don't want to hurt yourself."

Her breath came heavy as she rushed into the bathroom, trying to shut the door, but it bounced back into her as he pushed his way inside.

"Calm down, Eden, or I'll have to administer a sedative." There was laughter in his voice as his eyes moved over her body, taking in the naked flesh she scrambled to cover.

"No—please. Leave." Eden couldn't make the words come out forcefully enough as she backed into the shower, but there was nowhere to go.

She screamed then—as loud as her lungs could project as she wrapped her arms around her chest and huddled in the corner of the shower. He tipped his head toward the door as if he was trying to listen for someone in the bedroom. She felt her stomach roll, and before she could stop herself, she was puking in the shower. His lustful stare turned quickly to one of disgust.

"I'll be out here if you need me." He sank into the shadow of her room.

Everything suddenly became silent as she hunched in the shower for several long moments until she was sure her stomach was settled, and she realized she only had the soiled jumper and panties on the floor. She dried herself quickly and put the dirty clothes back on. She would not go back into that room naked—of that, she was determined.

As the day's first light shone through the window, she stood from her crouched seat against the door. She expected him to force his way in at any moment, but Marsha would be here soon. She just had to wait him out, but as the silence persisted, she wondered if he had gone. Once she gathered the nerve to exit the bathroom, she found it empty, the heavy metal door closed and locked. No sign Gilmore had ever been there except the shame she felt and a small piece of paper covering the camera mounted near the door. Her heart sank when she considered the apparent premeditation of Gilmore's attack. Maybe he'd thought she would be passed out from the medication? Had he done this before? She tried to reach up and remove the paper, but she was too short, and when she tried to drag the table over, she realized it was bolted to the floor, just like the bed.

She sank into the corner of her room and cried. That's where Marsha found her not long after.

# Chapter 16

Layla
Before

L ayla arrived early as Olivia's complaints filled the hallway. It's too hot; it's too cold. She wanted to sit next to Ben, and the other seat should be left empty. Eden fielded each complaint with grace and a fixed smile, often nodding to assure Olivia that she'd heard her.

When they were alone, Eden nearly collapsed from her effort. "Why did I do this again? Remind me next time to have a Zoom dinner. At least then I can mute her."

Though Eden smiled as she spoke, Layla watched as she fussed with her hair and bit her lip—she was nervous, or maybe excited.

"I got your back. And yes, I won't allow this to happen again." Layla winked. "Can I sit next to her, please? Just to piss her off." Layla raised her interwoven fingers in mock begging.

"I would give her this house right now if I thought it would get her to shut up."

Eden had spent most of the previous day preparing dinner and appetizers, ordering alcohol, and stringing elegant lights in the yard. In her juvenile way, Olivia kept demanding to know what the fuss was. "I don't like surprises—" And everyone knows, it's all about her.

Layla stood at the back doors observing the guests as they quietly mingled under the twinkling lights strung from the pergola. The sun sank over the lake in a palate of deep golds, and the air was damp but not too hot—the perfect night for a storm.

She had to get Olivia alone, to plant the seed. After overhearing Olivia's remarks on the phone, Layla knew the tension was at the breaking point between Eden and Ben. Even though they seemed to have rekindled something only a month ago, they had relaxed into the same old behavior of avoidance and ignorance since Eden found out about the baby. It was clear to Layla that Eden had no plans to end this farce of a marriage, but maybe Layla could help her along by using the most unlikely ally ever. Olivia.

When it was time, Layla followed Eden out onto the patio carrying the food. Ruby Milton, Eden's adoptive mother, smiled up at Eden as she set plates of food onto the table. Ruby was small and fragile, but she had a firm handshake at seventy-five, and her affection for Eden was obvious.

Jim and Cynthia Wyatt sat across from Layla. She didn't know what she'd expected when meeting them, but it wasn't what she found. Ben's father was wearing blue jeans, his mother in flip-flops, happily chatting with Ben's coworkers. Eden had explained Ben's rise from meager means, and Jim and Cynthia confirmed it; but more so, Layla wondered how two nice, unpretentious individuals could raise two people who were so consumed with themselves.

Olivia's voice screeched over all the conversations as her

arms draped over the seemingly random empty chair. Last night at dinner, she had thoughtlessly suggested to Eden that they hire a chef for her next visit because her stomach was sensitive to undercooked vegetables and overcooked meat. Layla thought the meal was perfect. Eden had excused herself so many times due to morning sickness that Olivia had quietly suggested to Ben that she might have a drug problem. It had taken every ounce of Layla's willpower not to put Olivia in her place then and there, but she needed Eden to make her announcement first. She didn't want to ruin this night for Eden.

"Okay, everyone. Dinner is served." Eden waved toward the food. Her skin looked pale, and her lip trembled. Was she sick again?

Olivia muttered about the late hour for dinner and how starved she was. How could that be after all the hors d'oeuvres she'd horsed down?

"This looks fabulous, hun." Ben pulled Eden into a half-hug and took his seat at the head of the table. Everyone began passing the food around.

"When will you come out to Hollywood, Eden?" Olivia pulled a napkin onto her lap, elbow resting on the white table-cloth. The topic had come up last night, outside of Eden's presence.

Eden's smile was tight. "I think Ben might have mentioned something about this fall."

"I'll be getting some well-earned time off in November. Maybe we can have a California Thanksgiving," Ben suggested.

"That would be awesome. I know some excellent restau-rants in the area, and I could show you all the great hangouts. I have a roommate, so you'll have to get a hotel." Olivia eyed her brother with an exaggerated frown about her unfortunate situation.

"Well, I don't know if I'm going to want to fly in the fall." Eden's voice was low; her lips bowed in a soft smile.

"Why's that?" Olivia asked, eyes narrowed. The transformation was so fast Layla had to do a double take.

"I'll be in my third trimester by then." Eden's voice was clear as a bell now. Ben's smile froze on his face, then melted into a look of confusion.

Layla had assumed Eden had prepared a speech or worked on some elaborate announcement, but there it was, flopped into the conversation like one of the side dishes being passed around.

Everyone at the table stopped talking for several long beats, and then chatter broke out in loud congratulations on the warm summer air. Only Ben, at the head of the table, couldn't form words with his gaping mouth. Eden was smiling and thanking her mother and in-laws, avoiding Ben's gaze. Olivia looked between the two, her brow furrowed low, almost hostile.

Finally, Ben broke the spell, produced a broad smile, and beamed at his wife. "This is great," he announced to the whole group. While standing, his knee hit the table, sending a tremor down its length, and everyone reached for their drinks to keep them from spilling over. "To Eden," he said in a cheery tone. "To getting what you've always wanted."

The chatter dimmed again as Ben drank his entire beer before coming up for air. Froth lined his mouth as he smiled at no one in particular.

\* \* \*

Layla offered to help Eden get the dessert. She was dying to ask her why she had made the announcement the way she had. There was no love lost for Ben, but Layla was having a hard time watching him afterwards. He was drinking way too much and embarrassing himself with rude jokes and obnoxious laughter. She didn't know if he was celebrating or scared. She absently wondered how he reacted to Malinda's pregnancy announcement.

"No, that's okay." Eden pressed a hand to her arm. "Relax. I have it all ready."

Ben was chatting with Olivia and had ignored Eden following her announcement as she accepted congratulations from all the guests. He absently grabbed Eden's hand and randomly let it go again as if he was trying to communicate something to his wife without saying the words.

After Eden was gone too long, Layla decided to go in and help her anyway.

Quietly she crept toward the kitchen, where she could hear Eden's soft frenzied whispered curses as she pulled ice cream out of the freezer and removed the cake from the refrigerator. Layla stopped, backed up into the shadow of the doorframe and watched.

Eden seemed to stare at the glinting steel of the knife for a long time before picking it up. Without warning, she slashed at the smooth white frosting and slammed the blade down into the cake over and over. Crumbs scattered the counter and nearby floor in puffs of dark chocolate crumbs until she finally grew tired. Eden's eyes blazed with silent fury as she looked around at the mess.

Feeling nauseous, Layla retreated out the doorway and back to the table. Her mind was unable to reconcile the two people Eden could be. Moments later, Eden returned with the ice cream and a broad smile on her face, sending a wink to Layla.

"Sorry everyone—so clumsy I dropped the cake."

# Chapter 17

Eden

31 days until review hearing

Gilmore was back the next day, waiting in her doorway to take her to her appointment with Doc Jones. She tugged at her jumper, wanting to disappear inside of its baggy folds. Her mind was racing from disgust to embarrassment, finally settling on anger. The corner of her room seemed to pinch and squeeze her; his eyes held steadfast, a smirk on his face. Did he have no shame? He acted as though nothing had happened yesterday.

She rose slowly but rushed past him once she reached the doorway. The air smelled of French fries and sweat, and her nose wrinkled.

She would only look at him from the corner of her eye as he hit the down arrow for the elevator. Doc Jones's office was on the main level, and even though she preferred the stairs, Gilmore always took the elevator. Today, the thought of entering the small space with him, having no way out, was suffocating, and her breath began to hitch. The doors of the empty box rolled open, and she realized she was hoping someone would be inside. Her steps stuttered as she nearly asked him to take the stairs, but he was already waiting for her to join him.

As soon as the doors slid shut, she pressed further into the corner as he moved a bit closer.

"I hope you're better after that episode yesterday," he said in a sour-smelling whisper.

She looked up to see the steady blink of the red light on the camera. They were all over the building, and Gilmore must be aware of them. It memorialized their interactions, and she knew he wasn't stupid enough to do anything in front of one that functioned.

"I would hate to tell Doc Jones about what I found in your room." His hand fell to his side, his outstretched thumb brushed her leg, and she jumped away from him, sucking air deep into her lungs.

"What?" Her voice stuttered.

"I won't mention the other day if you don't. I would hate to tell Doc Jones the truth. That you hit me when I found that knife in your room, under your mattress."

She stared over at him, feeling every muscle in her body tighten. Her heart smashed inside her ribs; she was unable to form words in her defense. Was he blackmailing her? The thought was too hideous to consider. What else would he require from her besides her silence?

"Don't worry; I got rid of it," Gilmore said with a wink.

"Got rid of what?" Eden's mind was whirring.

"I've noticed the last few days that you're regressing. Maybe you need to go upstairs. Pump you with all kinds of drugs. You don't want that, do you, Eden? Maybe I could come visit you there—" He smiled, revealing stained yellow teeth as his thick pink tongue shot out of his cracked lips. The bell dinged, and he quickly stepped away from her as the doors slid open.

The sight of Doc Jones's door propelled her feet forward in an awkward shuffle. Gilmore's words kept repeating in her mind.

The scuff of shoes echoed down the hall as another orderly walked toward them with two patients in tow. The door to Doc Jones's office was ajar and voices filtered out into the hallway as she stood still, back to the wall.

"Gwen, you know you should have said something." A man's stern voice bellowed. "This is a huge conflict and how am I supposed to respond knowing you said nothing?"

"It was an oversight." Doc Jones sounded contrite. "It will never happen again."

"I can work with her." Doc Lucas's voice joined the others. Eden wondered if she should be listening to them as Gilmore shifted from foot to foot next to her, anxious to be on his way.

"Make it happen. And Gwen—" The man's voice moved closer to the door. "Don't let this happen again."

Before Doc Jones could answer the door swung open, and the unknown man and Doc Lucas rushed past them, neither noticing her still form as they walked in the opposite direction.

Gilmore guided her toward the door.

"Is everything okay, Eden?" But Doc Jones was looking to Gilmore when she asked, vetting any response through the orderly.

"Everything's fine," Gilmore assured her. Eden nodded at Gilmore, and she wondered what she had agreed to with the gesture. Was she assuring him she wouldn't say anything or was she deciding that she was okay?

"All right. Let's get started." Doc Jones held the door open to her, and Eden walked directly to her usual seat while the doctor retrieved some papers and a pen from her desk. Once Eden sat, and her eyes lingered closed for a second, she could feel the horrifying pinch of Gilmore's fingers on her breast. The wild look in his eyes as he witnessed her nakedness. She shook her head and let out a soft groan. He had calculated that attack —and she didn't think he would give up after one attempt. The sickening thought occurred to her that it was probably not the first time Gilmore had assaulted a patient here.

"What is it, Eden? What's wrong?" When Eden's eyes blinked open, she looked at Doc Jones and saw genuine worry on her face, maybe for the first time.

"It's nothing. I didn't sleep well."

There was a beat of silence as Doc Jones traced her lips with her pen. "You're already taking a sleeping aid—"

"I don't need to be taking anything," Eden snapped. Inhaling deeply, she continued in a more even tone. "I'm fine. I had a rough night." Add the last three nights to that list ever since Gilmore had done those things, the note—and the situation with Finn. It was all stacking up, adding to her stress.

Doc Jones appraised her. "You remember what I told you about the fastest way out that gate?" She pointed in what Eden presumed to be the direction out of this place. "Sleep deprivation is a trigger for psychosis. If you want to be whole again, you need to get sleep."

Whole again. How could she be complete after what she had done?

"Let's pick up where we left off last time."

Eden nodded and searched her recent memory, but she couldn't remember what they had talked about two days ago. "I don't remember where we left off," she said, too tired to pretend today. With everything going on, she might get tripped up.

That's what these sessions had become to her: a sort of test for her sanity. And she was failing.

"You mentioned your desire for a child might stem from your mother's abandonment of you." Doc Jones herself had suggested the association, but Eden didn't correct her. She'd learned Doctor Jones's games and how the doctor was manipulating her. She wanted Eden to think it was her idea rather than something she'd planted in Eden's head.

The wind howled against the glass, and the sunlight dimmed behind a cloud.

Ruby had told her the story about her birth mother when Eden was fifteen years old. Eden had long suspected she wasn't Ruby's biological daughter. Physically, they couldn't be more different. Ruby was pale, heavyset. In contrast, Eden had dark features and a slim build.

They'd been sitting at the kitchen table just after breakfast when Ruby explained the truth. "I think your mother was Cuban." Ruby's smile was gentle. "The nurses in the hospital called you Baby Jane after your mother left." Her mother had snuck out past the nurses and staff less than twelve hours after Eden's birth—never to be seen again. She didn't even give Eden a name.

It was silly, she knew, but her immediate thought was that her mother didn't love her. But how could she possibly know what her mother was thinking? Eden didn't know how old her mother was or where she was from. It turned out that the name and address her mother gave to the hospital staff were both fake.

"I think she was running from someone, maybe your father. She wanted to save you." That's what her adoptive mother had decided to believe, but Eden hadn't made up her mind, and she probably never would. But she always assumed her mother was bipolar too, and maybe she had come to regret leaving Eden behind. Eden knew all too well how the ups and downs worked with her mental illness, especially unmedicated.

Now, Eden realized with sadness that she hadn't thought about her adoptive mother in weeks. Across from her, Doc Jones cleared her throat. "Do you have a good relationship with your adoptive mother?"

"Yes. I love her very much, and she never treated me as if I didn't always belong with her. I guess I was just curious about my birth mother. And I wonder if it was hard for her to leave me there."

"Yes, well, these thoughts are normal, of course."

Eden nodded, not because she agreed with Doc Jones, but because she felt the doctor wanted her to.

"Do you think she's disappointed in you?" The question, so harsh and unexpected, made Eden flinch. "It's time for honesty —so you can heal."

Eden stared back at Doc Jones, unable to answer the question. But a response echoed inside her mind—yes. She did feel like a disappointment. She was a killer, after all. Ruby didn't have a mean bone in her body and had raised Eden to be kind to everyone.

"There is something I need to discuss with you." Doc Jones set aside her notes and pulled her glasses down off her face. Without them, she looked much younger.

"Yes."

"I wanted to let you know you will be seeing Doc Lucas from now on for all your one-on-one treatment."

Eden felt her stomach flutter. "Really?" She couldn't help but welcome the first positive thing that had happened to her in weeks, possibly longer.

"Yes. Doc Lucas and I happen to have conflicts with you

and another patient, so we have decided it's best to switch you both. It's the right thing to do. I will still be in charge of your release evaluation."

She might have jumped to the conclusion too quickly that this move would help her, but if Doc Jones was still involved in her release, Eden didn't believe she would be fair to her.

What conflict could the doctor have? Perhaps someone found out that she was working with Olivia? Eden shook off the thought; it was only a paranoid theory.

Raindrops tapped the window just beyond the desk, and the sun was gone, giving the daylight a nighttime appearance beyond the curtained windows.

"What conflict?" Eden asked.

"I can't discuss it with you, but I cannot ethically treat you because of a mutual acquaintance we have."

Was Doc Jones from Miami? Eden had lived in Cedar Lake for such a short time and had no memory of meeting her before she came to this place. But if she knew Olivia...

"Okay," Eden agreed. "Whatever you think is best."

Eden swung her legs down to the ground and began to rise.

"There is just one more thing I wanted to discuss with you before you leave for the day. I had to report this issue, and I want you to understand that it will require changing your status here at the hospital for the time being."

"Status? What does that mean?"

The doctor's frown deepened, and Eden could see it was bad news. She would probably have more restrictions and supervision. Maybe even more therapy. Her throat tightened, and she swallowed hard. Had Gilmore lied and told her about the imaginary knife he "found"?

"Can you explain this?" Doctor Jones held up a single piece of paper. Its ink stains cut through the lines; the author had pushed so hard while writing that tiny tears marred its surface —each letter crafted with hate.

She looked down at the note, speechless. It was identical to the one she had found in her room. *Kill you. Kill you. Kill you.* She pictured the tiny scraps of paper in the toilet bowl only days ago, rushing down inside and vanishing.

"I've never seen this before in my life." The words spat out of her in a defensive tone.

"Are you telling me you didn't write this?" Doc Jones asked, but not in a way that would make Eden believe it to be a sincere question—it was more of a challenge.

"I just—" She thrust the note back to the doctor, wanting to get rid of it. "No, I didn't write this."

"I wanted to see if you would lie to me." A single brow raised in her direction. To see her reaction—she was testing Eden. Was this a joke to her? She wasn't going to allow herself to be a pet in this woman's circus.

"I..." She heard shouts from the hall followed by heavy footsteps; someone running. "I don't know what this means." She was so sure she was telling the truth. If only she hadn't seen the same note, with the exact same words, only days ago—when she'd torn it up and flushed it down the toilet. Her thoughts wouldn't come into focus, scrambling over possibilities.

Doc Jones sat there saying nothing, and Eden felt the urge to fill the silence with her denials. "I'm sorry, but I've never seen this before. I didn't write it, and if someone told you I did, they're lying to you."

Gilmore must have done this. Was he already covering his tracks in case she decided to tell Doc Jones about his assault on her? Why was everyone here out to get her?

"I see." Doc Jones folded the note carefully, not taking her eyes off Eden.

"Where did you get this?"

"One of the orderlies cleared off your table after you were in the day room yesterday. They said you were writing in your journal, and when you got up, this fell out."

There was only one problem with that explanation: Gilmore left early yesterday.

# Chapter 18

Layla
Before

L ate-afternoon shadows danced as the sun streamed through the leaves of the maple trees beyond Eden's house as Layla sat in her car parked at the curb. Eden should have been here ten minutes ago, so they could plan the details of her baby shower, but she still wasn't home. It had been four months since Eden's announcement, and things had fallen into a rhythm again. Mum was the word on any marital issues from Eden, while Layla understood all too well what Ben was doing. It was clear from Olivia's reaction to the announcement and the conversation Layla had overheard her having that Ben wanted to leave Eden, but he had yet to follow through with any action, and the reason was probably directly related to Eden's announcement.

Layla's phone vibrated in her palm. "Hello."

"It's me. I'm still at the doctor's office. They're running

behind. I think someone gave birth or something." Eden's tone was low; she was probably in the exam room.

"No problem. I'm here, but we can get together tomorrow if that's better for you." Now that Eden was over halfway, things were moving along quickly. As her belly grew, so grew Layla's excitement. She rubbed at her neck to loosen the day's strain she felt bunched there. One of her coworkers had quit yesterday, doubling her current workload until they were able to fill the vacancy. Maybe she would be better off going home and drinking a big glass of wine in her bathtub.

"I'm sure you don't want to sit there and wait. It's up to you. You can meet me at that restaurant we like. The one across from the hospital."

From the corner of her eye, she saw Ben's truck rush past her car; driving way too fast, it bucked over the curb and jerked to a stop just outside the closed garage. Layla was holding her breath, sure the careening truck was going to slam into the garage door; her hand hovered over the door handle, ready to jump out, but she stopped herself.

"Layla?"

"That sounds good. Thirty minutes?" Either Eden didn't notice, or she didn't mention the tremor in Layla's voice. It was on the tip of her tongue to mention Ben's sudden arrival, but she didn't. What was he doing home so early?

"I hope I'm out of here by then."

"I'll keep the seat warm."

"You're too dammed good to me."

"See you soon."

Layla's eyes were riveted to the truck, phone still at her ear, when the door flung open, and Ben staggered out. His fingers nudged the door closed, but it didn't latch and popped back open about an inch. It went unnoticed as he moved to the front door, where after an agonizing attempt to unlock it several times, he was finally successful and disappeared inside. He must be drunk. Had he seen her siting out front? She wasn't sure if he would approach her or not if he had.

Layla continued to watch the house; its two-story white brick exterior shone in the sunlight, and the lake was the sparkling backdrop of an expansive green lawn that rolled down to the water's edge. The sun dipped behind the house, darkening the windows with shadows.

As she started the car and pulled her seatbelt on, she watched a light on the second floor turn on. It was the baby's room. Layla had never seen Ben go inside it, but perhaps that was because he was never home on her frequent visits.

His shadow filled the doorway, and she reached into her glove compartment to retrieve her binoculars. She scanned the neighborhood to see if anyone was watching her. This was different than watching him at Malinda's house. It was broad daylight, and these people knew who she was.

Seeing no one, she lifted the binoculars to her eyes, and Ben's features came into focus. His twisted sneer scanned the pale gray walls and animal prints Eden had bought off Etsy. He lurched into the room, and his head jerked from left to right before settling on the dresser. With one swift move, he knocked the sound machine, changing pad and lamp off the wood surface. His mouth hung open in a shout or howl.

What was he doing?

She watched as he turned toward the glider, yanked it onto its side, and kicked at it like a wild animal. He was destroying the baby's room. Gooseflesh rose on her arms and the base of her neck tingled. He began flipping the animal prints off the wall with a flick of his hand. It looked as though he was talking, but he was still alone in the room. Thank God Eden wasn't home. She cringed to think of what he might do to her if she were there. Stumbling toward the door again, he threw it open with such force that the doorknob jammed into the drywall. She had never seen Ben lose his cool before. The short episode made her want to look Eden over for bruises or scars. It had never even crossed her mind that he might be violent.

Tossing the binoculars onto the passenger seat, she put her car into gear, rushing away from that house and the animal that lived inside.

* * *

Eden entered the restaurant forty minutes after their call looking harried but glowing.

"Sorry." She planted a kiss on Layla's cheek and took a seat. "What's up?" she asked.

Layla was never very good at hiding her emotions, mainly because she didn't try. She'd learned long ago her feelings were worth sharing with the world around her—good, bad, or indifferent.

"La—" Eden began, but Layla cut her off.

Ben's actions tonight were unacceptable in Layla's opinion. She understood why Eden avoided talking about Ben with her —Layla could be pushy about the choices Eden made—but how could she not mention the bizarre behavior she'd just witnessed?

"What's going on between you and Ben? What's happened to him?"

"What do you mean?" She looked puzzled as she stared back at Layla. Was she ignorant, or was she only ignoring his behavior?

"Does he hit you?" Layla reached a hand across the table and cupped it over Eden's.

"What? No." Eden pulled her hand back, and it sank under the lip of the table. "Where is all this coming from?"

"I was waiting for you to come home, and Ben showed up. He was plastered and—" She paused, looking around the restaurant, expecting the server back at any moment. "I just watched him destroy the baby's room."

Eden's face paled, and her hand flew up to cover her heart.

"There's something very wrong with that man," Layla warned. "I'm worried about you and the baby."

"We'll be fine. I'm sure he's—"

"Just what? Venting?" Layla snapped. That was no environment to bring a baby into.

"I should go." Eden rose from her seat and, without another word, rushed out the front door. She was cradling her belly as she muttered, "Went too far." A fearful expression on her face.

# Chapter 19

Eden

30 days until review hearing

After her last session with Doc Jones, Eden couldn't stop thinking about the letter, about Gilmore's threats, about her situation which seemed impossible to navigate. She had come to two possible conclusions: someone was framing her to make her look dangerous, or the worst-case scenario—she wrote those letters and had no memory of doing so. If that was the case, Eden herself had no idea what she was capable of.

Jenkins walked Eden to the rear of the visitors center and into a small fenced in area where Layla waited for her. The late spring morning was warm, signaling summer's fast approach. Chaz had made a point of bringing the topic up three times at dinner last night. It was his favorite season and would allow him and some of the more docile residents to get outside. It was better than listening to Jinx talk about her mystery man, which frequently caused her to become irritated.

Layla stood from the bench where she waited and greeted Eden with a wide smile. Her arms were empty—no Finn again. She'd assumed he wouldn't be here, but the quick slash of disappointment assured her she had harbored some hope.

"Hi," Eden said as she approached.

"Every time I see you, you're looking better and better." Layla pulled her into a firm embrace. The spring jacket Layla wore crinkled with the hug, and Eden detected the delicate scent of baby soap.

"Thanks. A day feels like an eternity here." Eden looked back at her ward, the morning sun glancing off the beaten brick face as other residents scattered along the path in its crouching shadow.

Both women sat on the bench. "How are things? Are you still with that doctor lady you don't like?" Layla asked.

"No, actually. They told me yesterday they're moving me to a different doctor."

Layla's eyes grew wide. "Really? Why are they moving you?"

"I think she might have asked Doc Lucas because he needed help with one of his patients, and she knows someone that knows me. That's what she told me, anyways." Eden had a sneaking suspicion that Jinx might be the other patient. It was clear Jinx had an unhealthy infatuation with Doc Lucas, and he might very well be the mystery man she was so fond of mentioning.

"That's good. I'm glad. Who's the new doctor?" Layla asked, head cocking to one side. "Maybe things will move a bit quicker with them. Finn needs his mom back."

"I know. That's what I was telling Doc Jones, but she disagreed." A warm breeze picked up her hair and she tamped it down. "His name's Doc Lucas."

"Disagreed with what? That Finn needs his mom back?" Layla asked.

"No—not exactly. She wanted to know why I wasn't considering Olivia as a temporary guardian rather than you." There was a long pause as Eden pulled out a piece of bread she'd squirreled away in her pocket from breakfast and began littering it onto the ground. Several small birds flew down to feed, and Eden watched them.

"Did she mention why?" Layla's brow pulled down.

"I'm not sure. Maybe she believes that family is automatically entitled to custody." Though she had never said that, Eden assumed Doctor Jones was always on the opposite side of an argument that she was.

Any time Olivia popped up in her mind, she felt a wild frustration. And that led her back to the note Doc Jones had showed her yesterday. Was it possible she could have written it? Did she want to kill Olivia? She shook her head.

"What is it?" Layla asked.

"It's nothing. Just Olivia," Eden said as she watched Layla's hand twist around a gold necklace lying over her shirt. "We have to make sure she doesn't get Finn."

Layla looked around and back at Eden. "What do you have in mind?"

Eden felt her heart speed up at the seriousness displayed in Layla's face. Would she be on board with whatever Eden suggested? Even if people got hurt?

"I was thinking of money—quickest way to her heart," Eden said.

An orderly began walking toward them, lingering around patients, watching them. Layla leaned toward Eden. "Money might work."

Eden waited for the orderly to move on before she spoke. "I don't know what the doctor was thinking. She's never met

Olivia, and I don't think she likes me." Eden needed to let it go. Stop assuming the outcome of a case she prayed would never take place. She still had time, months in fact. She tried to tell herself she'd be out of here by then.

"How's Finn?" Eden's voice bathed in admiration and a touch of sadness. *How's my son?*

"He's doing well. He misses you." Layla's hands were restless in her lap. "Everything will be ready for when you're released. We'll live together in my new house."

"I heard!" Eden tugged on Layla's arm. "You made the plunge to single-family."

"Yeah. It feels almost normal again." Layla smiled. "I just need you back."

"Soon. That last visit was just a hiccup, but as long as you have Finn, I'm going to focus on getting better."

Willie sat at a nearby table, and his eyes blinked over at them.

"Are you still hearing voices?" Layla asked. The words came out awkward, as if she didn't want to say them.

Embarrassment flooded her even though she knew it shouldn't.

"No—not really." The truth was she wasn't sure what was real and what wasn't sometimes since they kept changing her medication, but it was manageable. Without knowing the standard for her release, she needed to do whatever she could to be normal again. Whatever normal was, it wasn't hearing voices; she knew that.

"That's good. Now that you have a new doctor, I'll put in a good word for you," Layla said with a wink.

Jinx shuffled along the sidewalk next to an orderly. Her eyes caught Eden's and she slowly began shaking her head. Eden looked away.

"There is something," Layla said reluctantly.

"What is it?"

"It's Olivia." Layla reached for both of Eden's hands and pulled them into hers. "I didn't bring this up last time because of how the last visit ended, and I didn't want to upset you further."

The sun glared off the water, and Eden squinted while throwing the last piece of bread onto the ground. She wished she could fly away like the birds who hopped in the grass, feeding happily.

"Did they tell you she's staying at your house?" Layla swallowed with effort.

"I heard." Eden didn't understand that part of the legal system, but knew Lauren was attempting several avenues of recourse.

"And..."

"And she stopped by a few times to see Finn." Layla's eyes fell away guiltily. "She told me someone from social services asked her if she wanted custody of Finn right after, ya know, the Ben thing."

"What?" This was the first time Eden was hearing about social services' offer to Olivia. Lauren should have told her about this.

"He's your son. I'm only his temporary guardian. I don't know what I'm allowed to do." She waved her hands in the air toward Eden's ward. "What authority do I have to keep her away?"

Eden filled her lungs. The truth was she didn't know; she was trying to keep her head above water in here. She would be sure to ask Lauren at their next meeting. Between Gilmore's attack and Jinx's odd behavior, she was too distracted to develop a plan to deal with Olivia, but now she would have to. And why hadn't Kendrick gotten back to her yet? It had been four days since she'd called and left him a message to come visit her. She would need his expertise in fixing Olivia.

"I'll talk with Jacob. He's the GAL," Eden said. "It can't be in Finn's best interest to have so much tension around him." Eden chose to adopt Jacob's favorite buzz phrase, *in Finn's best interest*. For just a moment, she glimpsed into what life would be like if Olivia were to prevail. It was an ugly, frightening thought. All love and affection withheld from Finn during the most crucial time in his life. To think of Finn being a pawn for money was terrifying. For all communication with her son to have to go through that woman was unthinkable.

"It would be different if I had custody, I think. I'm just his guardian."

"As far as I'm concerned, he's yours as long as I'm in here. You're making all the choices for him, not Olivia," Eden said fiercely.

Layla nodded. "I'm trying. It's not easy. I wish you were with us like we always planned."

Eden reached out and hugged her, pulling her in like a lifeline. "You're too good to me."

"It's just...you should see her when she drops by. She ignores Finn and sits on her phone half the time. Asking me not-so-subtly how much you're paying me to take care of him." Layla's cheeks flushed red.

A cloud moved over the sun, casting them in shadow.

"This wasn't how I pictured things would be." Layla sniffled and whipped away a tear.

"I know. Me either." Eden said. "We'll be fine. It's just a season. They've got me on the right medications now." It seemed surreal that they might one day let her walk out the front gate after she'd stabbed her husband to death.

"They did that before, too," Layla whispered. Eden

watched as Layla bit down on her lip suddenly considering her words.

"Before?" Something plunked into the water beyond them followed by a group of birds scattering into the air above them.

"You don't remember my first visit, do you?" Layla frowned. "Right after your arrest."

Eden shook her head. She had no clear recollection for some time after being found in that store.

"You were like you are now. You looked better; you were talking normally. You said you didn't hear the voices anymore, and then bam—" She struck her thigh with her palm, causing Eden to jerk back. "You—"

"I what?" Eden interrupted. Sweat gathered at the rim of her jumper and behind her ears.

"I don't know. You just started yelling, and when they came to get you, you were hitting them, telling them you would kill them and—"

"And what?" She considered the note that was given to Doc Jones, so ominous and filled with hatred. She couldn't forget who she was. The facts, when gathered, gave a clear picture of Eden Wyatt. *I am a mother. I am a survivor. I am a killer.*

"You said you would rather see Finn dead than lose him."

"No." She gasped, shifting back from Layla and her words. That couldn't be true; she wouldn't hurt Finn. Layla was a liar, and for a moment, she hated the woman—her friend the liar.

"Don't you remember the night you gave him to me? The night before you killed Ben?" Layla crying now, body shaking. "I don't blame you after what he did to you."

His daughter—and the paper trail she found that lead to his ultimate betrayal. The decision he made that ripped her heart out.

"You begged me to take Finn with me that night. You told me you would rather see Finn dead than with Ben."

"I wasn't well." Eden jerked up from the bench and looked around, feeling eyes on her. Panic filling her up like a glass of water, to the brim and rolling over the edges with nowhere to go.

"You told me you were going to kill him if I didn't take him away." She was pleading with Eden now, pleading for her to remember.

Eden's hands slammed over her ears. "Shut up. Shut the hell up." She was yelling now, and everyone was looking at her. The movement startled her as Jenkins hurried to them. How dare Layla do this to her? She must have misinterpreted what Eden was doing that night; she must have.

"It's not your fault," Layla begged. "It wasn't you—you're sick."

Eden closed her eyes and began to count slowly in her head, letting the calm pour in over her, but it was too late. She felt fingers wrap around her wrist. Jenkins looked between the two women.

"Is everything okay here?"

"I think she's having an episode." Layla stood. "I'm going to go."

"No—wait." She tried to pull away from Jenkins to reach for Layla, who was backing away, eyes wide; fearful.

"I'm okay. I'm getting better every day," she said, but her voice was too loud; she was screaming—a disturbing sound.

# Chapter 20

Layla
Before

en was absent when Layla arrived to pick Eden up at the house. It would seem Eden's ignorance was willful. When Layla asked her about Ben's rampage, Eden had explained that the nursery incident was due to his anger over a lost mediation job fueled by too much alcohol. No big deal, she had said. But it was. What would he do with a colicky baby if he had no coping skills for such rage? From infidelity to violence, it would appear Eden was willing to forgo common sense and rationality. But why? Was Ben holding some dark secret over her head?

Layla had arrived at Eden's house twenty minutes earlier. Now she sat at the island as Eden looked up from packing her bag.

"It's a boy," Eden announced with a beaming smile. Layla stared for a moment too long; she had been sure it was a girl.

"What! A boy. Congratulations." She looked at the ultrasound picture as Eden held it out. Why was she disappointed? She'd been unaware of any expectations she had until Eden's announcement.

"Yup, those are the boys right there," Layla joked at the circled genitals. "I thought you were going to wait to find out?" Layla's dream had been to learn the sex of her child at delivery. How exciting it would have been for her and Todd—except there was no baby, and never would be.

Eden gathered her bags for the parenting class that Ben had begged off. So, here Layla was, ready to fill in. She didn't mind. It was this or feed the fish or think about finally doing the dishes. It was harder and harder to go home to her depressing apartment each night. To the point that she had reached out to a realtor to find a house. It was time to move on.

"Ben wanted to know," Eden said, her eyes shifted away.

"He went to the ultrasound appointment?" Layla asked, shocked. As far as she was aware, Ben hadn't gone to any of the baby's appointments, claiming it was a waste of time for both of them to be there. He would have to take off too much work. She knew he was still seeing Malinda. She felt bad about breaking her promise to Eden, but she was obsessed with these diseased relationships.

"Yes. He went," Eden said, but Layla knew she was lying.

"Why are you lying to me?"

A kiss of color stained Eden's cheeks as she moved toward the door, trying to escape Layla's stare.

"We're going to be late, and someone has to put the diaper on the doll," Eden announced.

* * *

"I know you're lying to me," Layla continued when they were in the car. She wanted to drop the subject, but she needed answers; something had to break this stalemate they found themselves in. Eden searched for music, intent on ignoring her until finally, she spoke.

"Okay. Fine. Ben didn't go to the appointment with me. I went alone. Is that what you wanted to hear?"

"No. It doesn't make me happy to see you stay with him, but I don't want you to feel like you have to lie to me either." Layla shut the radio off. "You can tell me anything; you know that."

Eden considered what Layla had said but didn't respond.

"I've been following him." The words burst out of Layla's mouth. She kept her eyes on the road, unable to look over at the passenger seat where she could sense Eden's fury. Tension grew with the silence, and her fingers twisted against the leather-wrapped wheel, bracing.

"Stop the car!" Eden demanded. "I asked you to leave it alone."

"He's still seeing her." Layla didn't have the luxury of tact at this point. Eden was already furious with her. Now that Layla had finally made her confession, she didn't feel any better: it was just as bad as she thought it was going to be. Maybe even worse, because she knew Eden had told her not to, and now, she was betraying her trust for a second time.

"Take me back home," Eden snapped.

"I'm sorry—"

"Are you? I don't think you are. Why do you care if my husband is running around on me? How does that affect you in your little bubble?"

Layla resented the insinuation that she was isolated from grief, from betrayal, but she

considered what Eden had said. Why did she care what Ben did if Eden didn't care? She couldn't fix the world. She couldn't even seem to fix her own problems. But she felt she owed Eden her loyalty even when it was something Eden chose to ignore. Deep down, she knew it was because she wanted Eden to leave Ben, and Layla would be there for her when she did.

She pulled the car to the side of the road as the truck behind them honked. They were only three blocks from Eden's house, and she began gathering her bags and pushed the passenger door open, prepared to walk back home.

"Please, don't do this. I'm sorry. I can't stand that you're with him after everything he's done to you. I shouldn't have been following him after you asked me not to. I don't know why I did it." It was the truth, bare and unhelpful.

"I know who I married. It's you who has no idea about him."

"Why are you staying with him?" Layla's voice was on the edge of yelling. She wanted to understand what was going on. Something had come between her and her friend since Eden had come back from Miami. Things had changed.

"I want to make him pay." Eden's shoulders rolled forward as she stared out the front window.

"Pay for what? How?"

"It doesn't matter anymore—he's leaving me." Eden's words were so quiet that Layla found herself leaning forward, all the fight seeping from her. Layla swallowed down the memory of Olivia at the poolside and what she had said. It had been a long time coming, and Layla felt sick to think that Ben wasn't just screwing Malinda—that he might actually love her.

"Leaving you?" Layla said, disbelieving. "Why didn't you tell me?"

"Why didn't you tell me you were following him?"

"I don't know. I guess I didn't want you to be mad at me." Was that the truth, though? "Stay," Layla said while reaching for Eden's hand.

After a long moment, Eden pulled her leg back inside and drew her bags onto her lap.

"I haven't figured out what I'm going to do. I don't have a job, and Ben's hired an excellent attorney, Lauren Ross," Eden said, deflated. "He said he's just waiting until the baby's born, then it's over." Tears were streaming down her face now. "He's moved most of his things out of the house. Said he's going to sell it."

"Oh, sweetie." Layla pulled her in for a hug. "You have me. You and the baby will come to stay with me."

"In your tiny apartment?" Eden laughed.

"I have some money saved, cuz; what the hell am I gonna spend money on?" Layla said. "I'm already talking to a realtor. And when you two get on your feet, you can move on."

Eden nodded her head. "I'm sorry. I should have told you."

"You need to take him to the cleaners. For an eleven-year marriage and his cheating—he has a daughter to prove it."

There was a long stretch of silence while Eden took several deep breaths.

"Can I ask you something?" Layla said. "I've been wondering for a little while now."

Reluctantly, Eden smiled. "Sure."

"What happened in Miami?"

Eden turned to her and lied for the third time. "Nothing happened. Why do you ask?"

*   *   *

After Layla got home from the parenting class, she tossed her bag onto the battered coffee table facing the brightly lit fish tank. She dropped some food in and pulled out the baby shower planner she had purchased. She was never this person who bought a planner for a party. But then again, she'd never been asked by anyone to plan a baby shower for them. Colored tabs separated the items, baby games, food, and guest list.

Grabbing a beer from the fridge, she took a seat in the well-worn La-Z-Boy. She realized how badly she needed a new place as she glanced around. How had she fallen into this trap? Life had just seemed to settle into a routine, and she forgot about having fun, living life, and, maybe most important, love. She loved Eden like a sister. While it was true she had a brother, they barely talked, and she had herself to blame for that one. She should reach out to Richard—reconnect. She brushed the idea off as quickly as it arrived. She needed to get this shower done; then she could think about her issues.

She pulled the organizer open to the guest list and found Ruby Milton's address and phone number listed first. She checked the clock: 8:30 pm. She dialed her number.

"Hello," said a gravelly voice.

"Hi. Is this Ruby?"

"Yes."

"It's Layla. We met at Eden's house." Layla felt the familiar sense of guilt as she was again prying into Eden's life. Wasn't that what true friends did, even when it was unwelcomed?

"Oh, yes. From the dinner, right?" Ruby said warmly.

"Yes. we met there."

"How are you? Is everything okay with Eden?" Ruby's voice was suddenly concerned.

"Yes. Everything's fine. I'm calling to ask you for some shower ideas. What you think Eden might like."

Ruby immediately warmed and began reciting all of Eden's favorite things. When there was finally a break in the conversation, Layla said, "She told me she came to see you this past summer. How was her visit?"

There was a pause, dead air on the line. Had Layla made a mistake?

"Yes. She came here for about a month if I recall."

A month—that wasn't right. How sharp was Ruby's memory? Eden was gone for three months.

"What did the two of you do?"

Another pause.

"She wasn't herself. She just stayed around the condo. She usually needs rest after an episode." An episode? "I think she and Ben might have been having some issues—she wouldn't take his calls all month."

"Ruby, what do you mean, episode?"

There was a deep breath over the line. "Eden has episodes of mania. It hasn't happened in years, but I don't think I'd ever seen her that bad before. She usually takes medication, but she told me she stopped taking it when they were trying to have a baby."

Layla considered Eden's brazen change after returning from Florida. Having sex with Ben while Layla waited on the porch, the wild mood swings, the destruction of the cake. After the fact, Layla should have recognized that her friend's behavior was not merely mood swings, but a mood disorder.

"Was everything okay—did something happen during her visit?" Layla blurted.

"I think you should ask her that."

# Chapter 21

Eden

28 days until review hearing

Compared to the peaceful silence of her room, the day room was a cacophony of noises, voices, and frenzied motions. Perhaps it was because she'd spent the last two days in her room. After Layla's visit, she couldn't summon the energy or the drive to pretend with these people. Jinx and Chaz were already holed up at their usual table when she arrived. Gilmore slunk away to join the other orderlies posted in a corner, talking among themselves as if there wasn't chaos all around them. Gilmore made plenty of space on their short walk, and she couldn't help but think he was up to something, plotting. Two can play that game, she thought bitterly.

"There she is," Jinx cooed and patted the vacant seat next to her. Eden sat wordlessly. Today was a bit of a struggle. She had searched her journal for any signs of new writing, worrying the stiff pages with her fingers—there was nothing out of place. She kept assuring herself Gilmore was the one setting her up with the notes, but she wasn't convinced. He was absent the day someone from the staff had given Doc Jones the forged message—someone else was trying to make her look dangerous. It was either that or she had to come to terms with the possibility that she'd actually written them.

This morning her relief was short-lived due to her agitation and lack of sleep. Her legs felt heavy, and her eyes burned from the sunlight streaming through the wide window. The voices around her, although loud, were incoherent and almost frantic.

"You look like hell," Jinx said, almost giddy.

Eden smiled as though Jinx had paid her a compliment, too exhausted to participate. She needed a way to steer the conversation to what she wanted to tell Jinx, but she had to be patient. Someone as smart as Jinx would see through what she was doing.

"She's right," Chaz said, but wasn't even looking at Eden. His shoulders pulled back near his ears as he looked around the half-full room, forever scanning. Two card games were running, if one could call it that, and several residents were leaning in their chairs as though they had fallen asleep in mid-sentence. Others paced the floor, muttering loudly.

"Yes. She usually is," Eden said. Jinx smiled back at her, but it wasn't warm. Her eyes were reading the lines on Eden's face as if they were telling her something. This was a trait of Jinx's that always unnerved Eden. Doc Lucas's deep voice moved down the hallway past the day room. Jinx's head snapped to the sound.

"I can't believe what they're doing to me," Jinx snarled.

Eden focused on the palms of her hands as they rested on the table. She refused to meet Jinx's gaze, sensing the woman was keen on her discomfort and somehow seemed to taste it—like a fine wine or a good dinner.

"I don't think she knows, Jinx. They had to drug her the last two days," Chaz said.

How did everyone seem to know about her? As she collected the images of half-functioning adults, she wondered why Chaz and Jinx were so different. Was it possible they were faking it? Sometimes she felt like she was faking it. Shouldn't all these people, including herself, be in prison for life rather than in a hospital?

"Is it that stupid friend of yours? Every time she visits, you end up flipping out. I can tell this about people," Jinx bragged as she slumped back in her seat, one arm hanging down. "She's playing you like a whore." Jinx snorted a laugh, proud of her dig.

"You don't even know her," Eden snapped, realizing only too late that defending Layla would only make Jinx increase her attacks.

"Can we talk about me for a minute?" Jinx asked. Chaz sighed from his seat, apparently not welcoming the change of subject.

"Sure." Eden twisted her fingers in her lap—she needed to get Jinx to bring up Gilmore, or at the least Doc Lucas.

"They moved me to Doc Jones." Her voice dripped with disgust, eyes narrowed at Eden. "I think they know what's going on with the good doctor and me."

It was definitely Doc Lucas, then. The real question now was, was there any truth to what Jinx hinted at—an inappropriate relationship? If so, Eden's plan to get rid of Gilmore once and for all would probably work.

"I think they know what's going on between us, and they want to keep us apart."

Eden's heart beat fast. She could feel Jinx's eyes searching for the truth in Eden's face. It wasn't her fault the doctors had switched them—did Jinx know Eden was the patient she was traded with?

Eden cleared her throat. "Really?" She frowned, hiding her giddiness at the all-too-perfect setup. "It's funny that you mention that because I heard someone talking to Doc Lucas in the hallway on my way to meet Doctor Jones the other day."

"Who?" Jinx's eyes were wide, and she snatched Eden by the hand.

"Gilmore." Eden's eyes shifted around the room, searching him out, but he must have slunk away. Eden nodded gravely at Jinx, who watched her. Jinx was suspicious enough to pull the picture together, but maybe Eden needed to be more direct. "He's telling them all about how much you love Doc Lucas, how unbalanced you are." Eden frowned as if to telegraph that she herself didn't believe this.

Jinx shifted forward so fast Eden flinched back in her chair. "Why would he do that?" It was an accusation more than it was a question, but Jinx's eyes floated away as she thought about what Eden had said. Chaz's mouth dropped open—a worried expression on his gaunt face. Eden willed him not to say anything that might contradict her.

"But why the hell would Gilmore throw me under the bus like that?" She was whining now. "I promised I wouldn't say anything —" Jinx gasped, and her fingers curled around the lip of the table.

"Promised what?" Eden asked. Her heart began to pound harder—had Gilmore done something to Jinx too?

Jinx appraised her for a moment. "Nothing. Don't worry about it. It's best to steer clear of that perv if you can." She winked at Eden, and a flush of heat moved up Eden's neck.

There was a pregnant silence as they looked between each other, and Eden felt they might be enemies—she couldn't tell.

"Eden." Someone called her name from across the room

and inwardly she groaned. No—this couldn't be happening, not now. "Eden."

Jinx's jaw muscles tensed as Doc Lucas made his way to their table.

"Ready to go?" he asked her as she stood on wobbly legs.

"Yes," Eden stammered and moved to his side. She pictured Jinx rising to follow them out of the room, a crazed, jealous look in her eye, a knife clutched in her hand. When she looked back over her shoulder twice, Jinx was only smiling and waving goodbye, but she caught Chaz's horrified expression as he looked between the two women. She hadn't dared to tell Jinx about Doc Lucas, and now she realized that had been a big mistake.

*　*　*

"Have a seat," Doc Lucas said with a wave of his hand. She sat on the soft leather sofa facing his desk and a single chair, where he sat. She was surprised at how quickly she'd been moved to Doc Lucas.

His office was so much different from Doc Jones's. Instead of certificates and accolades, his had children's drawings. The soft scent of sandalwood lingered in the air.

"You have children?" Her eyes shot to his ring finger but found it bare.

"These are patients' drawings." He delicately avoided answering her question.

This office felt warmer, not as sterile as Doc Jones's, and Eden knew she was talking to someone who cared. He crossed his jean-clad legs and smiled.

"How are you today?" he asked.

She nodded. "I'm okay."

"Are you sleeping?"

She almost gasped when she thought of how she must look. Had she even run a brush through her hair? She pulled her long dark hair past her shoulders and smoothed her oversized jumper down her belly.

"I'm having a little trouble sleeping," she said to excuse her appearance. "I wasn't expecting to have an appointment so early."

"It's okay, Eden. As you know, Doc Jones and I have decided I will be your primary doctor, and I didn't get a chance to tell you before now, but I'm under the impression she mentioned this new arrangement with you."

"Yes, she did." She looked up to see his unerring stare, and a stirring began in her gut.

"Okay. Because this is our first meeting, I'd like to hear about you."

When she finally spoke, it felt like the first words she'd spoken in months, or maybe it was what she said that was like the breath from an unearthed coffin. "I'm here because I killed my husband eleven months ago." The words sank into her as though she'd never considered them before now.

"No. I want to know about you, Eden. I know why you're here."

"Oh, okay." She was fumbling now. "I'm a—was a teacher up until about two years ago. When Ben and I first started trying for a baby, I had too much stress, and seeing those kids every day—" She crossed her legs at her ankles and watched as his eyes flicked down to catch the motion.

There was a long pause. She didn't want to talk about Ben. "I'm adopted."

"Let's talk about that." Doctor Lucas perked up. "Do you get along with your adoptive parents?"

"Just me and my mom. Yes, I love her very much. She was an older woman when she adopted me." Eden found herself rubbing her belly, a habit she'd fallen into since pregnancy; she clung to the comfort it offered her. It was as if she associated any good thing with Finn.

"She's nearly eighty now and in poor health. She wanted to come up for Finn's birth, but I told her we would come see her once Finn was settled." If she had let her mother visit, would that have changed anything? Ruby wouldn't have let her do anything so terrible. She would have found a way to stop Eden. Like she had in Miami. She recalled the tear-filled reunion at the hospital when her mother came to get her. The breathy confession she'd made. And like all bad things Eden had done, Ruby forgave her again, bringing her back from the edge.

"Do you remember giving birth to Finn?" Doc Lucas asked, intruding on her memory.

Eden's fingers grasped her ankle and pulled it toward herself like she was stretching. "Not really. I know Layla was there, and I think I remember seeing him for the first time." She let out a breath. "Is this normal? My memory gaps."

Doc Lucas's head tilted to the side as he spoke. "I've worked with several women who have either suffered from postpartum depression or psychosis. It's normal to have lapses in memories when there is a break from reality. According to my notes—" He skimmed through some papers. "It looks like there's a witness statement in the file that said you were exhibiting symptoms of paranoia, sleeplessness, and delusions."

"Witness?"

"There were some officers' statements from the day of your detention, a few patrons in a grocery store, and a family friend." He listed them off without giving her any names. Who was the family friend? It couldn't be Olivia; she was family. Eden wanted to ask but didn't want to bring attention to her obsession with her sister-in-law. It was better to deal with Olivia directly and keep conversations regarding her to a minimum.

"I don't remember any of that stuff. I think it was a while before I even knew I was in jail—" She squinted as if physically looking into her past but finding nothing—just a void.

"I'm going to give you a sleep aid."

She opened her mouth to object, but before she could, he held up a hand. "Eden, I can tell you haven't gotten any sleep. This isn't a setback; it's a step forward. Have you ever heard the term 'sleep begets sleep?' Your body is stressed, and it's going to trigger another break."

"Another one? But..."

"Yes. You are at risk, and you need to learn to manage this, not run from it. Not fake it 'til you make it."

Her guilt caused her to drag her eyes to the ground.

"Out of all the women I've worked with in similar situations, they're all different. I can't tell you when you're going to get better, but if you work with me and take my advice, I'm sure you'll make it. I know you miss your son, and I want to get you back to him as soon as possible." He smiled.

"Why do I feel like I'll never get out of here?" She felt the shift then. The walls were moving inward, her lungs too small to hold any of the breath she desperately needed. Would she always be a risk to Finn? Layla's declaration came back to her. *You said you would rather see Finn dead than lose him.* Now Doctor Lucas said the monster was still inside of her, ready and waiting for a moment of weakness to take over her again.

He was next to her then. She felt the sag of the cushion and his hands pressed to her cheeks, as a man might embrace a woman before a kiss, but her mind was sluggish, and she didn't understand what was happening. She could smell his soap, and his hands were soft against her cheeks; she heard his voice, a far-off sound, calling to her.

"Look at me. Breath. Big breath." He demonstrated an

exaggerated breath. He didn't look scared or even anxious. She followed his directions.

Sights and sound began to come back into focus, and she was staring into his eyes. It was so intense; she couldn't look away. She wanted to lean into him, kiss his lips, feel his arms around her and welcome the comfort it would bring. He must have interpreted the desire written on her features because a moment later his hands dropped away, leaving a void behind.

"Are you okay?" he asked, not moving from her side while still managing to create distance from her.

"Yes." She was breathless.

"Good." He frowned. "I would hate to have you faint on our first visit."

"I—"

A knock sounded from the door, startling them both, and he stood.

"One moment." He strode toward the door, and Eden dropped her eyes as she continued to ease her breaths in and out. She tried to ignore the attraction she felt for him—it wasn't right. He was her doctor, but she couldn't help herself.

The door squeaked, and she heard Jinx's voice from the hallway, muffled but recognizable.

"I need to see you," she pleaded. "Please. I need you back. I can't work with Doc Jones, and we have something—special."

"You need to go back to your room or the day room. Where's Gilmore?"

"I'll let you do whatever you want," she said. "I'll let you—"

"That's enough. I'm no longer treating you. You're with Doc Jones now," he snapped. "Gilmore." Eden heard heavy steps on the floor, running toward them. "Take Ms. Nelson to her room, please."

*I'll let you do whatever you want.* Had she said that or was Eden hearing things? If Doc Lucas was the mystery man, then was Jinx telling the truth that they were involved in some sort of affair? Jinx cussed, and there were shouts and muffled thumps. "You can't do this. You can't make me fall in love with you and then get rid of me—" Her voice cut off as if silenced.

Several moments later, Doc Lucas returned. He took his coat off and threw it over the back of the desk chair as though he'd forgotten she was there. When he turned abruptly to see her on the couch, his cheeks were red.

"I'm sorry you had to hear that, Eden. We'll pick this up again on Wednesday." She had never seen him look so flustered before. She stood and moved quickly to the door.

"I'll go then," she mumbled, and when he didn't reply, she let herself out into the now empty hallway. Jinx knew Eden was here, and therefore wanted her to hear her accusations. Was it possible she was trying to warn Eden?

# Chapter 22

Layla
Before

Two days after her conversation with Ruby, she had a newfound determination to find out what was going on with Eden. Why hadn't Eden told Layla she had a mood disorder? Did she not trust Layla? She was now sure her friend was probably hiding other things. That was why she found herself outside Eden's house.

The dim light of dawn shrouded her movements as mud clotted against the insoles of her boots, producing a soft sucking sound as she crept alongside the house. The early morning air bit against her exposed skin as she opened the side door into the garage with a key Eden had given her.

Darkness swallowed her, and her heartbeat settled into its normal rhythm. If a neighbor spotted her, she would be fine. She made sure it looked like she belonged here, though she didn't.

Her nerves were strung tight this morning. She had

debated making this stop on her way to work but was overcome with worry. Eden hadn't returned any of her phone calls all week, and she was due soon. So, Layla had parked on the street and watched as Eden left the house, her body hidden under a peacoat and her head smothered by a wool hat. Strands of black hair whipped around silken flesh. Layla had the urge to exit the car—to demand to know what was wrong—but she resisted. Had Ruby mentioned Layla's telephone call to Eden? Layla couldn't let Eden find out she had gone beyond following Ben to actively spying on her.

Maneuvering through the dark garage with the ease of someone who lived there, she took the four short steps to enter the kitchen.

Every dish was in its place in the expansive glass cabinets, and the polished sheen of the subway tiles gleamed under the overhead lights. Fresh flowers placed on the center of the granite countertop added a splash of yellow to the earth tones surrounding them. What an excellent housekeeper Eden was. Layla allowed herself to imagine the three of them living in this house—laughter echoing through its vast, elaborate halls. But it would never happen. Ben was selling the place as soon as Eden had her baby, as far as Layla was aware.

Layla's eyes lingered on a wedding photo. Ben's arms wrapped around his perfect bride. Eden, younger, smiling with bright eyes, was breathtaking. It would have been perfect, but Ben didn't deserve her.

She passed through the hall that connected to the two-story foyer. Her ultimate destination was the long, elegant staircase that climbed to the second floor. The lacquered railing was smooth and cool under her damp palm.

Once at the top of the stairs, she moved to the double doors leading into the master bedroom. The pale blue and beige walls and the cream-colored rug provided a sense of luxury. Not one item seemed out of place. The comforter wrapped the king-sized bed, and an image of Eden and her husband entwined together surged in her head. Ben's head lowered to draw her nipple into his mouth, and her body arched toward him. Then the image morphed into Malinda with Ben. She pinched her eyes shut, trying to squeeze the picture out, but it didn't help.

She entered the walk-in closet, and her hand drifted to Eden's clothes, hanging from the rack. Different textures and fabrics pricked her skin. Soft silks and cashmere, rough wool and tweed.

She looked past clothes and under the boxes of shoes lining the shelves. There was nothing out of the ordinary on Eden's side, but Ben's was sparse. She felt a pang of sadness. Maybe Eden was attempting to cope on her own.

She left the closet and looked through Eden's drawers and nightstand. Nothing that could give her any indication of what was going on. Again, Ben's dresser was half empty. The likeliness of the marital split made her giddy.

She left the room and made her way to the nursery. It was spotless and ready for Finn. That was the name she had chosen. Eden had been beaming when she told Layla.

Everything in his room was as it should be, except for a large hole in the wall behind the door. She recalled the day Ben had torn through the room in a rage and Eden's quick defense of his actions. It wasn't right for her to let such an offense go without repercussions.

She reentered the hallway and wandered down to the other end. The house was familiar to her by now. She had even slept in the guest room on occasions when Ben was out of town and she'd had too much to drink, which at one time was often.

Olivia also stayed in the guest room on her previous visit. Her short stay for the announcement dinner had turned into three weeks of being pampered by Eden's gracious hosting.

At the end of the hall, she opened a door into a room she had never entered. It looked like it was an office or a reading room of sorts. She pushed inside and looked around. Eden had tastefully decorated it in pale teal and gray. Potted succulents lined the shelves, now gathering dust.

This must be where she went to relax. A well-worn chair sat near the window where one could look out on the lake while reading a book.

Sitting on a small table next to the windowsill was a photo album. She pictured Eden up late at night, tears filling her eyes as she tore through the memories of her once-happy marriage. Wishing it could all work out, knowing it wouldn't.

Layla took a seat in the chair and pulled the album onto her lap. The cool faux leather was smooth against the pads of her fingers. Opening the first page, a chill entered the room, and she wanted to throw the book away from herself. The images were disturbing: burned, cut, and marred photos occupied the spaces. Page after page, each more terrible than the last.

A door closed, and the loud echo of shoes on hardwood came from downstairs. She rushed out the door and pulled it shut behind her. Someone was on the stairs, moving in her direction. Her eyes were jumping around to find an escape when Ben's somber face appeared.

"What are you doing here?" His tone was friendly, but his eyes betrayed his suspicion.

She looked down to see that she was still clutching the damned photo album. "Eden asked me to grab some stuff for the baby shower." Had he seen the album? Did he know what was inside?

By the brief dismissal that followed, she assumed he didn't: he forced a smile and looked past her at the closed door. "Okay. I just stopped by to grab some things," he said and walked into the master bedroom. Without a goodbye, she hustled down-stairs and out of the house.

Once in the safety of her car, she set the album on the seat and wondered if Ben and Eden were talking enough these days for word to reach Eden that Layla had stolen her photos. If that's what you could call them. She peered inside the front page again, and it dawned on her for the first time that there might be something very wrong with her friend—she was dangerous. She should warn Ben, she thought, but instead started her car and drove off.

# Chapter 23

Eden
26 days until review hearing

She watched the residents wandering around the yard three floors below her window—none doing anything in particular, just pacing the grass or slumping under the trees. Marsha had left about an hour ago, according to the small cordless clock on her nightstand. She'd brought Eden's medication and asked how she was today. It was clear to the nurse right away that Eden hadn't slept any better last night, even with the assistance of new sleep medication. That was fine with Eden—she was too scared to sleep, knowing Gilmore could come in at any time and touch her. She shuddered when she considered the possibility.

She hummed softly to drown out the thoughts in her head, pulled out her note to herself with the things that she knew to be true, and read it over. She was a mother, she survived, and she was a killer. Last night while lying alone, she'd told herself she wasn't a killer, but it was too late; she knew it was there, written with a shaky hand. She couldn't run from it. If only she could focus on Finn now and not on all the other noise around her.

"Time to go." Gilmore's voice interrupted her thoughts. She jerked her head to the door, but he wasn't standing there. He was only inches behind her, and she hadn't even heard him come in. He reached a hand out to touch her, but she jerked back.

"Don't touch me." Anger thrashed through her, and she kept her eyes trained on him. "Don't you dare touch me ever again."

His mouth dropped open for a split second and shifted just as quickly into a smirk. "You're crazy, lady. I don't know what you think I was doing. It's my job to make sure you get to where you need to go."

"Yes. But it isn't your job to touch me. Ever." She rushed to the door and didn't turn back to him until she was in the hallway. He strolled in her wake, not in any hurry to get her to the visitors center. She didn't wait for him, just kept walking to the stairs.

"I ain't taking the stairs. I walk all over this building all day —I'm not looking to get more exercise."

"She can go down with us." Marsha stood behind them with Larry, a new guy. "We like the stairs, don't we, Larry?" The quiet new arrival nodded at the ground, his eyes wide.

"Whatever—I gotta get to my break anyway." Gilmore stomped off toward the elevator, and Eden took a deep breath as she followed Marsha.

"Thanks." Eden descended the stairs slowly, thinking of Jinx with each new step. Her head peeked down the narrow opening to the series of stairs below. It would be painful to fall down them or be pushed by some psycho. She had stayed in her room yesterday after her appointment with Doc Lucas, afraid of Jinx's wrath, but she knew she would eventually have to face her. The earlier conversation with Chaz came to mind and she wondered what might happen next. She had no proof that Jinx had killed this other resident; Chaz could be trying to get a rise out of her. In which case, the lies Eden had told about Gilmore wouldn't help her. She was counting on Jinx's vindictiveness.

"Eden, hold up a second." Marsha pulled to a stop, and Eden trekked back up three steps to stand in front of the woman, Larry behind her, whistling quietly as his head bobbed gently.

"Is everything okay with Phil?"

"Who's Phil?" Eden asked.

"Gilmore. The orderly that usually walks with you."

"Everything's fine," Eden snapped. "What do you mean?"

Marsha reached out and touched Eden's shoulder. "Has he done something?"

"No—nothing." Eden's eyes flitted away. "I just don't like him." It was the only answer her tired brain could come up with, and she couldn't even manage to make eye contact with Marsha to see if she was buying it or not.

"Okay—you know if something happened, you can tell me, right? No matter what he said."

"What do you mean, no matter what he said?" Eden risked a glance at the nurse.

"If he threatened you," Marsha said point-blank.

Eden shook her head, and they continued in silence until they reached the day room where Marsha dropped Larry off to Lynsi, who put him in front of the TV for *Law & Order*.

As Eden peered inside, Jinx waved to her from next to Chaz. Despite all her fears Jinx looked happy to see her; or was it all an act?

* * *

157

Kendrick's bulky frame stood as she entered the visitors center.

"It's so good to see you." He held out a hand, but she ignored the gesture and hugged him. He smelled like worn leather and mint gum and was no less than two feet taller than she was. His arms swallowed her in a hug, and she felt his chest shake from his soft chuckle.

"It's nice to see you too," Eden said.

They each took a seat. Their table was somewhat secluded, with only two other visitors in the center.

"I'm glad you got my message. I need you for a job. Well, two," Eden began, not knowing how long she would have to explain. When she'd decided to bring Kendrick in on damage control, she was fearful it might be too late. Maybe that was the case, but she had to try and fix the situation before it got worse. She could have quickly done this over the phone, except Jinx had told her they recorded all the calls coming in and out, therefore she wanted to see Kendrick face to face with her request.

Kendrick pulled out a small notebook from his back pocket. He had told her when they first met that it was a habit he had formed when he was a police officer for five years. He quit the force because, in his words, "It's a messed up world we live in." He stumbled into PI work and found that he enjoyed the flexibility and still got to solve some people's problems.

"Whatcha got, girl?" His pen poised.

"I need you to look into my sister-in-law. Her name is Olivia Wyatt, and she lives in Hollywood, California. Lauren told me she's been at my house for the last six months. Something about Ben giving her use of it or some nonsense excuse. Olivia's telling me I have to evict her if I want her gone."

"Then why don't you?" Kendrick asked. "I can't see you having any qualms about that."

"I want her there. It's better I—we—know where she is for now."

"Okay—check out the gold-digger," Kendrick said. "Boy, do I remember her from the last job I did for you." Eden had hired Kendrick to find out if Ben was cheating. He had let her cry on his shoulder the day he delivered the news of Ben's daughter's existence. The moment that shaped her last spiral. "And what's the second one?"

"There's a woman here—Nina Nelson. Just check her out for me. Basic stuff—why she's here," Eden said in a low tone.

"Nina Nelson—" Kendrick clucked his tongue. "Now that's a name I haven't heard in a while." His features took on a sad quality.

"You know her?"

"Yeah. I guess maybe I knew at one point that she was here." He looked around the room as though physically making the connection. "She isn't someone you forget."

"What happened to her? Why is she here?"

"Three years ago, she killed her lover—and I mean she mutilated his ass and abducted the woman who she blamed for the end of their toxic relationship. It was a messy ordeal for a quiet place like Cedar Lake." He shook his head. "She isn't right, and I would steer clear of her if I were you."

"She's from Cedar Lake?" She felt her muscles tighten.

"Yeah. Her whole life."

There was a beat of silence as she thought about what he'd said. She was a killer just like Eden was—Eden couldn't judge her from where she sat.

"There's one more thing." Eden shifted toward him. "About our last job—"

Kendrick nodded.

"I need you to do me a favor and get rid of everything you sent me. Shred, burn, delete and destroy. All the emails, and bank statements. All Ben's paperwork you compiled—the pictures."

"Done."

"And there's a phone and a photo album I need you to get from the house when Olivia isn't there." Eden's hands shook. She couldn't let anyone, especially her sister-in-law, get ahold of them.

He held up his hand, eyes wide. "What are you getting me involved in?"

She felt her frown deepen. "I wouldn't do anything to get you into any trouble—I promise. It's just after you told me about Ben, I was upset. I defaced our wedding album, but I don't want anyone to see it and get the wrong idea." Like think she'd planned on killing her husband all along.

# Chapter 24

Layla
Before

L ayla received Eden's frantic call at 4:00 pm.

"You have to come, please." Eden's voice seemed to carry through gritted teeth.

Shamefully, her first thought was that Eden had killed Ben. An image of her friend standing over her husband's lifeless body flashed in her mind. But it turned out she was in labor. Layla had spoken with Eden only a few times since finding the defaced photo album at her house. The original chilling experience had softened as she considered what Ben had put Eden through. Cheated on her, had a child with another woman. Frankly, Layla felt Ben had gotten off easy, as it now appeared he was having his happily ever after with Malinda while threatening to evict his wife of eleven years soon after she was to give birth. They were just pictures. Eden needed to vent and that's all it was, Layla told herself.

"I've got my bag packed; I have to stop by the house and

grab it. Hang in there, mama. This is the best day of your life."
Their lives. They were in this together.

Ever since their argument on the side of the road, Eden had
made excuses for not getting together, and Layla didn't have the
energy to argue. At least the baby shower had gone off without
a hitch, but they had only seen each other twice since then, and
it was because Layla had found an excuse to drop by and Eden
was too polite to kick her out. This was the bonding experience
that would mend their relationship.

Now, as she took the stairs up to labor and delivery with
Mylar balloons flapping behind her head, she couldn't keep the
grin off her face. Eden would be a mother—it was beautiful,
and Layla was invited to be a part of the occasion. What if Ben
was there? She hadn't seen him since that day in the hall where
she had lied to him and stole Eden's album. She had forced
herself to examine the whole thing and, once she finished,
buried it at the bottom of a closet she never used, trying to
forget the images and how disturbed a person would have to be
to do those things.

When she got to Eden's room, she was propped on her bed,
gripping the rails—with only a nurse in sight. No Ben.

They had talked at length about the birth plan Eden
wanted, but it had already gone sideways. The music Eden had
worked on for months was not playing, and she'd expressly
indicated she wanted a water birth.

"You're doing great," Layla said, automatically throwing
her bag down on the chair and releasing the balloons near the
window. She rushed to Eden's bedside, pulled her hand off the
rail, and held it in hers. "Do you have your music? Did you
bring your plan?"

"No—" Eden grunted past pressed lips.

"It's a big one," the nurse added as she watched the
machine to the right of the bed. Its lines wiggled and peaked on

the screen. Eden's grip tightened, and Layla found herself huffing through the contraction as if it were her own.

"Whatever you want to do," Layla whispered in her ear. "I'm here for you."

Tears rolled down Eden's cheeks, and with her free hand, Layla blotted them away.

"Ben's out of town on business. I think he planned it this way," Eden said once the contraction subsided. Her lower lip trembled, and she looked exhausted.

"How long have you been here?" Layla's tone was chastising.

"Since seven this morning."

"Why didn't you call me?" It was nearly 6:00 pm.

Another contraction began to build, and Eden's face contorted with pain, red and sweat-covered.

"We were going to do the water birth, maybe use the birthing ball..." Layla's voice trailed off as she recognized that her disappointment wasn't helping.

"I was so excited I forgot all about the plan." Eden grunted.

"She's too far gone for that now. Won't be long," the nurse said, smiling.

"Never mind, everything is perfect. You're going to be a mom." Layla brushed Eden's long black hair away from her face and pressed a cold cloth to her forehead.

"Pressure," Eden gasped.

"It's time. I've already paged the doctor," one of the two nurses announced as more staff entered the room in a flurry of activity.

\* \* \*

His scream, she remembered, was the most beautiful sound she had ever heard. She watched the doctor pull him up, his scrunched face red and angry looking. His limbs and head were covered in a fine white film. Eden's hand went limp in hers, and both women looked at each other. Love, so indescribable, filled her until it ran over as she looked between her best friend and her baby. Something she never thought possible after Todd had left her.

"You did it." Layla leaned in and kissed the top of Eden's head. "Congratulations, he's perfect."

"Can I hold him?" Eden reached for him.

One of the nurses swaddled him and placed him on Eden's bare chest. Tears, silky and sparking, coursed down her cheeks. Eden's hand cupped the back of his tiny skull as she gazed down at him. No one deserved it more than Eden, but they were in this together now. Just the three of them.

Eden pulled him to her breast, but he fussed until she settled him on her chest.

"We have to deliver the placenta," the doctor said. "The nurses will need to get him cleaned up and checked out."

"Will you go?" Eden asked. Layla's eyes followed the wrapped baby around the room.

"Yes. Of course," Layla said. Her heart raced as she watched the nurse take Finn. She pulled her phone out and snapped pictures of his weight and size as the nurses recorded them. He was so perfect with his swollen features and plump cheeks. His lips were a small cupid's bow as he pursed them, searching for food. It was a joy; it was agony. Knowing she would never have a child of her own.

When they were finished, she finally gained the courage to ask, "Can I hold him?"

"Yes." The nurse lifted him gently and placed him in Layla's arms. The weight of him was perfect against her ribs, and she gently bounced him. After the doctor was finished, she walked to Eden's bedside.

"Seven pounds eight ounces of perfection," Layla said, enjoying the warmth that was spreading at her side.

Eden's tired eyes gazed over at her, and she smiled.

"Thank you so much for being here. I know I've been a brat," Eden confessed. "It's just this stuff with Ben has me stressed out."

"Shhhh. Let's not ruin this. It's just the three of us now." Layla handed Finn over to Eden's waiting arms. As soon as he was lifted away, she missed the curve of his tiny body next to her. She took a seat in the chair next to the bed and watched while Eden nursed him.

"What's his name?" a nurse asked, setting Eden's paperwork down on the table next to Layla to help Eden find a more comfortable position to nurse.

"Finnigan Wyatt," Eden cooed down at her son, tapping his nose with the tip of her finger.

"Oh, honey. You left this spot blank." The nurse pointed out a space on a page that Layla couldn't read.

"No—it was IVF. Sperm donor." She spoke quietly, her eyes darting away from Layla's as Layla shuffled back from the bed, stunned. Eden never told her she underwent IVF. Had she used an egg donor? Suddenly, Ben's anger made sense. Was it possible she went ahead with IVF without asking Ben, while she was in Florida?

The nurse nodded and took the paperwork with her.

When they were finally alone, Layla asked, "What was that all about? You used an egg donor?"

Eden looked down at Finn, lying in her arms, while shaking her head. "It's Ben. I think you were right. He isn't a good guy. And I'm scared."

"Scared of what?"

"I'm scared that he's going to take him from me—he's going to take my son."

# Chapter 25

Eden

25 days until review hearing

"I miss you, Mom," Eden said. A sigh rumbled over the phone line. It had been far too long since Eden was able to hear her mother's voice, months. She wanted to be with her, snuggled in her heavy embrace. *Do you think your mother's disappointed in you?* "I'm so sorry Mom." Tears slid down her cheeks and she pressed the rough cuff of her sleeve against her eyes.

"I'm sorry. I wasn't there for you when you needed me," came the reply.

Eden was inclined to tell her mother it wasn't her fault, but the words died on her tongue. They would do nothing to appease her mother's irrational guilt.

"So, tell me how you're doing now?" Ruby asked. "How's the treatment—are you getting everything you need to get well?" This seemed like a conversation they'd had many times before—because they had, and anger roiled in her for continuing the dysfunctional cycle. But could she have gotten pregnant with Finn if she had taken her lithium?

"Yes. I have an excellent doctor, and I think I'm improving." It was a hope, but it was what she clung to. Doc Lucas seemed so sure of her success; she allowed herself to hope.

"That's great, Eden. Now, tell me about Finn. And why haven't I gotten any pictures?"

Guilt, immediate and sharp, speared her. She hadn't even thought to send her mother pictures of Finn. Being locked away so consumed her she forgot the world had moved on. All things didn't begin and end at Middle State Psychiatric Hospital.

"I'm sorry—it's just, I'm trying to figure things out," Eden said. "I'll talk to Layla soon and ask her to send some. It's tough to get things done when you're not out and about."

"Don't worry about me. I'll reach out to her. I have her number."

Eden felt a smile pull at her lips. "I love you."

"I love you too, honey. When you get out, consider moving back down here with me." It wasn't a question, it was an option, and Eden had already decided that was what she was going to do. She hadn't shared this with anyone, including Layla, for fear of upsetting things and how they were going, but nothing good had happened in Eden's life since moving to Virginia, and she was more than eager to leave the past in the rearview. She wasn't entirely sure how that would work once she was released —if she would have to check in with someone, like a probationary period.

"Someone came by the house a few weeks ago, looking for Jane—"

Her words echoed over the phone line, and suddenly Eden could feel the humid Miami heat as she'd deplaned. Her heart had skipped as she walked quickly through the terminal to her rental car. While on the plane flying down, she had wondered what she was doing. This was dangerous, but the need would not go away. Ben had done the unthinkable, and she had to make him pay—but under all her seething anger, the excitement seemed to grow, the wild edges of mania had crept over her, and she welcomed it to take the place of her pain.

She had removed the burner phone from her bag and sent the text:

*I'm here—where to meet up?*

Almost immediately, she received a response:

*Lounge 52 @7pm.*

"Are you there?" Her mother's voice brought her back.

"Yeah, I'm here." She took a deep breath. "Who stopped by?"

"He said he was an old friend."

"Old friend?" Eden sat straighter. "Did you recognize him?"

"He was tall, dark hair. He had a nice smile. Handsome. Dressed very nice."

It wasn't surprising that the man didn't tell Ruby who he was. Hell, Eden didn't know his real name—that's what happened when you met someone on the dark web. It was a gamble, but one could find anything from drugs to prostitution to hired killers in the anonymous space of the Tor relay. The man had insisted on vetting her before making the introduction to his boss. But the meeting had never taken place. At 6:30, she had sent a message to the mystery person:

*I can't do this—sorry.*

After sending the message, she had checked into a hotel four blocks from her mother's house.

"I told him I didn't know a Jane, but then I thought about

the nurses at the hospital, and how they started calling you Baby Jane. Are you in trouble, Eden?"

Jane was the name she'd gave herself on the dark web when she communicated with him.

With age came wisdom, and Ruby had no shortage of it.

"I'm fine. Why would you ask that?"

"I'm not sure. He mentioned Finn and wanted to know how you were doing. If you were planning on another visit to the area."

"Finn? Did you mention Finn or did he?" There was a long pause over the line until finally Ruby spoke.

"I might have—I can't remember." She sighed. "Is he. Is the man—dangerous?"

How had he found Ruby when Eden had been so careful? She always used a burner phone, she called herself Jane, and she took all the necessary steps to protect her identity on the dark web. She knew now that she'd underestimated the man's resources, assuming that once she canceled the deal, he would go quietly into the night. Why did he now want to find her? It had to be about money, that's what these people were all about. He lost a huge job when she sent that message.

"It's fine. Just someone I used to know, that's all." Her explanation was sorely lacking, and she caught sight of Gilmore lingering nearby, his sharp look indicating her time was up. She needed to cut her conversation short.

"Mom, they're here to get me. I have to go now. I'll call you again soon."

"Okay, dear. I love you."

"And Mom. Don't answer the door if that man comes back."

* * *

Gilmore dropped her off in the day room, where she found Chaz at their usual table and joined him. It was raining again, and the light shining through the window was like dusk rather than midday.

"Where's Jinx?" Eden kept her tone casual as she scanned the room, expecting Jinx to appear near the television or bathroom.

He shrugged.

"Can I ask you a weird question?" Eden watched Chaz's eyes bounce around to settle on her for half a beat before continuing to move around the room.

"Sure."

"Is there a way to communicate with people on the outside? Not the phones or by letter. Another way?" Eden thought of the man at her mother's house. If Kendrick was able to retrieve her cellphone, where his number was stored, she would call him—pay him to back off. She shivered when she thought of her mother standing next to a killer and not even realizing it. Jinx told Eden she had a cellphone. What Eden didn't know was how she got it. Was it a privilege Jinx had earned?

"Lemme think about it and get back to you."

She wasn't sure what that meant—he either knew or didn't —but she let it go.

Willie shuffled cards endlessly while staring out the window and Gilmore returned from his smoke break to stand sentinel over the room, his eyes settling on her for a beat too long.

"I hope Jinx comes back soon," Chaz said, his finger scrubbing at something unseen on his shirt.

"Where has she been?"

Chaz's eyes narrowed at the table as he considered her question. "I don't know. She didn't mention anything to me."

The words came out in a rush, and his foot thumped against the floor. Was he lying?

"Do you think Jinx will try to hurt Gilmore?" Her speech was low, her eyes trekking around the room. She had no time for her usual tact; Jinx could show up any minute. Eden needed to know if her plan would work.

"Why would she hurt him?" Chaz asked.

"Because he's the reason she was moved away from Doctor Lucas, remember." She tried not to sound frustrated but wondered if Chaz was listening to her at all. "Would she hurt him like that woman she pushed down the stairs? What was her name again?"

"Jaybird—and I didn't say she pushed her," Chaz whispered. "She was pretty too."

She tried to follow his words, to understand what he was talking about, but she didn't.

"Eden Wyatt," a voice called.

She looked up to see Doc Jones in the doorway, and she stood without being summoned. Anxiety needling her at the sight of the doctor's face. She hadn't seen Doc Jones for several days, and she was only now realizing, as she approached, what a relief it had been.

"Ace of space, ace of spade. The Deuce," Willie chanted quietly as Eden passed.

"Doc Lucas and I need to speak with you in his office," Doc Jones said and turned into the hallway. Heat flushed Eden's skin as she tried to keep up with Doc Jones's strides. The damned medication slowed her down, made her trudge rather than walk the halls of this place.

"What's this about?" Stress spiked through her at the doctor's ongoing silence. "I don't understand."

Doc Lucas rose from behind his desk, a rare frown on his

face. Doc Jones joined him across the room as Eden walked toward the sofa. For a split second, Eden expected Doc Jones to put her arm around Doc Lucas, but instead, he sat, and she stood next to him, giving Eden an impression of who was in charge of this meeting.

"Eden, have a seat." Doc Lucas nodded to the sofa.

"What is it?" Her voice panicked, she looked between the two, begging for an explanation. She sorted through her recent memory. What had she done now?

"Is there something you want to tell us?" It was Doc Jones who spoke.

"Like what?" Tension moved up her spine, and she sat on the edge of the sofa—a flight reaction to their scrutiny. "I have no idea why I'm here."

There must have been something in her shocked expression that eased the tension coming from them both.

"This was brought to our attention today." Doc Jones held up a metal fork. "Are you going to deny that you hid this in your room?"

Her tone was level and almost friendly, taking Eden off guard. She was sure she had checked every square inch of her room this morning for any other notes; she would have found the utensil.

Instead of answering her question, Eden asked, "Who found it?"

"That's hardly important."

Doctor Lucas continued his silence, making it clear he wouldn't defend her, and she stumbled over the disappointment.

"I think—" She couldn't tell them about Gilmore. What if they didn't believe her and he carried out his threats? At this point, they might assume she was using a convenient complaint of harassment to get herself out of trouble instead of telling the truth. She had less than a month to go until her mandatory 45-day evaluation was due. "Someone could have put that in my room."

"Why would someone do that, Eden?" Doc Jones seemed impatient now. Maybe the woman was expecting Eden to rush to confess.

Eden shrugged, unable to do anything else. "Where was it found?"

Doc Jones's eyes traveled down to Doc Lucas, but he looked at Eden. "It was found in your room, under your mattress," he confirmed.

"And a staff member collected it today." Doc Jones authenticated the discovery. It would be so much easier if it were just Eden and Doc Lucas working on this. At least he showed some interest in helping her.

"Which staff member?" The words were forceful, angry. She could picture Gilmore sneaking into her room to deposit the fork under her mattress. She was dangerously close to yelling his name. He couldn't be allowed to get away with this.

"It's not important who told us," Doc Jones said.

"I don't know who gave this to you, but I promise I didn't hide that." Eden was looking at Doc Lucas. "I don't want to hurt anyone."

"We have no choice but to change your status, you know," Doc Jones said with pursed lips as if she had won the war. She was officially putting Eden back in her place. It was always one step forward with ten steps back, and she was running out of time.

She didn't say anything, only nodded. She would do whatever they told her to. Whatever made her better. She had second-guessed herself about the note they had found, but surely she would remember hiding a fork in her room.

It was hard enough for her to try and understand what she

did to her husband all those months ago, stabbing him to death in their own home. But now, she was like a ticking bomb that could explode at any moment, and when she thought of the man in Miami who came by her mother's house, she was reminded of what she was truly capable of.

# Chapter 26

Layla
Before

A work commitment took her away the week after Finn's birth. She assured Eden she would beg off the trip, but Eden told her not to, that everything would be fine. So, after the plane touched down and she found her car in long-term parking, she rushed over to Eden's house to see them, forgoing even the short trip to her apartment.

The garage door yawned open, and Ben's truck was missing from its usual spot when Layla arrived. Eden hadn't mentioned Ben once during their minimal phone conversations, leading Layla to assume they had truly separated.

When she entered the garage, empty boxes containing diapers, a baby monitor, and a Pack 'n Play lined the wall, along with several bags of garbage. Loose trash littered the floor from animals scavenging the bottoms of the bags; the smell momentarily overwhelmed her as she passed. Had Eden forgotten to close the garage? She tried the interior door, the knob turned in her palm, and she pushed it open.

"Eden," she gasped. The pungent smell of sour food hung in the air. Flies buzzed around the counter where dishes were piled high in the sink, and food containers were abandoned on the granite countertops. Dead flower petals sloughed off under weeping stems, and clothes sagged on chairs and stools.

Something fell to the floor behind her, and she jerked around to empty air. What had happened here?

Boxes and bags stacked against the patio doors like a barricade. As she slowly rounded the counter, her toe caught the edge of a package, and she nearly stumbled into a mess of unsorted baby clothes. The curtains hung closed against the massive wall of windows in the two-story living room. Dust from the unwashed surfaces floated through the air.

The faint cry of a baby cut through the silence. What was she going to find up there? Her heart sped up, and she took the stairs as fast as she could. Finn's angelic voice echoed down the hall.

"Eden?" Still no response as she pushed open the door to Finn's room. Inside she found him writhing in his blankets, his face red and wet from crying. Didn't Eden know that Finn shouldn't have stuffed animals and blankets in his crib? He could succumb to SIDS. Layla scooped him up. "Shhhh. It's all right now. I've got you." His tiny body shook in her arms, refusing to settle.

She bounced him gently as she walked to the master suite. Both doors were closed, and she knocked gently. "Eden, it's me."

She pushed the door open to a dark room. Goosebumps rippled over her arms as her eyes tried to adjust to the darkness. She stopped abruptly when she bumped gently into something that felt like a body, just standing in the middle of the room.

"Who let you in here? What do you want from me?" came a shriek. Layla backtracked toward the doorway and flipped on the light with a trembling hand. In the glow of the bulbs, Eden covered her eyes from the light, but only for a moment. Her long, once-silky hair was matted and greasy; her clothes hung loosely from her thin frame. "Did he send you? Did Ben tell you to come here?" Eden was advancing on her, eyes forced wide, hostile.

"Eden, it's me. It's Layla," she said; hearing the panic in her voice made her cringe. Eden paused halfway to her and tipped her head to the side. She took a deep breath and closed her eyes, and when she opened them, they were filled with tears.

"Thank God you're here. You're here!" Eden's face crumpled into sobs. Her hands moved to cover her face again.

"Honey, what happened?" Layla used her free arm to hug Eden to her. "You should have called me—I would have come to help you."

"I'm sorry," Eden cried out. "I didn't know what to do."

"It's okay. I'm here now." Finn continued to whimper against Layla's shoulder. "The baby, he's hungry. Are you nursing?"

"No—I had to stop. He was biting me—biting my breast." As if Layla wouldn't believe her, Eden pulled her tank top down to reveal two engorged breasts with scabbed nipples and produced a hoarse sob.

"Oh, honey. I'm here. I'm here," Layla chanted and went to smooth Eden's hair back. "I'll just get Finn fed, and we can talk, okay?"

Eden lifted her shirt to cover her injured breast and nodded. Her fingers shook as she pulled the hair away from her face. "I must look a mess."

Layla tried to maintain her casual composure. What was happening to Eden? Was she like this the whole week Layla was gone? One thing was for sure, there was no way Layla was going to leave Finn with her now until she snapped out of this funk.

"It's nothing. I'm here now. Take a shower, relax, then come downstairs. It'll be right as rain now that we're all together."

\* \* \*

Layla found the baby carrier in Finn's room; she cleaned the kitchen after feeding him a bottle of formula, and now he was sleeping against her chest. She was shocked at the state of the house, and when changing Finn, she noticed he looked a bit thin and had an angry-looking rash on his bottom and legs. Eden was neglecting him. She swallowed the immediate anger and told herself Eden must be overwhelmed.

"Thanks," Eden said from behind her. She had taken a shower but, to Layla's shock, had put on the same soiled clothes that smelled sour and were marred with spit-up.

"Don't you have any clean clothes?"

Eden's eyes went from Finn resting against Layla's chest back to her face and shrugged.

"It's been bad. Really bad." Eden's eyes tracked around the kitchen to the back doors. "I haven't slept in days—I don't know what happened." Layla had moved the boxes to open the doors and get some fresh air inside the house.

"What are you doing?" Eden hissed when she noticed Layla's effort.

Eden rushed past and slammed the doors shut. Then she began to re-stack the boxes in front of the doors once again. "He'll see it open. He's always watching. That asshole," she snarled.

"Who?" Layla asked, clutching Finn to her. Eden began

peering out of the curtains hanging in front of the glass doors. Her head was bobbing left and right to get the perfect view of whatever she was looking for. "The neighbor. He and Ben are talking, you know. They want to put me in the nuthouse," Eden said in a rush, the words tumbling out of her mouth as she continued to scan the yard. "Plotting, you know."

"Who?" Layla asked again, confused.

"The guy who lives over there?" Her index finger hooked to the right. "I see Ben over there all night, drinking and having sex with all those women, just to rub it in my face. Laughing at me."

As Layla watched Eden, her heart sank slowly into her stomach, where an ache began. There was something very wrong with her friend. Layla wasn't sure what to believe.

"How much sleep have you gotten, dear?" Layla asked, closing the space between them slowly. Eden's head jerked up and, for a second, she seemed to have forgotten Layla was there.

"None. I don't think. Finn's a hungry baby," Eden said with a note of sadness in her tone. She quickly went back to her task of glaring out the window, and Layla moved to the sink to wash the dishes. All the while, she felt Finn's warm body snuggled against hers. She couldn't leave him here with Eden like this. Should she call the doctor? Yes, that seemed like the prudent thing to do. The moment she could break away, she would call the helpline at Eden's doctor's office and ask what she should do.

"Where's Ben?" Layla asked.

"Hell if I know. He's planning on kicking Finn and me out of the house soon, probably. Maybe that's what he and Martin are always talking about. I see them pointing their fingers and laughing." Eden snorted loudly. "Can you believe that, Jane? They're laughing at me."

*Jane.* Should she correct her? Eden paced but looked over at the window often as if she expected someone to storm through at any moment, past the boxes and randomly strewn items.

"Has anyone been helping you out?" Layla asked.

"Who. Who's going to help me? Ben?" Eden's tone was livid. "Just wait until I see that asshole... Just one time, that's all it'll take."

Eden pulled up next to her at the sink, close enough that Layla felt her breath hot against her cheek, and she whispered in a childlike voice. "I hear them talking." She tapped her temple with her finger. "You know what they're saying... Kill Ben, Eden. Kill him." And she craned her neck back and laughed. She laughed so hard tears streamed down her face.

# Chapter 27

Eden
24 days until review hearing

Gilmore passed Marsha as she was leaving Eden's room. His features were hard and angry. "I gotta take you to the phones before breakfast."

She gathered her things under his watchful stare. She was sure to search for notes or other contraband—finding none for the second day in a row. Take that, Gilmore. She wanted to tell him she was onto him. That just because she'd fought him off didn't give him the right to continue to bother her—but she didn't. It looked like he was in a horrible mood, and she took comfort in the thought that things were only going to get worse for him. As she walked past him in the doorway and into the hall, she felt his hand brush her hip, and she jerked away from his touch, sending him a glare.

"Freak," he muttered and closed the door. Heat spilled into her face, and anger fired into her veins, but she walked in frustrated silence behind him as if she were a dog on a leash.

She'd requested to use the phone last night but was denied and told she could make the all-important call this morning. They were restricting her communication to twice a week and room checks every day. They had stopped short of giving her two orderlies for escorts around the facility, the one punishment she would have welcomed. Doc Jones must be so pleased with herself now that Eden had hit yet another setback in her treatment.

Gilmore pressed the button for the elevator, and she felt her palms begin to sweat as she twisted her fingers into knots. The door opened, and Doc Lucas smiled at them. "Going down?" he asked.

She felt relief pour through her as she nodded.

"I got her, Gilmore, if you need to get to the cafeteria."

"I do. Thanks," Gilmore muttered and turned on his heels. Relieved, she stepped inside.

"How are you today, Doctor?" It felt like something a regular person would say. He looked at her as if he could read her thoughts, the way he always did, and she wondered if he knew he did that.

"You look rested."

"I slept better last night." The new sleeping aid they gave her last night knocked her right out. She'd gotten five hours of solid sleep, an unusually high amount for her.

"Where was he taking you?"

"I'm going to the phones." She smiled weakly.

He hit the button for the first floor and relaxed into the opposite corner of the elevator. She looked down at her new jumpsuit and tugged at the cuffs. At least she'd showered and brushed her hair today. It was humorous how much care she'd once taken with her hair and makeup, and now she was just glad to be clean.

"Are you okay? With Gilmore, I mean?"

"Um. I don't understand." She couldn't look at him but could feel him watching her—probing.

"You're pale as a ghost—you look upset." He stalled as if he was searching for a different word but only settled on "upset."

She swallowed. "I don't know." That wasn't an answer, and she knew it, but the door was opening to the first floor, and three people were waiting to enter. She followed Doc Lucas to the nurse's station, where the bank of phones was located.

"I don't like him." It was the best she could do.

"Why?"

She shrugged as he pulled the door open for her, and she smelled the mold from the aging carpets.

Doctor Lucas took one more look at her and smiled. "I'll see you soon."

She watched his receding form move toward the day room. She didn't want to notice his perfect jawline or how his jeans hung on his hips, but she couldn't take her eyes away. What was she thinking? She was turning into Jinx, she thought with disdain.

She cleared her throat and picked up the phone, dialed, and listened to it ring.

"Eden, is that you?" Layla asked. Her voice sounded off—wrong somehow.

"What is it? Are you crying?" Eden asked and looked around the small empty space. She caught sight of Lynsi walking next to Chaz. His shuffling gait was slow and deliberate, as if he didn't want to go where she was leading him. His eyes caught hers, and he quickly looked away.

"Oh, honey. I miss you so much," Layla said.

"What is it?"

"It's Olivia." The words burst out of Layla like a volcanic eruption. "She's been harassing me—us."

Harassing? The word bounced around before she could

grasp its meaning, and even then, she couldn't understand what Layla was saying. "What do you mean?"

"She's coming by the house, uninvited. Trying to get a feel for what kind of child Finn is." She spoke the last words slowly to indicate how absurd the thought was. "Asking me what items she should take if she were to get custody."

"I told you, he's in your care. You can send her away. In fact, I want you to. I don't want her around my child." Eden's voice was growing too loud, her breath heavy. This was exactly how their last visit had progressed.

"I did. I mean, I will. I'm just so worried. She told me last time..." Her voice trailed off and Eden pictured her sad face. "I know she's hired someone to get custody. He's good—excellent. He said if I don't let Olivia see him, then the court will consider that in their ruling over who gets custody."

"He's probably lying to you." But Eden felt defeated. Lauren had told her the same thing the last time they spoke; something about facilitating relationships with other family members.

"I don't want you to be mad, but I asked her what it would take to make her go away." Layla's voice was an eerie whisper. "Like you mentioned before."

Go away. Yes. That's what they needed, for Olivia to go away, and money was the quickest way to her heart. It wasn't Eden's original plan, but now that she thought about it, it was probably safer than the alternative: finding someone to persuade her to walk away.

"She mentioned fifty thousand dollars." Layla cleared her throat as two orderlies were making their rounds near Eden. After they passed, Eden spoke.

"Give the bitch what she wants."

"I don't have that kind of money," Layla said with apparent shock.

"I'll talk to Lauren. I want you to make it clear to her that she will get cash, and she needs to go away." This would work, and Eden didn't care about the money. There would be plenty left after all this was behind her. She would spend every last cent if it meant Olivia wouldn't ever get her son.

"Are you sure? I think she's just trying to play us. What happens when she spends it and needs more?"

Olivia would be a thorn in her side for the entire time she was in here, but it wouldn't be forever. All she needed to do was buy a little time.

As long as Kendrick found that phone—everything would be okay. She was nervous that she hadn't heard from him. How long did it take to find a cellphone and photo album? She'd given him explicit directions about where she hid them. It had been two days.

There was also the issue with the items found in her room, but if her suspicion was correct and it was Gilmore, he wouldn't be a problem much longer.

"Make the offer and tell her I'll need a few days to take care of it with my lawyer. I'll make it available to you," she added.

"Only if you're sure," Layla said. "We can try to find another way."

What other way would get Olivia out of the picture but death or money?

"No. This is what I want."

Several moments of silence ticked past before Layla changed topics abruptly. "How are you feeling today?"

"Just taking it one day at a time. No more Doc Jones—so that's good."

"Hallelujah, the witch is dead," Layla sang.

"Yes, my new doctor is amazing. He's kind and warm—"

"And cute?" Layla laughed.

"How do you know that?"

"I can tell by how pitchy your voice gets when you talk about him." Layla laughed.

Eden didn't want to ruin the moment, but something was nagging her, a question she needed answered.

"I'm sorry about our last visit. It's just with that horrible doctor and my orderly here, I can't seem to get any peace these days."

"What orderly?"

"It's nothing." She brushed Layla off. "There's something I need to ask you about, and I'm ashamed to say I have no memory of the incident."

"What is it?"

"I need to know more about that night." Need. She couldn't stop thinking about her recent conversations with Layla about the time surrounding Ben's murder. There were so many things Layla had told her that, no matter how hard she tried, she couldn't remember. The need to know how it all culminated in Ben's murder was eating away at her and Layla had been the only person around her at the time.

"Don't worry; I didn't tell them anything. Not even the police," Layla replied in a whisper. "Just like I promised you."

Eden felt her throat tighten. "Promised me what?"

Layla took a deep breath. "I didn't tell them about how you told me you were going to kill Ben days before it happened."

A buzz grew in Eden's ears.

"I had to protect you," Layla said.

All Eden could hear was the soft crackle of air over the phone, and she wondered if what Jinx had told her was true—that the phone calls here were recorded...

# Chapter 28

Layla
Before

T he house was like a silent hull at night, with the occasional muffled creaks from Eden's quiet movement in the darkness up and down the hall and stairs at all hours of the night. Layla slept in the guest room at Eden's insistence. She knew Eden wasn't sleeping at all. Finn, on several occasions, cried in his crib until Layla got out of bed to feed him. She didn't mind. But her concern grew with each passing minute and the soft slap of bare feet on the hardwood—there was something very wrong with her friend.

Layla had called Eden's doctor earlier that day and asked what she could do for Eden. They told her it was customary for sleep-deprived mothers to have mood issues and anxiety. In fairness, Layla hadn't informed the doctor that Eden might be delusional. She didn't want Ben to get wind of the situation and come take Finn away.

But Eden's behavior was too concerning to ignore. Before

Finn was born, Eden had insisted Finn would sleep in her room in a bassinet until he was three months old. She wanted him to be near in case he needed her. But for some reason, he was now sleeping in his room, all alone. Eden acted as if he wasn't there most of the time, ignoring him completely. What would happen when Layla had to go back to work once her vacation days were over, and Eden was alone with him?

After he finished his bottle, Layla rocked him back to sleep. A shadow fell over the doorway, and Eden peered in. She didn't come inside, only watched from the hallway.

"What are you doing?" Eden asked, genuine curiosity in her tone.

"He was hungry. I thought I'd help you get some sleep—so I fed him."

Eden's hair hung down past her shoulders, limp and dark in the shadows. "I was checking on the neighbor's house. He's still up in his garage making all kinds of noise. I didn't want him to wake the baby, but I guess he did." She sounded as though she was grinding the words through her teeth, her hands in tight fists at her sides gently bumping off her thighs.

"No, sweetie, he was hungry. He was crying for some milk."

Eden looked down at her breast and back up at Layla without answering. It appeared her breast milk was leaking through her shirt, but Eden ignored it.

She snorted. "He usually sleeps through the night."

A new sense of dread moved over her. He was less than a month old; he wasn't sleeping through the night. Why would she think such a thing—unless she was ignoring him.

"He gobbled down a whole bottle, and now he's back to sleep," Layla said. "See."

Eden only nodded and walked toward the stairs. Was she neglecting her son because she was sleep-deprived and angry at Ben? Well, it wasn't Finn's fault. Layla looked out the window into the darkness where only the moon gave its light. What happened to a person's mind after days or even weeks of sleep deprivation? Tomorrow she would have to confront Eden about this, and they would take her to see someone. Maybe a specialist for post-partum issues. She could tell the doctor that she would stay with Eden and Finn until she was better—no need to involve Ben.

Layla kissed Finn on his smooth cheek and put him back in his crib.

If the neighbor was making so much noise, why hadn't Layla heard? She descended the stairs and walked to the kitchen. As she neared the back of the house, she saw more boxes had been stacked at the back door; the heap hovered at five feet or so. A chair had also been dragged over to the mounting pile.

Layla pulled the curtain back and looked outside toward the neighbor's house.

"Can you hear them?"

Layla clutched her chest and cried out as her eyes searched the dark behind her. Eden stood in the shadows of the kitchen, a drink in hand. "They're up all night, partying and making noise."

Layla peered outside again. The two-story single-family home was just in view from her position. It was dark and silent; only a single glowing porch light signaled any sign of life. They could be on vacation for all she knew.

"Eden. You're not well." Layla turned from the window and moved toward her at the kitchen island.

"It's because they put something in the water." Eden sloshed her glass into the sink, and a crash of breaking glass shattered the silence.

"I mean, I think you need to talk with your doctor, sweetie," Layla said as gently as possible. "Because you aren't sleeping. I think what you need is a long rest. Would you like that?"

Eden began to sob. Her petite frame crumpled to the ground, and she hugged her knees and rocked back and forth.

"Oh, sweetie. It's okay. I've taken off the next week at work, and I'm going to stay with you. Don't worry about a thing, okay?" Layla pulled her into her arms, and Eden didn't resist. "When was the last time you were out of the house?" She'd noticed groceries were running low; this, too, was unlike Eden. At least the old Eden.

"I haven't left since the delivery."

"What about Finn's checkup?" Layla recalled the small card with a pastel yellow giraffe on it. The appointment was three days ago.

"He doesn't need an appointment. He's fine," Eden said weakly.

"Don't you worry about that," Layla said. "I'm going to take him tomorrow, and you can rest here all day." She mentally calculated where there might be sleeping medication in the house; didn't all homes have some? Layla used to take some after she was diagnosed with depression when Todd left her.

"I need some sleep," Eden begged. "Yes. I need to rest." She stumbled trying to rise to her feet, and Layla helped her to the stairs. Eden's body gently bumped the railing as if she were drunk, and her toe caught the edge of the runner at the top, but Layla grabbed her before she fell. She was as light as a feather, and Layla recalled that she hadn't seen her eat anything since arriving yesterday.

Eden's room smelled of stale air and urine. Once she got Eden into the bed and pulled the covers up, Layla went into the bathroom and closed the door so the light wouldn't shine into the bedroom. Cosmetics, medication, and other items were littered on the white granite countertop. Clothes were heaped in piles and hung from the shower door.

Inside the medicine cabinet, she found some sleeping pills, and she filled a glass and went to Eden.

"Honey, here. Take this; it'll help you sleep." She took a seat on the edge of the bed, and Eden moaned in rejection. "You need sleep, or you won't be able to take care of Finn."

Eden shot up to sit at the mention of her son. "Where is he? Did Ben take him from me?" She looked around frantic and wide-eyed. The thought occurred to Layla that if Ben were to stop by and see Eden in such a state, he might actually take Finn away with him. Eden would get nothing in the divorce, including her precious son. Layla couldn't let that happen.

"That's not going to happen," Layla promised.

"He stopped by and told me what a pigsty the place was and said I don't deserve Finn. He told me he would call the cops if I don't get out of his house, and he would keep Finn—that way he won't have to pay child support." Eden was crying now, her small frame shaking in the shadows. "You have to take him. Take him away from here, or I'll never see him again." Eden was on her knees, begging now, pulling at Layla's shirt. "Take him to your house. Ben won't know where he is, and he'll be safe with you."

It dawned on her that Eden might be imagining this visit from Ben; Layla hadn't seen or heard from him since before the baby was born. But if there was even a tiny chance it was true, she needed to act. She didn't think this was the best idea, but she wouldn't be able to convince Eden of that.

"Of course, I'll help you. I'll need to get some of his things," Layla said as she thought. Car seat, Pack 'n Play for him to sleep on because the bassinet wouldn't fit in her car.

"I'll leave in the morning." The clock on the nightstand

read 2:00 am. It was too late to wake him and take him for the drive.

"No—he could be coming now. Please, if you ever loved Finn or me, you'll take him now." She was frantic. "I won't be able to sleep until I know he's safe."

"Okay. I'll go pack right now." Layla held out the pills she had found with the glass of water. "Take these, and I'll go pack. We'll be gone before morning."

Eden took the medication and sank against Layla's shoulder. "You're a true friend, Layla."

It didn't take long to gather all the things he would need, saving Finn for last. She couldn't help but think it was her dream inside of a nightmare. Her best friend was having a mental break, but to help her, she would be a mother of sorts. He wasn't hers, of course, but for tonight she could pretend. And tomorrow, after Eden had a whole night of rest, she would come back, and they would work on their plan together.

# Chapter 29

After her call with Layla, her mood lifted as she followed a nurse to the day room. They were moving toward getting rid of Olivia and she felt the stress seeping from her a bit.

Shouts moved down the hall, and the scrape of wheels on the floor. Eden closed her eyes and pictured the cart wheels from the store—the strangers staring at her. She inhaled deeply and opened her eyes as a group of paramedics rushed past her, pushing a stretcher toward the stairwell near the day room. The nurse put an arm on Eden's to be sure she wouldn't try to cross in front of them as more fire personnel followed.

"What's going on?" Eden asked the nurse. The patients in the day room were frantic as some covered their ears with wide palms or shouted as the last of the paramedics and firefighters passed.

"Someone's fallen down the stairs," the nurse replied with a solemn look.

"Are you kidding?" Why had she said that? "Who?" Cool air from an open door rushed past her and she drew her arms around her torso.

"I don't know."

Eden watched as a man she didn't recognize exited the door from the stairwell with two people behind him. Jinx smiled wide at the firefighters lingering outside the door, while Chaz cast his eyes to the ground, a grim expression on his thin face. *Someone's fallen down the stairs.*

Eden felt the gentle tug of the nurse pulling her toward the day room. Just as she crossed the threshold, she heard voices loud behind her.

"Head trauma—"

"Move those people—"

"Watch his airway."

Eden turned to see two men and a woman rushing past with the stretcher where Gilmore lay still as the dead.

It was an hour before Jinx and Chaz made it to the day room, dropped off by the same man who had led them away. Eden kept her eyes on Jinx's easy movement and cheery mood. Eden was still trying to come to terms with what had happened. She'd known what she was doing when she lied to Jinx, but had never considered what it might feel like for Jinx to do exactly what Eden was hoping for. Kill Gilmore. There were no tears or sadness, but a lump of some emotion—guilt maybe—that hovered at the back of her mind. She had done this—no matter who ultimately pushed him.

"Well, look who it is." Jinx leaned in on pointed elbows

after Eden plopped down next to her. "You got a new suit, makes your boobs look huge." Her eyes grew round as she looked down at Eden's breasts.

Eden coughed. "The other jumper was getting too big." She pulled the suit away from her chest as if to create more room, self-conscious of her apparent effort.

"You look good," Chaz said, though his eyes darted past her.

"Did you guys hear about Gilmore?" Eden asked, studying Jinx's face. One side of her mouth quirked up into a kind of grimace.

"He's a real perv. Always trying to touch the women. I heard he got one of the ladies on the fifth floor pregnant while she was high on all the drugs." Jinx giggled, and Eden thought she might be sick.

Eden wanted to steer the conversation back to Gilmore, but Jinx's hand jutted out so quickly Eden didn't have time to react as her fingers pinched Eden's nipple through the thin fabric of her jumper and cheap bra.

"Oh, he likes you, I bet. You're just his type." Her tongue licked the edges of her mouth, and Eden pulled away from her with a shout.

An orderly was already crossing the floor. "No touching, Nina. You know the rules."

She batted her lashes at Lynsi. "Sorry. My bad." But she laughed as she took in the horror that must have been written on Eden's features. A sudden coldness sank through her as the pain from Jinx's pinch swelled in her breast, and she looked away in shame—knowing everything had changed. With Gilmore ticked off Jinx's list, would she turn her attention to Eden next?

# Chapter 30

Layla
Before

When her eyes cracked open to Finn's growing cries the following day, everything looked new. Her grungy apartment was a little brighter; the early hour was a blessing and not a curse; the birds were singing louder and with a sweeter melody. She rushed to the Pack 'n Play she had set up only three hours earlier and scooped up his warm, wiggling body.

"I've got you," she soothed and walked to the kitchen, bouncing him on her chest. He stopped crying as his tiny fist jammed into his mouth. "Hungry little man."

He grunted, and her heart melted. She had to get Eden the help she needed, and the best way to do that was through Ben. Two birds, one stone. What would be perfect was getting Ben out of the picture entirely. Her mind was whirling as she finalized her plans to do just that.

\* \* \*

That afternoon, Layla asked her neighbor Betty to watch Finn while she went out. Everything was in place, and she needed to get over to the house. She wasn't sure, but her bet was on Eden either being in full recovery, in which case she would need to do nothing, or being an utter disaster, in which case Ben would be the key.

She packed a small bag at her apartment with the necessary items: her prescription sleeping pills and a change of clothes.

\* \* \*

As she walked up to the house, it looked silent and sad in the fading afternoon light. It had lost its sparkle. She was almost frightened to go inside and see the state Eden was in, but she had to do it.

After ringing the doorbell several times with no answer, she pulled the key out of her pocket and unlocked the door.

"Eden," she called. No answer. She had been able to clean up most of the mess in the house the last two days, except for the growing pile of things at the back door. She ignored the mess, went to the house phone, and dialed Ben's work number.

A woman responded on the second ring. "This is Patty; how may I direct your call?"

Layla lowered her voice and asked for Ben Wyatt.

"I'm sorry, Mr. Wyatt is in a meeting for the next hour. Can I take a message?"

Perfect. "Can you tell him his wife called and ask him to stop by the house after work?" Layla wasn't sure if the message would surprise or shock him. She had no earthly idea what was going on with Ben these days. And now, with Eden's condition deteriorating, she had to act fast, or the window would close forever.

She trudged up the stairs and into Eden's room. It was dark, and the curtains were still drawn, but she could see Eden wasn't in bed anymore.

"Where have you been? Did you see Ben outside? He's been driving by all morning, yelling obscenities out the window at me. He's the devil," Eden's garbled voice said from behind her. Layla turned quickly, and a nervous laugh escaped her mouth. Eden displayed two fingers at the back corner of her skull like horns. Her eyes looked sunken and red. Layla wasn't sure if she'd been able to sleep at all based on her appearance.

"I'm going to take care of all of it for you; you don't need to worry about him anymore," Layla said, wrapping her arms around Eden.

"What are you talking about? He's never going to go away, not without Finn. I can't stand to lose him; I went through so much to get him." She wept in Layla's firm grasp, and Layla led her back to bed.

"I've brought you something to sleep. Have you eaten yet?"

"I don't know." She looked so fragile as Layla gazed at her. The same glass of tap water was on the bedside table, looking untouched.

"Did you sleep at all last night?"

She nodded. "Yes. Some." She sounded eager now.

Layla closed her eyes for a second to ask herself if she could do this, but the image of Finn in her arms that morning pushed her forward.

"Take these; they'll help you relax." Layla produced a bottle from her bag and shook out three pills. It was probably the max amount she should give her.

Eden opened her mouth, and Layla dropped all the pills onto her tongue and handed her the water.

"I'm going to cook dinner for us, okay?" Layla added while lowering Eden to the bed and pulling the covers up to her chin.

"Dinner? Sounds nice." Eden's voice was so soft. Layla walked to the closet and found a sweatshirt hanging in the back and a pair of ballet flats on the floor. The shoes were snug, but they would work for the short time.

She closed the door softly behind her and made her way downstairs. She hated how her heart ached at her friend's utter vulnerability.

*I can do this. I must do this.*

An hour after Layla gave Eden the sleeping pills, the doorbell rang. She rushed to the door and opened it; hopefully, it wouldn't wake Eden or cause her to investigate. She nearly dropped the knife she had pulled into the middle of her back when she saw him standing on the stoop.

"Layla?" He was handsome and put together as always. "I got a message that Eden asked me to stop by." He looked —happy.

Layla nodded and pulled the door open. "It was me who called." Her voice was all wrong—too high pitched. She cleared her throat.

"Oh, what's up?" he asked, moving into the house. He was a big man, probably six feet three inches, but she had the element of surprise, and as soon as the door clicked shut and he walked past her to survey the mounting pile at the patio door, she lifted the knife and drove it into where she knew his lung to be. It cut into him with almost no effort, but her hands immediately dropped away in horror. Leaving the black handle jutting from his back.

Air hissed out of his pressed lips like the can she used to clean her keyboard at work. His big arm came around to grab at the knife, but he just seemed to flail, unable to reach. He stumbled toward the kitchen, and she pulled the knife out and stabbed him again. He had too much energy—too much spirit. What if he got away? She stabbed again, this time finding the other lung. She didn't have the stomach to make this last much longer. She needed it to be over.

"Heeeellppp—" He dropped onto his knees, and she stood over him as he tried to crawl. Her hands were shaking, covered in blood, as she fell back onto the seat in the foyer, at one point covering her eyes from the sight of him, until, finally, his labored breathing stopped. When she opened her eyes again, he was still, his head craned at an awkward angle. She nearly puked when she pulled the blood-covered knife out of his back and used a towel to clear her prints from the handle. The pool of blood grew rapidly under his body, and she was sure to step in the growing puddle of red liquid.

She had to do this for Finn—

She mounted the stairs and crept into the master bedroom again, the knife flush with her leg. She moved to the bed where Eden lay still, her breathing deep and rhythmic.

Carefully, she lifted her friend's hand, placed the knife into her palm and squeezed gently. Just as she did, Eden gasped and sat up sharply.

"Shhhhh, it's okay, honey. It's me. It's okay." Layla's voice was shaking like her hands; she dropped the knife, and it fell to the floor with a soft thud.

"Layla?"

"Shhh. I have to go out and get something from the store, honey. I'll be back before you wake." Layla's voice shook, and she flinched at the sound.

Moaning, Eden fell back onto the pillow, and Layla used a discarded shirt to pick up the knife. She pulled off the blood-stained sweatshirt, dropped it on the floor, and put the shoes back in their place. As she made her way down the stairs in her

stocking feet, she was careful not to step in the bloody footprints leading to the bedroom.

Before leaving the house, she changed her clothes, grabbed
all her things, and slid the knife back into Ben's back.

Time to get back home to Finn, her son.

# Chapter 31

Eden

22 days until review hearing

A slight euphoria woke Eden. It came early that morning and painted the sky brighter with the soft glow of golden rays. She knew that Marsha was giving her lithium each morning—so why did she feel the crisp, bright edges of mania moving over her? How did she wake to a dreary mess of a life one day, and everything seemed full of possibilities the next? It had been two days since Jinx pushed Gilmore down the stairs. Perhaps her excitement was due to the peace she found in his absence.

Lauren was waiting for her in a private conference room—the same as her last visit. The polished older woman wore a vibrant yellow shirt that matched Eden's rising mood. It should have alarmed her, but she ignored her internal warming, wanting to feel good again.

Ever since learning of Olivia's plan to take Finn, Lauren

had been working on a way to stop her. Or at least that was how she'd described her efforts to Eden.

"There's no way she'll back down now, but we're prepared," Lauren said. "Kendrick reached out to me about some information he found on Olivia's finances. He told me to let you know he's planning a visit soon."

"Thanks," Eden said.

"And I've got all the witnesses you mentioned. All have agreed to testify on Layla's behalf. Opposing counsel has agreed that your mother may testify by phone."

Her lawyer's words hardly put her at ease, even if she was confident that they would prevail. She wanted to trust her, but this was too important to entrust with anyone. She would need to make sure Olivia was taken care of herself—or pray she would take the money and go.

"I've been doing this a long time; I don't think the court is going to discount your wishes entirely. I need more information on Olivia. What can you tell me?"

What did she know about her sister-in-law?

"I didn't see her much, but she stayed in contact with Ben weekly. I think she would ask for money, but I'm not sure." Eden searched herself for objectivity. It wouldn't help anyone if she slung bitter words with nothing to back them up. "She's lived out in California since she graduated from a northern university—I can't remember where she went. She works for a doctor's office—assistant, I think."

"Why would Olivia make such a poor guardian?" Lauren cut off Eden's response—a nice way of saying she wasn't interested in the mundane details of Olivia's life. What could she say about Olivia then?

"She hates kids. She's told me before many times, and she always mentions not wanting them when we happen to be around some."

Lauren settled back in her chair and eyed Eden. "What is it she has on you?"

There it was—the question she feared. She wasn't dancing around it, but her mind refused to go there. Now, she had to— didn't she? If she wanted to protect Finn, she had to tell Lauren everything—well, maybe not everything.

"There was an album I kept at the house." She was hoping Kendrick had found it and not Olivia.

Lauren's brow quirked up. The statement was obviously not what her lawyer was expecting.

"It wasn't anything really, just some pictures of Ben and I that I—" The words wouldn't come out, and her eyes skittered around the room.

"Defaced?" Lauren guessed.

Eden nodded. "It was nothing. I was mad at him because he was cheating on me. He had a child with another woman." Her voice was rising higher. She couldn't finish what she was going to say; it would make her look even worse.

"Okay—that's not evidence of a plan to kill someone," Lauren argued to herself.

"That's all I can think of. There's nothing else." But there was, and she hoped Kendrick had been able to find it. She had to get that phone back. The one she'd used to communicate with a hitman. Even thinking about it seemed surreal. She knew she should have gotten rid of it once she returned from Miami. Even though she assumed, deep down, that she had done the right thing that night—even in her manic state—she wanted to keep all her options open.

"You're sure?" Lauren eyed her.

Eden swallowed a lump in her throat as she considered telling Lauren the whole truth, Miami and the plans that led her down there, but she knew she wouldn't understand—no one would.

"It's important to keep in touch with me and let me know if you can think of anything else," Lauren ordered. "And I'm going to be catching up with your doctors to find out how things are going here. Have you had any issues?"

Issues. She thought of the note. What could be worse for her defense than new allegations of her threatening to kill someone else—most assumed the intended recipient of the letter was Olivia. Lauren seemed to catch a hint of her struggle.

"What is it?"

"Ummm." What could she say that wouldn't make her look horrible? "Someone said they found a note that I supposedly wrote."

Lauren's brow creased. "What did it say?"

Eden was intentionally vague but knew someone as sharp as Lauren would catch on. "A note that threatened to kill someone." The response sounded so unbelievable Eden winced. "Not by name, but there is a strikingly similar situation to what Olivia and I are going through."

"Did you write it?"

Eden was shaking her head vigorously. "I swear."

Lauren looked thoughtful for a moment, and Eden wondered if she should tell her about Gilmore. About her suspicion that he'd been retaliating against her by making her seem dangerous. She recalled his lifeless body being wheeled past her.

"I'll talk with Doc Jones and find out what's going on."

"I have a new doctor now."

"Why?"

"I'm not sure. I think Doc Jones had a conflict, whatever that means, and another doctor needed to move one of his patients."

"Who's your new treating doctor?" Eden told her, and Lauren wrote down Doc Lucas's name. "Great. I'll get in touch with him and see what's what. In the meantime, my office is putting together our argument to keep Finn with Layla. There is one other option I think you should consider."

Eden eyed her.

"Layla will be a party to our suit as she is the current guardian—though not on paper. But if you're willing to sign custody over to Layla, it will make it harder for Olivia to prevail."

Sign over custody? Eden felt a weightiness in her chest as she considered Lauren's idea.

"At least to the court, it will be a more permanent solution."

"What would happen when I get out of here?"

"Well, you would petition to get custody back. But Layla would only need to sign an order changing custody back to you, and the court would sign off on it."

Eden was nodding her head.

"As long as you trust Layla, I think that might be our best avenue."

Eden knew Layla would never do anything to hurt her. She'd stood by her through all of this and would always be a part of Eden and Finn's life. "Yes, I trust her."

Eden was sitting next to the barred windows an hour later in the day room. There were only three others in the room, and the sound of voices hummed through her. The television played softly on the nature channel, Willie's favorite to watch after lunchtime.

No one was talking about Gilmore being gone. It shouldn't surprise her; most of the people here didn't understand a whole world was happening outside these doors. Gilmore's slip and fall investigation was officially underway, and Eden was prepared to answer any questions they might have.

As if summoning her from her thoughts, Jinx's cheery tone cut through her peace. "There you are."

Eden turned to look up at her standing only inches away, a broad smile on her face.

"Hi," Eden managed to say and tried her best to smile, but it pulled and stretched oddly over her face.

Jinx lowered herself into the chair next to Eden. Her eyes were glossy and wide as she looked around the room. "I had to take a step back for a few days. Reassess everything going on—new meds. That sort of thing. What did I miss?"

Her face was open and genuine. Eden suspected she was up to something.

"I've missed you." Jinx's hand held her chin. "I saw you in visiting the other day. You didn't say hi."

Eden looked down at her hands. She had waved to Jinx, but she didn't see, and Eden didn't want to start an argument. "Yeah. I was preoccupied. Who's the man you were with?"

Jinx seemed genuinely surprised at the question. "That's my lawyer. Alex. Hunky, right?" She threw her head back and laughed, but it didn't sound right, as if it got caught up in her throat and came out thick and slow. "And the best part is he's working my case for free."

"What case? Custody of your daughter?"

Her eyes narrowed at Eden, and for a second, Eden felt herself shiver against the coldness in Jinx's stare. "No, nothing like that. He's appealing my case for me. I was framed by this horrible bitch." She twisted a lock of red hair in her hands so hard it pulled away from her head, but she didn't seem to notice or mind the pain it must be causing, and Eden found herself wincing.

"This bitch Jamie killed the love of my life and tried to set me up for it. Now I'm here with these drooling idiots, and she's walking around having babies—" Her face twisted into an angry heap, and for a second, Eden thought she was going to spit, but just as quickly, her features turned cheerful again.

"This Gwen chick's a real ball-buster. I don't know how you put up with her for so long."

Eden felt her brow pull low. "Gwen?"

"Doc Jones."

Eden suspected a pending question about Doc Lucas, but Chaz slunk into the room and spotted them.

"I miss my dreamboat, ya know." She winked at Eden as if they were sharing a secret. "He's such a good lay."

Eden's cheeks flared, and she looked away.

"I—"

Chaz interrupted Eden. "Where have you been?" His eyes traveled past Jinx while he found a chair.

"Shut up and listen. My lawyer got me some new phones. Do you need one?" she asked him, her eyes leveled on his though he wouldn't look at her.

"Sure. Same price?"

Eden could have used a phone, but she didn't want to ask Jinx. After their last encounter, she wasn't sure how unstable the woman was or if Jinx was planning on retaliating because Jinx considered her a threat when it came to Doc Lucas.

"Yeah, baby needs a new pair of shoes. Doctor Dreamy needs a little reminder of what's so sweet," she said with a sly smile, her eyes sliding over to Eden.

"What are you talking about?" The words tumbled out before Eden could stop them, and Jinx jerked her head to look at her.

"I need to buy some new clothes. I'm never going to get him back as long as I look like this." She picked at her worn jumper.

A silence fell over all three. There was no other way to let the topic come up naturally, so she went for it.

"Were you with Gilmore when he—fell?" Eden asked Jinx.

Jinx's head tipped slowly to her shoulder, an exaggerated move, and Chaz flinched.

"Yes—I was, but I wasn't the only one." Her eyes turned on Chaz as if to communicate. "Chaz here was with me, weren't you Chaz?"

"Yeah, sure. I was there."

"You should have seen it—his feet flying out from under him." Jinx laughed loudly, and Eden shifted back in her seat. Eden couldn't look at her and see the derangement simmering inside. "When we went down to see him at the bottom of the stairs, he was drooling blood and muttering. We probably should have gone to get help—" Jinx turned back to Chaz. "Maybe next time."

# Chapter 32

Layla

22 days until review hearing

She didn't want to do it—to kill another human being or frame her best friend for murder—but eleven months later, she was holding Finn in her arms, and she knew she would kill Ben all over again if she had to. What she hadn't seen coming was the prosecutor basically letting Eden get away with murder because she was technically insane at the time. Layla's own statements to the police days later would cement her get out-of-jail-free card when she explained her friend was hallucinating and acting odd. She'd always assumed a not guilty by reason of insanity ruling was much harder to get than it was for Eden.

"Mommy's going to love you forever, little one," she cooed as she hugged him tightly. They were on their way to the park; she strolled, savoring the feel of him next to her. She would meet up with a group of women—those she used to envy only a year ago, but now she was one of them. They were chatting about their children near the monkey bars as joyful screams filled the air. Before, Layla had avoided looking over at the community playground, but now it was filled with fond memories. Even though Finn wasn't walking yet, he would come to love it here. A niggling voice told her they didn't have forever. When Eden got out, she would take Finn, and Layla would be alone again. She couldn't let that happen.

The walk was short, and by the time she arrived, she was sweating inside the baby carrier. She dropped the shoulder straps down and held Finn to her chest. He giggled and looked around with curiosity, taking in his world.

"Layla, hi. I was just talking about you," Becky said as she stood with two other women. "I was retelling your story about how your accident at forty-two years old turned into this beautiful little man."

Layla smiled. She loved to tell the story. "Accident isn't the word I would use—more like a miracle." She laughed with the other women. "I thought I couldn't have children, but the universe had other plans. After years of trying, I separated from my husband of ten years. Maybe that was what did the trick." Layla thought of her husband's daughter and inwardly smirked. "I was seeing this guy just for a short time, and here he is." She motioned to Finn. "It's such a blessing. The happiest time of my life."

"Good for you, honey. We all deserve our bit of happiness. Now that we're on three, I might have gone too far." Becky laughed at her own joke. A year ago, Layla would have been resisting the urge to spit in the woman's face for saying such a thing, but now that she was a mother, she pretended to laugh along—even sounding genuine.

"How long have you been in the area?" the other woman asked. Layla remembered the pretty blond woman was named Jamie, and a newborn rested on her chest. If she remembered right, Jamie had mentioned she was married to the police officer who'd arrested Eden the day after Ben's murder. Drew, his name was. What a small world.

"Almost six months now." Layla recalled finding her perfect little house. What would happen when Eden got out of the hospital? On her last visit, she'd looked so much better. But Layla could see the raw edges of paranoia and wondered what was behind it, not so she could help her friend—but to feed that paranoia, to buy herself more time with Finn. She had even managed to set her off the last two visits, but it wasn't going to be enough. It wouldn't be long before they let someone as harmless as Eden Wyatt out of detention, and Layla felt a squeeze of panic. There had to be a way to make sure Eden stayed locked up. She would kill again if that's what it took. She'd even pulled some old strings with Doc Jones—ornery witch that she was. But someone at the hospital had figured out their connection and moved Eden. Eden had lucked out there, but Doc Jones was still in charge of Eden's final evaluation. This gave Layla hope that she and Finn could stay in Virginia. If not—she was researching some underground networks for battered woman in Europe. Just in case she and Finn had to leave. A year ago, she'd spoken with a woman who ghosted her ex-husband into the network with their two children. He would have killed her if she stayed.

There was much more to be done before this was all over. Layla was moving everything into place, and she had Eden on her side, advocating to keep Finn in her care. And soon he would legally be Layla's son.

Waving goodbye to the ladies an hour later, she walked the short distance back to her house. She took her time and breathed in the fresh air, watching the birds take flight from a stop sign. Then she saw it: the outline of a person in the driver's seat of a black pickup truck. It wasn't unusual to have people lingering on the street, but this was the third time she'd seen this person in so many days. Were they watching her? She thought of Olivia and her demands. Olivia wouldn't be so easy to get rid of, and she couldn't be trusted. As she passed, she got a good look at the license plate as the truck roared to life and pulled slowly away from the curb.

If Layla was one thing, it was cautious, and she believed things happened for a reason. There was something up with this person, and she needed to find out what.

She watched the truck circle back toward the playground before she went inside; the man from the truck had parked and was getting out, making his way over to her new friends.

She pulled her cellphone out of her pocket and dialed.

"Hey, friend."

Layla rolled her eyes. "I need to come over."

"You got some money for me?"

Layla could hear the intake of breath and wondered if Olivia was still smoking in the house. "Yeah, fifteen grand, like we discussed." If only Olivia knew how much Eden had actually agreed to, she'd be livid.

Olivia laughed. "This was too easy. Thanks for the suggestion."

Layla bit the inside of her cheek as she recalled the first time the idea of getting Olivia involved had popped into her head.

The day of Ben's funeral had been a cool spring morning. Olivia's skin had looked plump as she stared down into the grave of her doting brother. She had been so sad, Layla thought.

A small group of mourners had gathered around the freshly turned earth; its sweet stench filled the air. His casket had been cherry-stained wood fitted with gold hinges and handles. It had been suspended above the hole as the crew worked to lower him down into the mouth of the grave. She forced herself to reconcile that the body in the wood box had once been her best friend's charismatic, energetic husband. That night crept back to her, and the strangled sound of his plea echoed in her ears. It was the guilt, nothing more. She didn't believe in ghosts but had felt a chill on her right. When she looked over, Olivia had moved up beside her. She wore a large black floppy hat and glasses—very dramatic.

"I can't believe she killed him," Olivia had whispered, her tone filled with sadness. "Now what? His money just sits there while she rots in the loony bin?" Layla's mouth collapsed open, but Olivia ignored her and continued. "He didn't even put me in his will." And just like that, Olivia revealed herself. "Even his mistress got some money."

People still lingered near the gravesite. Some tossed dirt or flowers over the casket and silently moved on. Malinda's tall, elegant figure stepped forward to the edge and dropped a deep red rose as tears streamed down her beautiful face.

"I should get some of that money." Olivia seemed to chew on her tongue, creating a pinch in her cheek.

Being so close to this vile woman made Layla's skin crawl, but when Olivia continued, Layla found herself moving a bit closer. "Can you believe someone from social services wants me to take their kid? They called and asked if I was interested." Olivia was shaking her head, and Layla felt her heart beat faster.

Layla could have puked at the foot of his grave at that moment if not for her sheer determination to keep her emotions hidden. It was best not to let a person like Olivia understand your weaknesses.

"What did you tell them?"

"I told them I don't want a kid. I live in a two-bedroom apartment with a roommate." She huffed, always the victim.

Layla eye's pinched shut in a gesture of gratitude.

"But now that I'm thinking about it, it might just work. I bet I could get all their money if I kept the kid. Then I could afford a nanny and my own house." Her eyes shone with excitement as she considered this option.

"Thank you all for coming." Ben's father spoke as he held his wife's arms. Her eyes were glossy and vacant as she stared out at them.

"He was our light." Mrs. Wyatt sniffled at his side. "Come to the house for drinks and refreshments."

The crowd slowly scattered toward the line of cars on the dirt path that wound through the cemetery.

"That's not how it works," Layla said. "You won't get anything unless she agrees to give it to you."

And that's when she got the idea. She could use Olivia to put pressure on Eden to sign the papers. If not for pressure, Eden would have been okay with the current arraignment. What Layla wanted was Finn as her son—legally. So Eden couldn't walk back into his life one day and take him back. It had happened to her once already, and it was a miracle she'd gotten out of that situation.

Now, Layla would deal with Olivia—get her out of the picture with a few bucks. "You can afford a ticket back to Cali," Layla said curtly.

"Maybe—what time you wanna stop over?"

*Maybe?* "Eight—"

"Whatever. See you then." Olivia hung up.

She bit the inside of her cheek as she patted Finn's back. He had fallen asleep again, and she paced the living room as she decided her next move. She needed to get into that house and find what Eden was hiding. Something had happened in Miami, and Layla was going to find out what. The problem was she had no idea what she was looking for.

# Chapter 33

Eden

19 days until review hearing

Jenkins walked her to the meeting she had been waiting for. The last time she spoke to Layla, she had agreed to make a deal with Olivia, but since then, Eden had heard nothing. Did Olivia take the money? Would she go away as promised? Layla, Jacob, and Lauren watched as Eden entered the conference room, where she took a seat next to Layla.

"Oh, good. Let's get started," Lauren said as Layla reached over to grasp Eden's hand. It was the most comfort she'd felt in days. The jittery feelings that preceded mania had continued, and she'd considered telling Doctor Lucas but kept putting it off, enjoying the uplift in her mood; the feel of energy throughout her hummed.

"Okay. We have the recommendation from the guardian at litem and the order asking for Layla Hughs to have full custodial rights of Finn." Lauren looked down at the papers in front of her. Eden had never dreamed in a million nightmares that it would come to this. Layla would take care of him—she loved Finn—but it didn't make it any easier to let him go, even if temporarily. This meeting made her think of her own mother sneaking out of the hospital not long after giving birth. But this was different; she wasn't abandoning Finn. She was trying to protect him.

"I'm recommending Finn stay where he is as long as it remains Eden's wish," Jacob said. "Though I do want you to know I will be meeting with Olivia tomorrow."

"What? Why?" Eden felt her pulse throb in her temples.

"This is how it works," Lauren assured her with a light touch on her hand.

"It's what I want; Finn to stay with Layla," Eden replied and felt a blush rise from her eagerness to get this over with. Olivia's face popped into her thoughts. Olivia's greed worn so casually for the world to see, as if it owed her something. "Until I'm released," she added. She hoped Finn would never learn of this moment.

"You understand that once you get out, you'll need to petition for your rights back. If Layla decides it's not in Finn's best interest for him to see you, you will have to take her to court." She felt Layla squeeze her hand, and when she looked up, she was smiling at Eden, reassuring her.

"I understand." Eden felt nausea ripple through her, and her fist clenched. She needed desperately for this to be all over before she stood and shouted that she had changed her mind.

"Lauren drew up an order; we can pass it around for everyone to sign." Jacob nodded.

"Are you sure you want to do this? We can take our chances against Olivia," Layla whispered to her. Eden thought about the money—did that mean Olivia had turned her down? She wanted to ask but she couldn't in front of the others.

"No—this is what I want. I would want you to have him if anything were to happen to me," Eden added. Her thoughts were shifting to Jinx: her recent bizarre behavior and her almost certain culpability in Gilmore's demise. It shamed her to think it was the first time she'd considered what would happen to Finn if she were to die in this place.

Layla nodded and began to sign the forms. It took Eden a moment to realize Layla had spit-up on her shoulder. How nice that must be. Before she could stop herself, she reached out to touch the soiled spot.

"Oops," Layla said, looking down at the stain.

It was too hot in the room. Eden felt tears prick her eyes as she looked down at the forms before her and picked up the pen with shaking fingers.

Once Eden had signed the last blank, she dropped the pen on the table with a loud clack. Somehow, relief swamped her. There was a chance the court would still favor a family member if Olivia wanted to push it, but it would cost her money and time. Hopefully, the fifty thousand dollars was enough to make her reconsider.

Layla stood and pulled her purse strap onto her shoulder over the soiled shirt. Eden felt disappointment stir inside of her. She wanted to visit with her, ask about Olivia, about Finn, but Layla spoke first.

"I have to run to Finn's checkup. I gave myself just enough time to take care of this and get him over there."

Eden was on her feet, too, and reached out to Layla. Eden hugged her hard, with more zeal than usual, and when she pulled away, she saw tears in Layla's eyes.

"It's okay," Eden said. "Doctor Lucas thinks I'm making progress. I'll be home before you know it." She winked at Layla, feeling the need to lighten the mood.

"Love you," Layla whispered and let her go.

Eden watched as Jacob gathered his things, and soon it was only her and Lauren left.

"Kendrick stopped by to see me. Can you make sure his invoices are taken care of?" Eden moved to sit next to her as Lauren finished organizing her papers.

"Sure thing," Lauren said. Her white suit looked soft and silky, her blond hair pulled tightly back into a French twist.

"He's going to be visiting me tomorrow to let me know what's going on," Eden said. "What about the house? I don't want Olivia there."

"Yeah, about that—" She stopped and looked at Eden. "She said she won't leave, and that Ben asked her to come stay when you had Finn—to help out. How far do you want to take this?"

Eden thought of the evidence Olivia claimed to have. Then thought of the frame of mind she was in when she was arrested. It could be true—she didn't know.

"Let me think about it." Her hands cupped her cheeks. "What about the money for Layla?"

"I sent it yesterday as you asked."

Eden nodded. Good. It would be so much better if Olivia were out of the picture, and she could work with Doc Lucas without this stress hanging over her head. There was a reason Olivia was still in Virginia, and it had to be about more money. Perhaps she was pawning items from the house. Ben's watches alone could pay for a year of living, even with the California price tag. Good, let her take all his things—all of Eden's too. There was only one thing in this world that held any value to her.

Yes, today, she would celebrate that her son was now safe.

# Chapter 34

Layla

19 days until review hearing

Today was the best day of her life. She stood in her kitchen as Finn nestled against her chest. She had rushed out of the signing that afternoon, fearful that her joy would spill out and Eden would understand the mistake she had made.

It was Friday night, and she had a date with her best little man to celebrate her official motherhood. Everyone had signed the papers, and he was now hers. Sure, Eden might eventually get out of the hospital, but Layla would be long gone by then. She'd slowly decrease her visits and keep in touch with Doc Jones to monitor Eden's recovery or her "setbacks" as they cropped up. And Doc Jones would be sure to find setbacks. Her marriage depended on it. When Layla had emailed the pictures of the good doctor with a man—not her husband of twelve years—the reply was fast.

*What do you want me to do?*

Layla didn't want or need Doc Jones to know who she was. Just that she was on the hook to be sure Eden never walked free. And, true to her word, the fork and threatening notes began to materialize. She pictured Eden's frantic explanations as she tried to explain them away, which only made her appear more paranoid and unhinged, Layla was sure.

The hard part was over, and now she could relax a little. She leaned down and kissed Finn's soft skin.

"I love you," she whispered.

Shuffling into her living room, the TV was playing in the background when she pulled the carrier down and slowly peeled Finn away from her body as his eyes remained closed. She laid him in the Pack 'n Play, not wanting to put him to bed for the night yet, even given the late hour. The only task left for the day loomed large from the center of the coffee table. The album she had stolen from Eden's house. She'd observed each of the torn and defaced pictures with anxiety last time, but now, as she sat on her sofa, a bottle of beer sweating on the coaster, the album made her feel safe. It was the insurance policy she needed, just in case.

She had to make sure Eden was put away for life, that she would never get out to take Finn back. All she had to do was convince someone that Eden had planned to kill Ben. This hadn't been part of the original plan either, but Finn had changed her life, and she couldn't imagine the long, lonely days without him. Eden wasn't going to stay with her no matter what she claimed. She was young and beautiful; she could get out and find someone new and move on with her life. Layla couldn't let that happen. It was an odd sensation to love someone you had to destroy. And taking Finn would destroy Eden.

She cracked the worn spine of the photo album, and her eyes traveled over the pictures: Eden and Ben's wedding.

Eden's tiny waist pulled impossibly tight into a corset top that blossomed into a long flowing dress. She was radiant, one of the most beautiful women Layla had ever seen. But she was weak, too weak in the end to protect what was hers.

The wedding photos became more grotesque and defaced as she continued to turn the pages. Their glossy surfaces were scratched or cut away, holes burned into the images. The defilement didn't end with Ben's pictures, but marred Eden's also, and Layla sensed the regret Eden had for ever meeting Ben Wyatt. Wedding pictures moved to honeymoon pictures, which had received the same treatment. Eden must have hated Ben in the end, but she didn't show it outwardly. In fact, Layla had no idea until she saw this album how much hate was welling inside of her friend.

When Layla finally got to the last page, she moved to close the book but caught sight of the corner of a piece of paper wedged into the album's spine. She tugged at it, and it pulled loose. A pink palm tree was displayed in the corner of notebook paper. A telephone number, and a single name, *Jason Sandoval*, was written in Eden's handwriting. Layla's heart began to thump; she thought she had just come across something essential but had no idea what it was. Eden had never mentioned a man named Jason to her. Was Eden seeing another man?

Using her phone, she discovered it was a Miami area code. She wanted to dial the number, but what was she going to say?

She opened her laptop and searched for Jason Sandoval in Miami, Florida.

Several articles from local papers popped up. *Rich Philanthropist Donates to Local Hospital*. She clicked on his picture. He was a handsome man. Black hair and dark eyes, much like Eden's, but that was where the similarities ended. Not a relative.

The following three articles featured the same man, but

much different headlines. *Local Man Acquitted in Murder for Hire*. Layla swallowed against a lump in her throat. *Murder for hire?*

She set her computer aside and picked up her phone. Dialing the number, she waited.

"Hello." Her younger brother's voice instantly brought back a memory, and she recalled the last time she spoke to him. He'd helped her out following her arrest, after Todd left. It had all been just a silly misunderstanding—a tiny white lie.

Now—she was back in the same situation. She needed Richard's help, and she would risk his ire if she had to.

"Hey, little brother."

"Long time no speak," Richard said. "Staying out of trouble?" The words had had a wholly different meaning when they were teens. Now they caused her to grimace at how disappointed with her he must be.

"I need your help."

There was a pause, and she sensed he wanted to say no to her because he thought she was in legal trouble yet again.

"It's no big deal; I'm not in any trouble," she assured him, and she could hear him blow out a breath through the phone line.

"Okay..." The lone word dragged out and seemed to be the best commitment she would get from him until he found out what she wanted. She would take it.

"If I gave you a name and phone number, could you look up who it is?"

Richard worked at a police department in southern Virginia, detective division, and his current job assignment was white-collar crimes.

"What's this for?"

She knew he would ask, so she recited her prepared answer. "Someone's harassing my friend, and she only has the number he's calling from. You know how I am with this stuff. I just want to know who's calling her. She's scared."

"Well, if someone's threatening her, she needs to call the local police."

"It's some creep, she thinks. He hasn't threatened her or anything. He's just, you know, passive aggressive."

There was a long pause, and finally, he said, "Okay—give me the number. I'll see what I can find."

# Chapter 35

Eden

18 days until review hearing

W hat sleep she got was broken and filled with anxious dreams. She was late for an appointment or left the house with no pants on. It was still a small sort of relief that she was dreaming at all. She'd used to have the most vivid dreams. Her slow return to what might be her new normal was welcoming until she found herself staring up at the ceiling for hours, the whisper of dread telling her that if she didn't sleep, she would go crazy again.

Then she thought about Gilmore—creeping into her room to touch her, his hand slithering out of the darkened corners. His snicker bounced off the space and whispered over her clammy flesh. But when she woke, she remembered Gilmore was gone—and he wasn't coming back.

\* \* \*

Kendrick stood when she entered the room, and she felt a calm come over her. It was still a shock to her that the man who'd brought such devastating news about Ben's betrayal had become such a good friend.

"It's nice to see you again." He smiled; white teeth contrasted his dark skin.

Eden sat across from him and reached a hand out to squeeze his. "Thanks for coming."

A stack of papers sitting on the table caught her eye, and her fingers itched to reach out and grab them. Information: she needed to know what was going on, what Kendrick had learned. She wanted him to announce that Olivia had packed up and moved back to California unexpectedly, but he didn't.

"I was watching your house and looked up anything I could find on Olivia." He shook his head. "That girl is about as interesting as a rock."

Eden frowned inwardly; he didn't find anything. She peered at a stack of pictures, the top of which was a shot of Olivia with her lawyer, Mr. Foster. His smug face frozen in time next to Olivia.

Since the last time Eden had seen her, over a year ago by her calculations, Olivia had put on weight. Her dyed blond hair was curled, and her makeup applied with a heavy hand over her deep scowl.

"This is her lawyer." Kendrick handed the picture to her, no doubt noticing her eyeing it. Eden nodded and took the picture from him.

"Did she drop the custody case?" Eden asked, feeling trepidation wiggle down her spine.

"I don't know anything about the courts." He frowned and sifted through some papers. "Olivia's been staying in your house since Ben's funeral." Kendrick handed over other photos. Pictures of Olivia by the pool—Eden's pool—sunning herself with a drink. Bile rose in Eden's throat. "All I know is there's a list of creditors and an angry ex-roommate looking to settle scores with her. There's nothing else."

"Did you speak with her?"

Kendrick shook his head. "I talked with a neighbor who said Olivia told her you planned to kill Ben because you found out he was going to ask for a divorce. Said Ben told her he was going to tell you right around the time you killed him."

Eden sat still and continued to listen. That was partially true. Kendrick frowned at her, no doubt taking her silence to mean she was guilty.

"There's another woman who's moved into Olivia's circle recently that I've begun tracking."

Her eyes froze on the picture of a woman carrying a baby—her baby, in the carrier her friend Jennifer had sent from Florida. Layla smiled and chatted with a group of women at a playground. The timestamp was four days ago.

"That's Layla, and my—" Her voice shattered with the strain of her emotions. She should have been using that carrier —not another woman, even if that woman was a friend. Jealousy, fierce and abrupt, surged in her. Eden was his mother, but he was just as unreachable as when she had tried and failed for years to get pregnant. "And my son, Finn," she finished.

She wanted to reach into the picture and pull the folds of fabric away to reveal his face. Layla was beaming, and Eden wondered if she'd ever seen that kind of smile on her friend's face before. When she looked up from the photos, Kendrick's mouth was set in a grim line.

"Why are you following her?" Eden asked. "Jacob already cleared her."

"I wasn't looking for her, but she stopped by the house a few times, and I picked her up on my radar."

Those must be the visits Olivia was demanding. "Was Finn with her?"

"No—she went alone."

"She went alone?"

Kendrick nodded.

"Olivia was demanding to have access to Finn, and I told Layla it was up to her if she wanted to supervise the visitations," Eden mumbled into her hand. She was confused by her anger. Layla was her friend. Someone she trusted. But this information made her feel betrayed.

"On all the occasions Layla visited your house it was usually late and for a short time. They would chat, and Layla would be on her way." Kendrick handed over more photos, these taken in the darkness outside of her home. Layla with Olivia in the backyard, or sitting in the kitchen. One might even mistake them for friends. Where was Finn during these visits? Did Scarlett spend the night with him? "Something is going on between them."

Eden scoffed at his suggestion but didn't say anything. He had no idea how much Layla hated Olivia, and how could he? Kendrick didn't know about the hush money either. Layla had probably been at the house to give it to her.

"How well do you know Layla?"

"What do you mean?" Spindles of fear shifted over her brain. How well did she know the woman to whom she'd just given custody of Finn?

"She changed her name—"

"I know," Eden snapped. "She was divorced several years ago. It wasn't a secret or anything."

Kendrick paused, waiting for her to settle again. "Yes, Hughs is her maiden name, but she changed her first name as well. Her birth name is Dianne Amelia Hughs." He pushed papers to rest by her unmoving hand. She wouldn't look at them while her brain tried to reason what it meant. There was probably a simple explanation. Maybe Layla hated her birth name and wanted it changed.

"What I'm about to tell you may be upsetting." He surveyed her from across the table, seemingly considering his options. The room was growing warmer, and she resisted the urge to fan her face with the papers and photos still in her hands. Her senses were screaming to stop listening to Kendrick, but her reasonable side told her she must keep going. She noticed she was sitting on the edge of her seat, subconsciously moving toward him.

"Okay—" she managed in a somewhat even tone.

"I spoke with some of the women in that picture; one of them is the spouse of my friend. She told me Layla claimed Finn was her son—a miracle child of sorts that she gave birth to last year." Kendrick frowned.

The air seemed to evaporate from her lungs as they shrank. She shook her head, but no command from her brain was forcing the movement.

"I don't understand." Her voice tumbled away from her like an ebbing tide in the quiet room. "She must be trying to fit in with the other mothers. It can't be easy to tell our story." As the excuse for Layla's behavior was crafted in her consciousness she was nodding. Yes—that must be it. She was trying to protect Finn and herself from scrutiny. These women were playdate moms; who the hell cared what Layla told them? She took several deep breaths as her brain processed this information.

"We should stop," Kendrick said. "I'll come back another time."

"No—" The word came out more forceful than she wanted. Kendrick opened his mouth to speak but snapped it shut again. "I'm okay. It's just, we need to watch her," Eden said, getting her bearings. She felt her mind gain traction. If there was even a chance that any of what Kendrick was telling her was true, she needed to know. She didn't want to believe Layla could betray her, but she didn't have the luxury of letting this go.

"I was also able to talk to a friend of mine in the PD in Cedar Lakes, Drew Turner."

Eden nodded.

"He's a good buddy of mine, and he shared with me that Layla was arrested just after her divorce a few years back; said she petitioned for her name change after the charges were dropped."

"Arrested?" The possibility that she'd just signed papers to give her son to a criminal overwhelmed Eden. "For what? What was she arrested for?" *Why hadn't the lawyers found out about this?*

Kendrick held up his hand to silence the barrage of questions. "Take a breath."

Eden forced air in and out.

"She was arrested in Virginia, but in another town—she was never charged. Her kid brother worked for the FBI at the time, and he pulled a bunch of favors. Given her explanation— the charges were dropped. She changed her name the next year when she moved to Cedar Lake as sort of a start-over."

Had she told Eden she wasn't from Cedar Lake? Perhaps Eden only assumed she was.

"What did she do?" She needed him to tell her, and he was stalling. Her breath caught against her fingers, panic closing around her throat. "Why was she arrested?"

"Kidnapping. The child was a neighbor of hers."

Eden blinked back at him as she reconsidered the entire friendship. They had met at a group for women who wanted children so badly that they couldn't cope. Was Eden's mental deterioration giving Layla a chance she'd been waiting for all along?

She was surprisingly calm as she took a deep breath and stared back at Kendrick. There was one thing she needed to know. "The phone. Did you find the phone?"

He looked around and slid something from his pocket over into her waiting hand.

# Chapter 36

Layla
17 days until review hearing

He was there again that morning when she backed out of her driveway to head to work—sitting behind tinted glass in the black truck. He didn't even try to hide that he was watching her. She wanted to storm over to his window and demand to know what he was doing, but she caught sight of her friends down the sidewalk and didn't want to make a scene. After her fourth call to Scarlett to check on Finn, the babysitter finally asked if everything was okay.

Later, after she was home from work, he was gone, only to reappear by dinnertime. After waiting almost an hour, she decided to call the police. She didn't want to do it, but what if he tried to kidnap Finn? The thought sent her swirling into a near panic. What if this man was involved in a kidnap for ransom scheme? To an outsider, Finn could run into all that family money.

"Nine-one-one, where's your emergency."

"1217 Market Avenue," she sputtered while keeping her eyes trained on the truck. "There's a man outside my home spying on me, and I'm terrified. He's parked on the street near my house. There's a child here."

"What make and color is the truck?"

"Black—Dodge, I think."

"Yes ma'am, I'm going to dispatch officers to your location; please remain on the line." She could hear murmuring and the sharp click of typing in the background before the woman came back on the phone.

"I'm going to ask you to please stay in the house and don't engage him. Make sure when the officers arrive, you remain in the house. They will come talk to you once they're done, okay?"

Layla's eyes trekked over to Finn and back to the window.

"Do you know the man?"

"No—I mean, I've seen him parked here before, but I don't know who he is." Should she have called the police sooner? What if he did something before they got here?

In less than seven minutes, the first police car arrived.

"They're here." Relief flooded her as the police car pulled up behind the man, the car's blue lights flickering in the fading daylight.

"Thank you," Layla said to the dispatcher and hung up without another word.

She watched as two police officers approached the man as he lowered his window. She was expecting them to pull him out and throw him to the ground, but instead, she saw the man's black arm come out, which one officer met with a handshake.

The man stepped from the truck and she watched him talk and joke with the two officers, hitching his chin toward her house. He was a big man, with a wide white grin. Another roar of laughter and finally, one of the officers, a Latino woman, approached the house. The officer couldn't have been over five foot one and a hundred pounds. Finn, now tucked against Layla's hip, happily chewed his hand as she swung the door open before the officer even knocked.

"Hello, ma'am, I'm Officer Ortiz."

"Yes. Hi. Thanks for coming so quickly." She pulled the door wider so the officer would come in. The other officer and the man watching her house were still beside his truck, talking loudly with sporadic laughter.

What were they doing? What if he was a police officer, and he was working undercover?

Officer Ortiz stepped inside, and Layla saw her eyes scan the area. Was that normal? Probably so.

"Ma'am—"

"Layla," she interrupted.

Officer Ortiz nodded. "Layla, the man outside your home is a private investigator, and he's working."

"What's he working on?" she exclaimed, hugging Finn a little closer. A private investigator outside her home—instead of relief, she felt something darker swirling up inside of her. Had someone hired him to keep tabs on her?

"I didn't ask, but he has the right to be on a public road." She paused, and her hand raised in the direction of the men on the street. "My partner knows him well, says he's a good man."

Was that supposed to make her feel better? And more alarmingly, how long had he been following her? What did he know?

"Who is he—investigating?" She almost said "spying on" but held her tongue. It was best to be friendly, and maybe Ortiz would share more with her.

Officer Ortiz looked her square in the eyes. "He didn't mention, and I didn't ask."

"Well, is that it then?" Layla's tone turned angry. An eerie feeling creeping into her, bearing the surety that he was there to spy on her, and the police would do nothing to help her.

"Yes, ma'am. If you need anything else, don't hesitate to call us back, but Mr. Morgan won't bother you." The officer paused at the door. "I don't know if he'll mind me saying this to you, but he's a good man. He volunteers for our RAD program and works with a local battered women's group to help them find new homes when they've been abused and need to leave." The officer's words hung in the air and Layla couldn't seem to articulate a proper response that didn't make her sound cold and indifferent. She didn't care what he did for other women. She cared why he was parked at her house at all hours of the day, spying on her.

Layla only nodded as the officer left the foyer and headed back to her cruiser. Repeating the name over and over in her head, she committed it to memory. Morgan. Morgan.

She slammed the door, and Finn fussed at her shoulder. "Shhhh, it's okay, honey."

But it wasn't. More troubling than his presence was the fact that someone had hired this man.

She pulled shut all the curtains and blinds in the house. She wasn't going to let his gaze touch her things or his camera lens document her life. She pulled roughly at them and trekked to each room. Was it Eden? Would she be in her right mind to hire someone to ensure Layla was taking care of her son? No—that didn't seem right. At their meeting the other day, Eden was putty in her hands. Eden didn't even suspect anything after she had left right after signing those papers, buying Layla's excuse about an appointment. Poor, trusting Eden lost everything that day and didn't know it yet. Layla stopped, yanked the last curtain closed, and looked down at Finn resting against her chest. Olivia might have the audacity to hire someone. Maybe look for a bit of dirt so she could squeeze more of Eden's money out of Layla.

Before settling on that thought, she picked up her house phone and called Olivia.

"I thought I'd be hearing from you," Olivia said before any greeting.

"I'll be by tonight."

"Fine, we'll talk then." And Olivia hung up.

Layla was going to have to speed things up.

The presence of Mr. Morgan quickly stole Layla's new joy. She had paced and watched him for the rest of the daylight hours. Until she watched his truck pull away. She wondered if he'd just went to a new spot to watch her. Finn was down for the night, and she was on her second beer when her phone rang. She couldn't risk going to see Olivia tonight. She would call and cancel.

"What did you find out, Richie?" Layla tried to keep her tone contrite.

"You know I hate when you call me that." Instead of the old banter they once shared, he sounded serious, almost angry.

She changed tactics. "I appreciate you sticking your neck out for me. My friend is distraught. This man called her three times yesterday."

Richard blew out a breath. "I'm sorry. I'm having a rough go of it today." He didn't offer any more explanation, and she found herself hoping he would move on without much of a to-do about it. She didn't need to hear about his problems—she had her own to deal with.

"Who did you say this woman was again? This is all pretty shady."

"A friend of mine. And what does shady mean? You're a cop—almost everything you deal with is suspect." This was true. They'd once had a relationship where they shared stories, and her little brother had seen some terrible things. Up until her arrest, they had been closer than they were now, and she wondered if he had used the last of his love on helping her out of that situation, and now had nothing left to give her. That was fine; as long as he helped her out, she was okay with the gap. She had made a gap with everyone in her life.

"He works for a man police believe was involved in at least five murders in the Miami area, but he's good, never been caught. No evidence, no witnesses. Jason Sandoval does all the vetting for possible clients."

"Clients for who?"

"His boss kills people, or so the intel says." Richard took a deep breath. "They suspect there is no boss, and Jason himself is a hired killer, but it's never been proven. The guy's a ghost when it comes to putting together a case against him."

"What?" She felt a flush of heat move up her neck as she stared down at the piece of paper. Sandoval was a hitman? Why did Eden have this man's number?

"Do you have any idea why someone would just have this man's number lying around?"

"From what I can see, the only reason I would speak with this man is if I wanted someone killed, and I had the money to pay for it."

Layla may have just stumbled upon Eden's dirty little secret. And just like that, Layla knew how she was going to bury Eden Wyatt in prison for life and take care of Olivia along with her.

# Chapter 37

Eden
16 days until review hearing

Eden stared out the window as beads of rain slid down in zigzags. Sitting on the sofa in the day room, where she'd been for the last hour. Thinking about everything happening to her. The notes, the custody paperwork she'd signed. Layla.

"I have something for you," a low whisper came from behind her. Eden twisted around so quickly that her neck strained, and she grabbed at her throat, silencing a cry into her cupped fingers. Jinx stood behind her, so close she could feel her breath on her face.

A picture of Jinx's emotional instability began to form in Eden's mind. Jinx competed with everyone to be the center of attention in every situation. Eden had wrongly believed it was male attention Jinx craved, but now she understood it was all attention. It was apparent from watching her twisted reality that she assumed everyone was competing with her too. Even though Chaz wouldn't dare look at Eden, Jinx began to show jealousy toward Chaz when he spoke to Eden. With this knowledge came new fear—how dangerous was Jinx? It had taken her no time at all to get rid of Gilmore for his perceived sin. And even though Eden's manipulation had worked out perfectly, she knew she had no control over Jinx's behavior, and that more than likely she considered Eden a threat.

A loud clap erupted across the room, and Eden jumped, already on edge. Rain pelted the window in a steady rhythm, making it hard to concentrate on what Jinx was saying. Even Willie sat quietly, entranced by the cascading water, none of his usual rantings. Eden folded her feet underneath her butt on the sofa and turned back to the window.

"Do you want one?" Jinx asked. "A phone. So you can, ya know, have conversations with people without them listening."

Eden shifted. Had Chaz mentioned to Jinx that she was asking about a phone? Her instinct told her to tell Jinx no—she didn't want one, she had a phone—

"Where do you hide them?" Eden thought of the phone that Kendrick had given her, which was now taped to the inside of the toilet tank in one of the common bathrooms off the day room. Even if someone were to find it, it couldn't be traced back to her.

Jinx shrugged. "Sometimes they do checks."

"I—" Eden, still rattled from their last encounter, tried to make sense of Jinx's behavior.

"What about your little friend? Wouldn't you like to talk to her?"

Yes, she would, but she didn't say so. At the mention of Layla, she felt a tightness in her muscles. She had tried several times to contact her lawyer since Kendrick visited yesterday. But what could even be done about it now? Since he'd told her, the edge she had felt had dulled with the medication. She told

Eva Mackenzie

herself she had time and not to worry about it. Everything would work out—Layla wouldn't hurt her; they were like sisters. It was most likely an easy story she told her nosy new friends.

Eden shivered, and Jinx's sharp eyes didn't miss it. "What's up with you?"

"Nothing. No, I don't need a phone. I'm trying to stay out of trouble." Yes. This was the right thing to do, and Doc Lucas would approve. Oddly, she was a little bit proud of herself.

Jinx abruptly stood and took the few steps to drop beside Eden on the sofa, causing Eden to shift. They both looked to the front of the room where Marsha and Lynsi were talking. Slowly, Jinx shifted her hands, and Eden felt the cool surface of plastic in her palm. She wanted to shake it away but couldn't move. Jinx's head dropped back on the sofa, and she turned away from Eden and lapsed into silence.

"First one's free," Jinx murmured and, in an ominous tone, added, "You gotta protect what's yours, just like I do." And with that, she stood and walked toward the door. Before she disappeared, she leaned over and said something to Marsha, who frowned.

The exchange raised gooseflesh on Eden's arms, and she could feel the weight of the phone in her hand grow heavy. Why did she take it? She told Jinx no. She cut her eyes down to the nondescript black phone. She rubbed it with her sleeve and dropped it into the sofa cushions. There was no way she was going to have anything to do with this phone—not after what Jinx had done to her. And it was clearer than ever—she had to take care of Jinx.

\* \* \*

240

Doctor Lucas sat in his usual chair; his manner relaxed as he listened. He took notes less often, instead watching her lay back on the sofa. She'd continued to look forward to their meetings, taking care to look her best. She didn't want to think about what was happening between them—she wrote it off as nothing: the lingering gazes, the heat in her belly.

"There's something that's bothering me." Eden shifted back into the deep sofa and crossed her legs. She liked how his office smelled familiar, like the angles of his jaw and his warm stare.

"Yes."

"It's Gilmore. Something I haven't told anyone." To her ears, her voice sounded shaky and weak. But Doc Lucas's glance was concerned and helped her continue. No one seemed to care that Jinx could have pushed him—no one was asking questions.

"I'm the reason he fell down the stairs. Or should I say was pushed."

He was alert now. His eyes sharpening—not warm any longer.

"Why would you say he was pushed? There was an investigation, and I think it's concluded. Tell me why you think this is your fault."

"Because." She looked away in shame. "I told Jinx he was the reason she was moved to Doctor Jones."

His brow furrowed. "He wasn't the reason."

She shook her head. "I heard him talking one day. Everyone knows she—" Her eyes looked down into her lap. "Everyone knows she loves you."

He frowned, and her heart sank to think he might be disappointed with her.

"I overheard him telling another staff member that he had to mention her obsession to Doc Jones, and right afterward, she was moved. I told her the truth when she asked me. Maybe I should have lied?" She paused for effect. "And she pushed another person a while ago."

"What other person?"

"You know. The woman who fell down the stairs—but it was Jinx—Jinx pushed her too."

"Who told you that Nina killed someone?"

"I don't remember," Eden said quickly. "I just know how she can be."

"A resident was killed, but the person who did it confessed a few days later. It wasn't Nina Nelson, or I guess everyone calls her Jinx." He didn't speak further on the subject. Why would Chaz tell her a story made up to make Jinx look danger-ous? Or maybe Doc Lucas didn't know how truly evil Jinx was, and Chaz would say anything to protect her.

* * *

Before they took her back to her room she asked to stop at the bathroom. She reached into the tank of the toilet and, with a sigh, retrieved her phone from the small bag she'd placed inside, and turned it on. She'd memorized Lauren's number. It had been a while since she'd used a cellphone. Her fingers fumbled over the screen, dialed the number, and she got Lauren's voice-mail. She almost hung up, but she needed to talk to her—

"Hey, it's me, Eden. I want you to hold off on the custody order if you can. There's something wrong, and I don't know what it is. Come see me; we have to figure this out." She hung up and, after a moment, put the phone back in its place and closed her eyes. Making the call caused raw paranoia over Layla's possible betrayal to set in. As if it confirmed her suspi-cions. It was only days ago she was fighting tooth and nail to keep Finn with Layla. Now she would have to wait, and if it came to it, do whatever she had to to protect Finn.

# Chapter 38

Layla
15 days until review hearing

I t was Tuesday morning, and she was running late again. Finn's teething had kept him up most of the night; worth it. She was rushing to get out of the house when her phone rang.

"Hello," she said briskly.

"Layla, hi, it's Lauren." The sound of wind rushed over the phone through an open window.

"Yes. Did I forget to sign somewhere?" Layla asked. She ignored the hiccup of panic. It was all over now; she just needed to stop freaking out at every little thing. Ever since she found the man outside her house, plus a hired killer's number in her best friend's phone—she had been overthinking everything. She wouldn't get caught.

"No—it's not that at all. Eden's changed her mind. She wants to leave things the way they are for now. With you being the primary guardian of Finn, she will let the court decide on custody based on the current situation." Layla halted in her tracks, hovering over the freshly mowed grass. This couldn't be happening; everyone signed the papers—it was done. "I don't think this will be an issue at all after speaking with Doc Lucas."

"Not an issue?" Doc Jones had said she was going to take care of this. She promised.

"I can't really say. Mr. Foster and I are also making arraignments to settle this."

What the hell did that mean?

She felt her pulse thrashing in her veins and took a deep breath.

"Oh, what arraignment is that?" Layla asked as casually as possible, but her voice sounded uneven and forced. Just a regular conversation with an ordinary person, she told herself, but her fist tightened.

"I can't say. I haven't had a chance to go see her in person, so I just wanted you to know my office hasn't filed the paperwork, and if Eden decides to move forward again, we'll have to draw up a new agreement."

"Has she hired a private investigator by chance?" Layla asked.

There was a beat of silence on the other end of the line as sweat gathered around her ears, and she rushed her sleeved arm over her forehead.

"I'm not aware of anyone—" Lauren's voice broke as if her phone had lost signal. "Why do you ask?"

"No reason." A quick response. "I'll go see her as soon as I can so we're all on the same page," she added.

"That sounds great. I know she'd love to see you."

But was that true anymore?

\* \* \*

Her cellphone rang again, and she half hoped it was Lauren calling back, telling her things had changed yet again. But Olivia's number flashed across her screen, and she took a deep breath before tapping the screen.

"Hey," she answered, not too excitedly. *Get it together, and don't screw this up now.*

"Where are you? We need to talk." There was quiet on the other end of the line when Olivia stopped speaking, and it made Layla question if she was being recorded.

"About what?" Layla would play dumb.

"Eden's stupid attorney just sent trespass papers to me!" Disbelief was plain in her tone. "No one's even living here, and I had to pay for cleaners to come clean all the blood out."

Layla cringed.

"It's a lot more than you'd think to get blood out. They charge extra. Biohazard and all."

"I paid you the money. Now go back to your life in California," Layla said as gently as she could, holding back all the words she wanted to say.

"I can't. I got evicted because I've been here so long; my roommate got someone else in there," she whined.

"I don't know what to tell you. It's her house."

"But she's in a loony bin." A lighter cracked to life. "She isn't even living here."

"What do you want me to do about it?" Layla's calm resolve was shifting away. She was trying, but dealing with Olivia was like working with a spoiled teen.

"Talk to her. She's your friend," she demanded.

"Okay—okay. I'll talk to her." She had no plan to bring this up with Eden at the next visit. Layla was more likely to park outside the house and watch while the sheriff's office put her stuff out on the curb.

"And I talked to my lawyer—"

"You mean the ambulance chaser you consulted?" Layla couldn't help the dig—even if it was untrue. Robert Foster was one of the best family attorneys in the area—eclipsed only by Eden's lawyer in court successes.

"Whatever. He's told me he knows the judge—they're buddies." Olivia took a breath—probably blowing smoke all over the custom sofa. "He said I could get way more than fifteen thousand if I were to get custody."

"What are you talking about? That money was hush money." Layla felt a vein pulse in her temple and sweat slide down her back. "It was to pay you to go away. Why the hell are you talking to him about it?"

"No, it wasn't—" There was a pause. "I need more now that I don't have a place to stay. I don't know how long it's going to be until they physically kick me out of here." She was rambling now, and Layla could barely hear her over the dull roar in her ears.

"You don't want to do this, Olivia," Layla said sternly. "I have custody of Finn now. You won't be taking her to court. I'll be the one at the table, and I know all about the kind of person you are. Don't you think Eden would spare any expense to prevent you from taking her son?" Layla almost slipped and said "my son." Hopefully Olivia's attorney didn't know about the custody order being rescinded.

There was a long pause as Olivia contemplated her words.

"I want more. Fifteen thousand wasn't enough. Rob thinks I should get half a million."

As though this wasn't about the life of an innocent child, but about how much money she could squeeze from Eden.

"Tell me why Rob thinks you should get five hundred thousand dollars."

Olivia huffed on the other end of the line. "He didn't say

for what, just noticed how desperate she was to make me go away once I filed the paperwork, just like you said."

A sharp inhalation was out before she could stop herself. "Did you mention that I helped get you the money?" Her tone was wrath-filled, and for a moment, she thought she was going to lose it.

"No—not by name, I said a friend."

"What the hell, Olivia? I helped you out. It's fifteen thousand dollars you didn't have before." She should have expected this, of course, especially because she had held back thirty-five thousand dollars just in case she and Finn needed to go on the run.

"I can always go pay her a visit," Olivia concluded.

"What?" Layla didn't catch what the bitch had said.

"I said I can always go talk to her myself. Tell her about how you and I came to our little agreement," Olivia said.

"You're blackmailing me?" Layla said, anger building inside of her. She pushed away the rage and focused. It didn't matter what Olivia threatened: she'd be dead soon.

# Chapter 39

Eden

14 days until review hearing

Outside her room, she heard the soft squeak of shoes against the floor as orderlies and nurses began moving around for the day. The pounding on a shared wall had started an hour ago and persisted, rousing her from a sort of daze—not sleep, but she hadn't been awake either.

Her journal rested right where she'd left it, and on impulse, she opened it and scanned its pages—nothing besides her thoughts she wrote last night. No notes or contraband had been found in her room since Gilmore's "accident."

"Well, hi there." She whirled around to the sound of Marsha's voice. "I didn't mean to scare you."

"It's okay," she stuttered. "I'm okay."

The nurse handed her two cups, the same as every morning.

"I saw Jenkins on his way up to get you for breakfast. You

okay with that?" The nurse eyed her, and Eden nodded a bit too emphatically. She had to self-talk now, gather all the information she knew in her mind—all her scattered thoughts were colliding with her calm exterior. Soon the staff would see her coming into mania. She didn't understand why, when she was taking the medication every day.

"I'll be ready." She made a show of making the bed, and Marsha left.

As she flipped the covers back, something clapped against the wall behind her. She scanned the floor, frantic to find the source of the noise. You're going crazy again, Eden—

Nothing was visible from the floor, so she sank to her knees to peer under the bed. She caught sight of a shadow of something lying next to the wall, and she pulled and stretched to reach it. Finally, her fingers grasped a smooth, plastic object and pulled it to her.

A phone, small and black, lay in her hands. Just like the one Jinx had given her yesterday. The one she had carefully left in the couch cushions in the day room. The sight of the phone now alarmed her. Was her mind so far gone that she remembered stuffing it between the worn cushions, but it wasn't true? She wasn't sure what she feared most—that it had never happened or that it had, and now there was another phone laying on her bed in its place. She wanted to hurl it across the room, but curiosity got the best of her, and with one touch, it lit up.

The phone was fully charged. She scrolled through the call log and noticed one number from yesterday. Her heart froze. She immediately recognized the Miami area code but didn't know who the number belonged to.

How had this phone gotten into her room? Her eyes raced around; she had to get rid of it before Jenkins showed up. But as she looked up from the bright screen, Jenkins' sharp features were staring at her.

"Ready?" As usual, he didn't attempt to cross into her room —but he looked down at the phone and back up at her, a frown bowing his mouth.

"You can't have phones in here." He held his hand out, and she nearly tossed it at him, wanting to be rid of it.

"I'm sorry. It's—" She didn't get the words out before he turned on his heels and left the room. Maybe he wasn't going to tell anyone. She moved quickly to catch up, wanting to explain herself further, but she couldn't figure out what to say before they arrived at the cafeteria.

Chaz was sitting alone, and after retrieving her food tray, she crossed the space to his table, taking a spot across from him. He liked his space more than the average person, and unlike Jinx, who seemed to enjoy the discomfort of others, Eden made sure to give him the space he required.

"Hey," he said, not looking up from his food. His shoulders hunched possessively over his breakfast as if someone might come up behind him and club him to death for it.

"Where's Jinx?" she asked scanning the room.

He shrugged and shoveled a chunk of pancake into his mouth. Willie shuffled in and sat down. "Cake. Cake. Cake." The big man cheered and slapped his palm against the table.

"You know she lied to you yesterday," Chaz said. His jaw worked up and down vigorously; food chunks spit past his open lips.

"About what?" she asked quietly. She didn't know if it was the cameras or the orderlies, but she felt someone was watching her, even though Willie and the new girl, Beth, were the only other patients in the room.

"I mean, she stabbed her ex-lover over twenty times. It was brutal," he said, matter-of-factly.

"She said she was set up—" But Eden never really believed Jinx was set up. She was sure there were some innocent people here, but not most. "Never mind."

"She blamed the woman she abducted for trying to steal him away."

"How do you know this?"

He shrugged again.

"Cake. Cake. Cake," Willie continued as Lynsi delivered his food, and only then did he fall silent.

"I know a lot of things. I listen—people think I'm not smart, I guess." He twisted his earlobe between his fingers almost roughly as he shoveled more food into his mouth.

"I don't think that," she said, and he glanced at her, so fleetingly she wondered if he had looked at her at all.

"She doesn't like you." He shook his head with three quick jerks. "Nope—just like the girl who fell down the stairs," he said, as if her official name was "the girl who fell down the stairs."

The one who Jinx probably killed. But hadn't Doc Lucas told her someone else had confessed to pushing that woman?

"Why didn't she like her?"

"Any time someone gets between Jinx and what she wants, they have to be eliminated."

"What did Jinx want that this other woman took?" She knew she was speaking in hypotheticals—Jinx assumed people wanted what she thought was hers. Doctor Lucas's easy smile flashed in her mind. Well, he wasn't Jinx's.

A guilty look covered his face, and the truth hit her like a punch to her gut. "It was you? Jinx thought this woman was taking you away from her?"

"I don't want to talk about her." His voice was strained. "I wouldn't cross her if I were you." But he didn't deny her statement.

"What happened to the woman she abducted?"

"She's okay. She almost killed Jinx, but she's still bothering her."

"The woman is bothering Jinx?"

He shook his head. "Jinx uses the phones her lawyer brings to call her—harass her. Penance, she calls it." As Eden looked up, Jinx entered the room, and Chaz's lips flattened to release a soft hissing noise. Her red hair was wild around her pale skin as she walked to them.

"Hey, slut." Her eyes narrowed at Eden. "And Eden." She laughed heartily at Chaz's scowl.

She seemed happy—too happy, like a manic episode after a deep low. Her cheerful mood was as concerning as her angry ones.

"What's up?" she asked, looking at Eden again.

"Nothing." Should she ask her about the phone? "I noticed —" The words wouldn't come out. The silence grew around them, and she felt her heart skip. She took a bite of her breakfast, and the food felt heavy and tasteless as she swallowed.

"Did you go into my room this morning?" Eden kept her voice low, and her eyes trained on Jinx for a reaction.

"What are you talking about?" But it looked like she was smiling. Eden found herself turning to Chaz, but she wasn't sure why. He wasn't going to help Eden out and make an enemy of Jinx.

"Eden, do you feel okay?" Jinx reached out and grabbed her hand. At first, Eden thought she was trying to comfort her, but then she began to squeeze, her nails digging into Eden's flesh. Eden tried to pull her hand back, but Jinx wouldn't let go.

"No touching," a voice called from the doorway, but Jinx didn't acknowledge it. Eden's fingers were turning red as she tugged and pulled back. Suddenly, Jinx let go, and Eden's hand flew back to hit something firm and round. Willie howled and covered his head with his fingers. The sound seemed to echo rather than muffle. Eden fell to the floor, a crack of pain scattering through her body.

"Ouch...Awwww—" he continued to howl as two orderlies made their way toward them.

"I didn't—" Eden began to speak, but Jinx jerked up from the table, her chair banging the wall behind her.

"She wouldn't give me my hand back," Jinx shouted to Lynsi. "I tried to, but she hurt me," Jinx whimpered, cradling her hand to her chest.

"What? No," Eden said. "She—"

"She's a monster, right Willie?" Jinx walked to the big man covering his ears, tears streaming down his red cheeks.

"She hit him too," Jinx insisted.

Lynsi looked at Eden, trying to make sense of it all.

"Are you okay, Willie?" Lynsi asked in a low, soft voice. Willie shook his head roughly, and she put a hand on his shoulder, which sent him further into a tantrum. "It's okay, Willie. It was an accident."

"Yes. I didn't know he was sitting behind me, and—" But no one was listening to Eden speak as they all tried to console Willie.

"Ms. Wyatt." Eden heard her name from across the room over the commotion. A man she recognized from the day Gilmore was injured stood next to Doctor Lucas. "Come with us, please."

She looked back at Lynsi, who whispered to Willie as Jinx advanced to Doc Lucas and the mystery man.

"She hit Willie, and she grabbed me." Jinx lifted an uninjured arm; both men looked from her to Eden, who shook her head. No one was giving her a chance to explain what happened, while at the same time, no one seemed concerned that she might have hurt Jinx.

"We'll take care of it, Nina," said the mystery man and gave Eden room to step past him into the hallway. Jinx argued from the other side of the doorway, but Eden didn't look back inside. Both men led the way down the hallway opposite Doc Lucas's office to an area Eden had never been to before.

The man ushered her into a room that was sterile and neat. Impersonal landscape pictures hung from white walls. She took a seat in front of the large wood desk; sweat slithered down her back, settling around her waist.

Both men stood outside the door for a moment, and she could hear their hushed low voices. The harder she strained to listen, the louder the rush of blood grew in her ears, drowning out their voices.

The man walked into the room and smiled at Eden.

"Well, Ms. Wyatt. I'm Peter Walker. I'm head of security at the facility. You may not remember meeting me before now." Suggesting that she had met him at some earlier time.

She studied his face, and thought the lines looked a bit familiar. His strong chin and plump cheeks made him look too young to be the supervisor of security.

"Hi," she mumbled. She felt the air shift behind her and turned to see Doc Lucas making his way into the office.

He took a seat next to her without a word as Peter began speaking again. "I'll get right to it; Lucas has a busy morning. Mr. Jenkins, your orderly, advised us that you were found with a phone in your room this morning. He brought it to my attention because that's what he's supposed to do. It would be best if you weren't upset with him. He was doing his job."

She found herself nodding, her stomach tangled in knots.

From her seat she could see the top of his desk where the phone rested in front of him.

"I didn't—" She felt her throat tighten. "It's not mine."

She didn't sound convinced. Yes, Jinx handed her that

phone, but she had stashed it. She had no idea what was on the phone she'd found on her bed. It wasn't hers, which made her feel all the more dread. Someone had left it there on purpose— like the notes, and the fork.

Peter's brow furrowed in deep wavy lines across his broad forehead, so deep that when his furrows unwound, there were still fine lines stretching over his skin.

"Whose is it if it isn't yours, Eden?" Doctor Lucas asked from beside her. Her hands bounced on her knees, and she forced them to stop. He didn't sound like he believed her, and maybe she didn't believe herself. How wild it must seem that she was accusing someone else of doing all these things to her and didn't know who nor why.

"I know this sounds crazy, but Jinx—I mean Nina—tried to give me a phone yesterday, and I told her..." She trailed off, knowing she would have to admit to her part in asking Chaz about a phone, and she knew they could hear it in her voice, but Peter waited for her to finish. As she looked over his face, she witnessed only disbelief.

"Then this morning, I found it sitting on my bed after I got out of the bathroom." That was true. "It's not mine. I swear." But it was defensiveness, not conviction, she heard.

"Then who sent these text messages?" Peter asked, using his fingers to turn the phone to face her. The screen lit up under the pads of his fingers, and she felt her breath hitch.

"I don't know," she said before she even had a chance to read them; the blue bubbles filled with letters blurred inside her mind. She couldn't make out what they said.

"The messages on here, several in fact, are to your sister-in-law, Olivia Wyatt, who consequently called to lodge a complaint with us and is threatening to get a restraining order against you."

Her heart skittered, a quick sort of tripping, and she reached her hand up to clutch her chest to restart it.

"I swear," she repeated and twisted in her chair to face Doc Lucas. Surely, he didn't believe this. But his defeated expression said it all. He was disappointed with her and maybe even mistrustful now.

"Wait, what do they say?" The moment that followed seemed to suck the air from her lungs. It was Peter's deep voice that sliced through the silence.

"Why don't you take a look for yourself."

He handed the phone over, and she realized her fingers were shaking. Her eyes found the text and slowly read the last one.

*You are going to die. I'm going to kill you.*

# Chapter 40

Layla

14 days until review hearing

She stood at the nurse's station, waiting for the too-skinny blonde to tell her what the hold-up was. She didn't have an appointment to see Eden, but she had never had an issue before. Now the nurse seemed unsure if she could visit. Her suspicion was turning into paranoia as she waited. Recalling Eden's eagerness to see her in the past caused a hiccup of anxiety to spill into her gut. *She knows something...*

Scenarios rolled through her head, none of which were good. Eden had backed out of signing over custody, and now she wouldn't see her. She paced the area and looked up every few steps to see if the nurse had returned.

"Doctor Lucas—here's your notebook. You left it in the break room."

Layla looked up to see a handsome man in a white coat flapping open over jeans and a polo shirt. Eden's new doctor.

She kept her eyes on him as he retrieved his notebook and looked down at a folder as he smiled and made small talk with the nurse, who was obviously attracted to him.

"Ms. Hughs." The nurse was back—pouting lips and all. "Eden isn't taking visitors today."

"Is she sick?"

"I can't say for sure—I was told she isn't seeing visitors today." The nurse dutifully repeated the same stupid excuse.

Layla turned with an absent nod. She couldn't ignore the apparent shift in her luck. She was losing Eden's support—she knew it. She walked toward Doctor Lucas. *Sometimes you have to make your own luck.*

On a whim, she said, "Thanks for helping my friend." Loud enough to catch his attention.

She watched Doctor Lucas's eyes turn to her. "I'm sorry. Do I know you?" His voice was smooth and deep. Layla could understand the appeal of a doctor like him and Eden's interest. She had only guessed he was handsome when she commented about his looks on their last phone call, but he was more attractive than she'd thought. It was almost disarming, and she forgot what she was going to say next.

"I'm Doctor Lucas." He held his hand out to her, and she shook it automatically.

"Sorry." She felt a blush rise on her cheeks. "I just got bad news about my friend, and I'm a bit worried."

"Oh." He frowned but didn't ask anything further, which forced her to bring up the subject.

"I'm here to visit Eden Wyatt, and they're telling me she isn't well."

He quickly covered the brief look of surprise on his face. "We all have our days."

"She talks about you all the time." Layla put on an uncomfortable smile. "You're her new doctor, right?"

He nodded his head. "Yes. She's coming along nicely."

This guy was too good at deflecting.

"So, she'll come home soon?" Layla said excitedly.

"We'll see."

"We'll see" wasn't good enough. He was trying to appease her with non-answers. What she needed to do was plant one little seed. To go along with the phone Doc Jones had promised to leave in Eden's room.

"I worry about her, and all this stuff going on with Olivia. Maybe when she gets out, it will all be smoothed over." She let the question ring in her voice, a worried expression on her stretched lips. She tamped down the instinct to raise her shoulders. "It's just—she can't stop talking about Olivia. But I'm sure you can deal with this new obsession. It's just—I don't want to tell you this, but I'm worried about what she might do—you know, if Olivia takes Finn away from her."

Doc Lucas's mouth hung open for a second.

"Yes, well. We'll make sure she's ready when she leaves Middle State, and her support system is going to be very important at that point."

She wanted to shout that Eden was dangerous, out of control, that she'd hurt someone again, but her doctor wouldn't buy that. No one knew how dangerous her friend was but Layla, and that was something she'd only learned after she found Jason Sandoval's number among her things; for all Layla knew, Eden would have killed Ben if Layla hadn't beaten her to it.

"It was nice to meet you," he said and began walking around her.

"Yes, nice to meet you." She watched him stroll down the hall, and she pulled her phone out of her pocket to write a text.

*Change of plans. Meet tonight.*

She walked toward the door and, before she pushed through, received a text reply.

*Bring money.*

She didn't need Doctor Lucas to sabotage Eden's stay here. She was about to kill two birds with her one stone.

# Chapter 41

Eden

14 days until review hearing

E den spent the rest of the day in her room. Now the sun sank into a black line beyond the window, into nothingness. A colorless, wild place that was humming at the edge of her consciousness. She didn't want them to see that she was on the edge of a manic episode. Her emotions were waking up, and her senses filtering through a sharper mind. She needed to focus all her newfound energy on the task of taking care of Layla, her "friend."

After Peter told her about the phone, she'd resisted the urge to ask Doc Lucas if he was disappointed in her. She had wanted to tell him someone was setting her up—but it all made her sound like she was going crazy. She would have to find out who was doing this to her first—get proof.

"We'll discuss this at our next meeting." Doc Lucas had paused and taken a big breath. "We may have to reevaluate your situation."

His words kept echoing in her erratic mind. She'd lost his much-needed support, and she didn't know how to repair the damage.

She drew her finger up to the glass and traced its clear surface. There was something niggling at the edge of her mind. Something she wanted to investigate—but she kept forgetting. Her mind jumped from thought to thought as the light faded to night, and she was vaguely aware that no one came to pick her up for her meeting with Doc Lucas.

The door clicked open.

"Do you want to eat in here tonight?" Marsha asked from the doorway. She looked harried—like she had to be somewhere. She didn't make eye contact as she went about giving Eden her evening medication.

"I'm not hungry. Thank you," Eden heard herself say but wondered where the words had come from. She was too hyper to eat.

"I think you should eat something," Marsha encouraged. "You've been in here all day. Doc Jones said you refused to see Doc Lucas for you meeting."

No—that wasn't right. Eden had never spoken to her. But instead of arguing, she remained silent.

No—she was sure she hadn't seen anyone since Doc Lucas dropped her off. After being caught with a phone that wasn't hers. The phone with the number in it—the Florida area code. Air sucked into her lungs with an audible pull, and Marsha's eyes narrowed.

"What is it?"

Eden shook her head. "Nothing—it's nothing," she chanted. "I just remembered something."

"Well, if you need anything, Jenkins is on until midnight."

"Okay—thanks." But Eden was already turning back to the window. Outwardly her features never changed, but inwardly she was frantic. The number from the phone—she knew whose it was, and she wondered how that number got in there, if not from her. Her heartbeat was pounding against her ribcage, and her head felt heavy. Maybe she should start asking about her medication. Holes, large and scary, were cropping up in her mind. She never took that phone from Jinx, but the phone they found in her room had the number of a killer on it...and someone had called him yesterday.

# Chapter 42

Layla

13 days until review hearing

L ayla pulled at the old sports bra she hadn't worn in almost ten years. It gouged into her back as she stopped on the corner to rest. She looked down at her watch as sweat slid down her face. She had to plan this just right, leaving nothing to chance.

She would need to catch her breath before heading down Lake Drive, which two police cars had turned onto half an hour ago. She pretended to stretch her calves, using the street sign to lean on, as she rechecked her watch.

Scarlett had agreed to come over early to watch Finn as Layla made some excuse for the need. The run-in with the police had to appear by chance. It would take a simple check to know Layla didn't pass by here on her way to work, but if she normally ran in the neighborhood... Everything had to play out just right. She took one final deep breath and began a slow jog down Lake Drive, where Eden's house was. Police cars lined the quaint setting, and she slowed. Yellow tape undulating in the breeze was strung from a vehicle to the oak tree and tied down to one of the lights leading up to the house's walkway. Neighbors lingered on their porches, trying to get a view of what was going on.

She slowed to a walk. She would have to make this count. The officers could use a little direction in their investigation, and she planned on giving them one.

"Can I help you?" a tall, lean man asked. He was casually dressed, but Layla saw the badge and gun hanging from his belt. She tried to see beyond him to the front yard, but a county van was parked diagonally, blocking her view.

"My name's Layla Hughs." She pointed up to the house as she caught her breath. "I'm friends with the owner of the house, and I know the woman who's staying here."

He said nothing, only looked at her until she continued speaking. "Is everything okay—you know, because of all this?" She raised her hands, indicating the police cars.

"I'm sorry, ma'am, but the woman who was staying here is dead."

She gasped and pulled her hand to her chest, only to find the gold necklace at her throat and twist it around her finger. "Oh, my goodness. What happened?"

"Ma'am, I can't discuss an ongoing investigation. What's your relationship to Olivia Wyatt?"

"I'm—um, it's a long story, but basically, her sister-in-law is my best friend. I'm caring for her son while she's—in a mental hospital for killing her husband." Layla forced a look of guilt onto her face as if she felt she was betraying Eden.

He looked at her with new interest. Perhaps he'd been expecting her to be a nosy neighbor who would be of no help.

"My name is Detective Drew Turner; do you remember me?"

Layla turned from the house and looked at him again. Sharp, icy blue eyes and a strong jaw. Yes—she nodded. "I gave you a statement about Eden after you arrested her."

He offered a sad smile. "Do you have a minute to answer some questions?"

"Yes, of course, whatever you need."

He moved her toward an unmarked police car and took out a small notebook from inside. He asked her general information that morphed into more challenging questions. "When was the last time you saw Olivia?"

"Ummm, it was last week, I think. She asked to see Finn, that's Eden's son."

"Did she seem okay when you saw her?"

"Yes. She seemed perfectly fine. May I ask how she died?"

"I can't say." How was she supposed to garner suspicion of Eden's involvement if this cop wouldn't tell her anything? She knew how Olivia died. She'd watched her stagger out of the house after a lethal dose of fentanyl found its way onto her wineglass.

She gasped again and shook her head. "This is just terrible."

He shifted back against the car, more relaxed now. "You know her pretty well then?"

"Yes. I've been stopping by. I have custody of Finn. At least for now." Layla frowned.

Drew's head cocked to the side with interest. "What do you mean by that?"

Layla made a subtle show of looking around and back to Drew. "Olivia was in a custody battle with Eden." Layla paused and bit the inside of her cheek. "Olivia called me the other day and even made the absurd claim that Eden sent threatening text messages to her, but I don't believe it. Eden doesn't have access to a phone."

Drew paused before asking, "Can I get your phone number so I can call you if I have any more questions?"

She gave him her phone number and implored him to call if he needed anything else from her.

"It's just so sad. Olivia was a wonderful person. I know Eden's upset about the custody stuff, but this—" She waved her hand at the house again. "This is such a tragedy." Her false words dripped with sadness. Poor, snotty Olivia dead, and she would make sure they knew who was to blame.

# Chapter 43

Eden

13 days until review hearing

When the door to the conference room opened, Lauren bolted up from the table and rushed to her. "Don't say anything. Okay?" Her eyes were searching as she waited for Eden to acknowledge her.

"Okay—" Before she could ask what was wrong, Eden saw a man's eyes trained on her. He was dressed casually, not like Lauren, in her red bottoms and suit. Fleetingly she thought how silly Lauren looked dressed like that in a place like this, but then it dawned on her; this was an unplanned visit.

"Hello, Eden. I'm Detective Drew Turner," the man said, rising from his seat. He was tall and broad, and his smile was genuine. The text messages—someone must have called the police. She was beginning to offer a defense when she felt Lauren's fingers dig into her arm.

Eden stifled the words through pressed lips and looked back to Lauren, who added, "Nothing."

Lauren tugged Eden to the table, where they sat. Yellow notebooks lay between the detective and her attorney.

"What's this about?" Eden asked.

"I'm here to ask you some questions about Olivia Wyatt." At a foot taller than Eden, he was no less imposing while seated. He looked familiar to her, but she wasn't sure why.

The silence filled in around them, and Eden's eyes tracked between the two. She felt her tongue twitch with the need to destroy the quiet, but Lauren's stern look said no. She knew now that she had become accustomed to living her life by the orders of others.

"Olivia Wyatt was found dead this morning at your property in Cedar Lake. I understand you knew she was staying there."

Eden began to nod but stopped abruptly. She looked to Lauren, who offered her discreet approval.

"Yes. I was told she's staying at my house."

Wait—dead. Her mind backtracked to what Detective Turner had just told her. Olivia was dead? She was ashamed of the relief she felt after the initial shock. She no longer had to worry about Olivia taking Finn. And as she sat across from the detective, she knew why he was here—he thought she killed Olivia. Her gut clenched at the evidence, circumstantial or otherwise, stacked against her.

"It appears Ms. Wyatt received a toxic amount of fentanyl. Did you know her to be a drug user?"

"No—" Fentanyl, what was that? She would have recognized the signs of drug use.

"Yes, well, we didn't find any paraphernalia in the house or any other indication that she used drugs, but somehow a substantial amount was found on a wineglass she used just before her death. Once she began feeling the effects, she must have panicked and rushed out of the house, but made it no further than the front yard, where she collapsed and died."

"Oh, my—" Eden's fingers flew up to her mouth. "How?"

"I was hoping you might be able to answer some questions about some text messages she recently received on her phone."

Eden felt heat flash over her skin. "I—"

"Don't answer that," Lauren snapped.

"You think I killed her?" Eden's voice was bewildered as his eyes focused on hers. He pulled out a piece of paper—on it a list of messages, photocopies of little round bubbles filled with text.

"This is your phone?"

She shook her head.

"Don't answer that." Lauren gave the detective a stern look. "We aren't going to get anywhere, Detective. You and I both know that phone is untraceable. My client denied sending those messages and insisted someone left the phone in her room while she used the bathroom."

Detective Turner looked skeptical as his head tipped to the side. She wanted to turn to Lauren and ask if it mattered if she claimed the phone or not. Didn't it still make her look guilty even if she continued to deny ownership?

"I don't believe in coincidences, Eden." He addressed her again.

She pulled her hands into her lap, and her eyes fell away from his. Even if Lauren would let her speak, she had no idea what to say. She wasn't even sure who'd put the phone there, though she had an idea. Someone at this hospital didn't want her to get out—someone setting her up. Jinx? She was the one who'd tried to force the phone on her in the day room. She was angry with Eden over her transfer to Doc Jones.

She remembered the day Jinx gave her the phone clearly. It looked exactly like the one found in her room the next morning.

But she had stuffed it into that couch. She never sent any messages... Then she recalled the phone number she'd seen moments before Jenkins took it away. The Miami area code. No one could have known that number but Eden herself. She'd told no one about what happened there, which made her doubt her innocence all over again.

"Her death is under investigation as a homicide until I can get some answers." He stood, gathered his folders, and nodded. "Ms. Ross, I'll be getting that warrant for the phone, and they're searching her room as we speak. Have a nice day."

The door closed softly behind him. They were searching her room, and she wasn't even sure what they would find in there. She was relieved that she'd left the phone Kendrick gave her in the bathroom. They would have found it in a thorough search.

Lauren let out a breath as though it was trapped. Only once Drew was gone did her attorney show any real fear.

"What are we going to do?" Eden asked.

"I don't generally practice criminal law now, but I have in the past. I can handle this for you."

"I don't understand. How did you know about the text messages?"

"Peter Walker called the police. It's required if there's a legitimate threat." Lauren didn't avoid Eden's gaze as she said it. She believed Eden sent the threats, and maybe even believed she killed Olivia.

"I spoke with Peter about it, and he told me what you said. That it wasn't your phone, and someone put it there." She noticed that Lauren didn't ask her if it was true. Perhaps it was easier to represent when ignorant.

"I didn't do this," Eden said, shaking her head roughly. "I'm locked up in here. How in the world could I kill her?" She thought of the single phone call on that damned phone. A call to a killer. It would take seconds to ask for the man to kill Olivia. *I don't remember calling him.*

"Something is going on here." Lauren stood and started pacing the area. She looked to each corner of the room, searching for something.

"Listen, someone here is setting me up. Trying to make it look like I'm—" She nearly said "crazy" but swallowed the word back down. "Dangerous."

Nervous energy sprang from each of Lauren's movements. "I saw the messages. It's not good. Why would someone be doing this to you? And who?" Lauren fired off. "We need to get prints off that phone." She was thinking aloud.

"All the people here have been handling it."

"You're right, that won't work," Lauren muttered. "What about the note?" She shifted back toward the table and looked at Eden. "Same thing? Someone's out to get you?"

Eden nodded, knowing how bad all of this made her look, as if someone had planned it that way. She rested her hands on her chin. Either way she played this, she looked guilty as sin.

"Have you spoken with Layla?" Lauren asked.

Eden began shaking her head. "Not for days."

"Layla seems to be cooperating," Lauren said pointedly.

"What does that mean?"

"I mean she was at the house this morning talking to Drew. Saying she would help in any way she could. Oh, and she just happened to mention the custody *battle.*"

Eden's thoughts tripped. "What did she say when you told her we weren't going to file the papers?"

Lauren was thoughtful for a moment. "I don't remember anything that concerned me. She wanted to know why you changed your mind."

"What about the kidnapping charge?"

"I wasn't able to ask her about it yet. I talked with someone over in Markham PD where the alleged kidnapping occurred, and they said it was kept very quiet, and they didn't think Layla was a risk to anyone."

Lauren pulled up short and looked at Eden. "I know she's your friend, but I think we need to consider something nefarious might be going on."

She didn't like where this conversation was headed. It was hard enough to ignore Layla's suspicious behavior without Lauren confirming her fear. Ever since Kendrick had told her Layla was telling people Finn was her son Eden had to rationalize her inexcusable behavior. Now it would seem Lauren was making a case against her best friend too.

"I assumed as much. She was the last one to see me before —" She didn't finish her thought.

"Let's not forget you're the one who went for help. She didn't." Lauren had never mentioned any of these thoughts before.

"What did she tell the police when I was arrested?" Eden asked.

"She recalled your condition. How you begged her to take Finn home with her because you were sure Ben was going to try and take him from you."

"That's true," she said. But was it? She couldn't pull up the finer details of her memory—just shards from broken images with no context. More questions tumbled through her head. Why didn't Layla take her to get help? As quickly as the questions came, they evaporated into the thickness of her thoughts.

"Well, I'm on the case. I'll get a copy of these messages and demand a list of people who had access to your room. Is there anyone here who doesn't like you?"

A lump grew in her throat, and her eyes jerked up.

"There is someone. It's a man who worked here. He tried —" She felt her cheeks flaring hot. "He assaulted me and told

273

me if I told anyone about him, he would say things about me—that I was dangerous."

Lauren's eyes widened, and her hand covered Eden's on the table. "Why didn't you tell someone? Why didn't you tell me?"

She looked away from the comfort she found in Lauren, ashamed.

"I thought he was going to get me in trouble," she said. "You have no idea what it feels like when no one believes what you say because they think you're unstable. I didn't think anyone would believe me." Tears pooled in her eyes.

"This is exactly what we need to be on the lookout for, Eden. This is very good." She took notes. "This has to be the person. As an employee, he would have access to your room and everything. Did you tell anyone about what he did?"

She shook her head.

"What's his name?"

"Gilmore. But there's one problem." Eden looked down at her toiling hands. "He had an accident about a week ago, and he wasn't here when the phone was left in my room."

Lauren looked disappointed. "What about the note? Was he around then?"

She nodded, then paused. "They found it just after he threatened me, but he left work early the day it was turned in to staff. I'm pretty sure I didn't write it."

"You didn't write it." It was a statement, not a question. She was telling Eden to lock her story down.

"If you don't have a recollection of writing it, you need to be more forceful. If you say things like 'I don't think so' or 'I don't know,' they'll jam you up."

She nodded. She was right. Eden had to take control of this situation and start fighting back. The problem was that she didn't know who she was fighting against.

"Okay. I have a good starting point. I'm going to get copies of everything and dig deep into this Gilmore guy."

"What should I do?"

"Talk only to me. If something comes up, make sure you take notes and let me know right away. It's best for me that I don't have any more surprises."

Lauren reached out and squeezed her hand. "Don't worry. I'm going to figure out what's going on."

# Chapter 44

Layla

10 days until review hearing

She waited three days after killing Olivia to visit Eden. To her surprise, Detective Turner hadn't called for more information. No worries. She would be ready and waiting for the inquiry to begin with all the correct answers formulated, but she must not seem too eager.

Layla's steps quickened until she reached Eden's building and ducked out of the midday heat.

"Layla Hughs here to see Eden Wyatt," she said as she approached the nurse's station.

"She's in the back; I'll call someone to take you out to see her."

Layla nodded and hung back by the wall. She could never get used to the sounds here; soft audible grunts seemed to belch from the chipped walls of the old building. Sometimes she could hear louder cries carrying through the dingy halls.

"Layla?" A female nurse with the name tag "N. Smith" approached. "Come with me."

She wasn't sure why the response from the nurse surprised her. Deep down she must have expected Eden to refuse to see her again.

She followed silently, out the back door and into the hot sunlight once again. Eden was perched under a large oak tree, and when she spotted Layla, she smiled weakly. She looked—anxious. Eden's hair was pulled back into a ponytail, showing her high cheekbones and almond-shaped eyes.

"Hi, honey. I came on my lunch break, so I don't have Finn." That was a lie, and she could read the disappointment all over Eden's appealing features, just like each of the last times she'd come alone. *He's mine now.*

"That's okay. I'm glad you could stop by." Eden didn't move to hug her or stand, and Layla slid down onto the weather-worn bench.

"It's been a busy week," Layla said as she looked out over the burnt grass and chain-link fences. It was depressing to think of living in this place. Layla reached out a hand and patted Eden on the leg, and she flinched away.

"How's Finn? Do you have any pictures?" Eden asked. Layla pulled out her phone and handed it over to Eden.

"He looks so happy." Tears slid down Eden's face as she stared at the pictures. Layla studied her expression and sensed that something about her was different. She twitched with energy and avoided Layla's eyes. Was Eden faking this apparently somber mood?

"He can't wait to be with his mommy." Layla tried for all the simulated enthusiasm she could manage and hoped Eden was too anxious to notice what a fraud she was.

"Soon. I talked with my lawyer. I think I'm making great progress, and she's going to make sure the review goes well."

Layla felt her heart sink. She wondered if the police had been by to talk with Eden about Olivia.

"You look amazing," Layla gushed. A lie. Sweat gathered at Eden's hairline, and her skin looked too pale.

"I feel a lot better. The medication, of course; I would have to stay on it, and it will be a battle for the rest of my life, but we can help each other." Eden's words sounded hollow. A lazy breeze brushed Layla's face as she looked away from Eden.

"I have some bad news."

"I know about Olivia," Eden said.

"I kind of figured someone would have told you. I didn't want to call with the news."

Layla took back her phone from Eden's outstretched hand. She pulled the phone into her lap, discreetly pulled up the audio app she had downloaded, and hit the red record button.

"Have you talked with Olivia?" Layla asked.

"Me? No. You talked to her, right? Did you give her the money? Lauren told me she never withdrew the custody petition," Eden babbled.

Greedy bitch.

"Look, I know you wanted her dead, but—"

"I didn't want her dead. I don't want anyone dead. I just want to move on with my life." Eden's voice rose. "I didn't like her, but that's no reason to want someone dead."

What the hell—Layla couldn't use any of this. She couldn't even edit it to be anything near a confession.

"Why did you stop the paperwork from transferring Finn to me? Was it because you knew Olivia wouldn't be a problem any longer?" Layla said in the softest tone possible.

"You think I killed her?" Eden gasped. She stood from her seat, looming over Layla, eyes wide. "I stopped the paperwork because I couldn't give him up."

"You know I'll take good care of him, right? I love him like he's my godson." She was careful with her words. Today wasn't the day to set Eden off. The sun shone at their feet but didn't touch them. Layla felt her tongue roll into her teeth, twisting her features.

"You've been good to us." Eden patted her shoulder and seemed to calm down. "Can I ask you something?" Eden sat slowly.

Layla forced a smile onto her face. "Sure."

"Did you kidnap a child?"

Air caught in her lungs. "Who told you that?" The sweat beaded on Layla's lip, and she didn't wait for an answer. "It was a misunderstanding."

Eden watched her closely, not like she had been the last few times Layla visited—much more aware. Her eyes narrowed at Layla, and Layla knew she couldn't brush this off. She had to tell the truth.

"My neighbor at the time was a piece of work. She was a drug addict and just a terrible mother. Her daughter Dalila would often cry, and I could hear it through the walls." Layla thought back to that day.

It had been cold, ice gathered on the bushes outside her apartment, glistening in the sun. One week after Todd had called with the news. He was going to be a father. Even though he was a state away from her, it felt like he had physically slapped her; him a father, and her a spinster old maid. Dalila had been crying so hard that Layla had had enough, and when she went knocking next door, Dalila answered in soiled clothes and with tear-streaked cheeks.

"Oh, honey. Where's your mommy?" She had been five years old, her big round eyes wide staring up at Layla; heart-breaking.

"Gone—out." The little girl had begun to sob again.

"For how long?" Layla had been on her knees, pulling her into a hug.

"I don't know. At least lunch and dinnertime now." Layla had looked past the girl to see a pile of food on the table, which she assumed was left out by her mother—feeding her like she was a pet dog rather than a five-year-old child.

At first, Layla had decided to keep Dalila in her apartment until her mother got home. She wouldn't leave her alone. Then, as minutes had ticked into hours and a day turned into three, Layla had not called the police. She should have, it was probably the best thing to do, but she just kept the little girl. Telling herself she would take care of her for a few days, that was all—no big deal. Until the mother, all cashed out and no drugs left, wandered home seven days later.

Seven days! Layla thought the police had known that she did what she did because Dalila's mother was a mess of a human, but what she had not told them was that when she had returned on the seventh day, banging on doors, shouting about her daughter, and Layla had answered the door, she had told the junkie her daughter wasn't with her. She hadn't meant to utter those words.

A week later, the police stopped by and asked questions because the junkie had filed a missing person's report, and Layla had crumbled. She told them what the woman had done and what she felt had been her obligation. They had arrested her. But after asking for her little brother's help, they had decided to dispose of her case. Her little brother only required one thing of her: to attend psychological counseling. That was where she had met Doctor Gwen Jones. And apparently, Doc Jones didn't remember Layla and had no idea Layla was blackmailing her with photos of the illicit affair the doctor had that Layla happened to stumble across on a day trip to an antique show the same year Doc Jones was treating her. She had followed close behind the couple, snapping pictures with her phone.

Now, Layla felt the familiar fear that at any moment she would have to give Finn back, just like Dalila. Eden's hearing was just over a week away. And for all she knew the police wouldn't tie Olivia's murder back to Eden. She was running out of time.

"You did it to save her." Eden's voice was low. Layla nodded her head and stared into her hands.

"She didn't deserve a beautiful daughter like Dalila, and there I was, no children. Alone. I just wanted to help, I swear." Layla wiped at tears streaking her cheeks. Real tears, she acknowledged.

"What happened to the girl?"

"She was placed in a foster home. I tried to get custody of her through the courts, but they passed on me. I don't know where she is now."

She felt Eden's hand on her shoulder, squeezing gently. "You did the right thing. It's just like with Finn and me. You saved that little girl's life, and you saved ours." But Eden's eyes were fierce—was she lying?

A big man walked past them, muttering into his hands, creating a sort of bird call sound.

"What do we do now?" Layla asked. She wanted to leave this place and never come back.

"We wait. I'll be out soon."

Layla forced a smile. "That's great."

"And we can all be together," Eden said. Layla had wanted that so badly before all of this, but now she knew she couldn't possibly give Finn back to Eden.

She didn't tell Eden what had happened to the little girl's mother. It was three weeks later that Layla had knocked on her door. She wanted to apologize for lying and ask about Dalila.

When the woman had answered the door, she was high. Drool leaked down her chin as she waved Layla inside. She was babbling and falling into the wall as she made her way down the short hall to the light streaming through the living room ahead. Before she passed the mouth of the hallway, she had collapsed onto the floor, and her eyes grew wide. "I can't breathe—I can't breathe—" It was so quiet that Layla had to crouch to hear. Her weak breath puffed against Layla's cheek.

"Little too much heroin, Tina?" Layla goaded. She looked into the living room and found an empty syringe next to a small baggie of brownish-white powder. Heroin: probably cut with fentanyl.

"Please. I can't breathe," Tina complained again, but then became very still.

Fentanyl, unlike heroin, can be absorbed through the skin, ingested into the nose and even into open eyes. So, Layla was careful not to touch anything. It attacked the respiratory system by blocking receptors in the brain. Tina was dying, suffocating to be exact. Layla's eyes caught sight of the small container of Narcan on the table, as if Tina was expecting to overdose. She let her eyes slide away from Tina's salvation, stood, and left the woman on the floor, wanting her to die. All Layla would have needed to do was open the container and spray the Narcan up her nose—it would save the woman's life. Instead, she used her sleeve to cover her hand and let herself out the door.

Layla considered the definition of a serial killer, and how she now met the classification. She quickly shut off that train of thought. She had to do what she did, didn't she? If she allowed the guilt to overcome her, she wouldn't be able to do what came next.

"That sounds nice," Layla murmured as she pulled away from the memory.

She stood and held out her hand to Eden, and she took it.

Both women strolled around the yard, and Eden begged Layla to bring Finn by to see her, to which she gladly agreed. It was almost enough to change Layla's mind about what would have to happen next. Almost.

* * *

Layla parked her car just outside Cedar Lake's police department. It was later than she'd planned on getting here, but she was running out of time. She grabbed the box from the back seat of her car and pushed inside the front doors.

A moment later Drew joined her. "Ms. Hughs. Come on back."

She followed him through the small office area where empty desks sat. A few uniformed officers were gathered in a side room as he opened a door bearing his name.

"Have a seat. What can I help you with?" He motioned toward a chair sitting in front of his desk, and she set the box at her feet.

"Thanks for seeing me. It's just. I was going through some things at the house, and I found something that I thought might be relevant."

His brow furrowed. "Regarding Olivia's death?"

"No—not her. Ben Wyatt, her brother." Layla tried her best look of remorse as she leaned forward and grabbed the item resting in the box. She handed it to Detective Turner. "I found this in Eden's office at the house. I wasn't looking for it or anything, but it alarmed me."

He opened the album and began flipping the pages slowly, his expression blank.

"You didn't know about this before?" he asked, looking up at her.

He was an intelligent detective. He always asked questions

quickly, while still gauging her response, so she needed to remain sharp.

"I found them weeks before the murder, actually, but I didn't think..." She purposely faded out. She knew there was nothing that could be done about Ben's murder. They couldn't legally retry Eden, but what Layla could do was make sure Drew found Jason Sandoval's number inside the album. She'd left it in such a way that he couldn't miss it. The last piece of the puzzle to frame Eden for Olivia's murder.

"Didn't think what?" He was waiting for her to connect the dots, but she needed him to do that. She rubbed the inside of her arms, feeling a sudden chill from his gaze.

"I didn't think it meant anything until what happened to Olivia."

"Do you think Eden had something to do with Olivia's death?"

"I don't know. She's made comments to me, but she's in a hospital. It's not like she could get up and walk out. I thought she was just venting her frustrations that Olivia was trying to get money from her."

"What money?" He moved forward in his seat, the first indication that what she was saying was getting through.

"Eden told me that Olivia agreed to drop the custody paperwork if Eden gave her fifteen thousand dollars." Layla looked down at her hands as if she was ashamed of Olivia's actions. As if the idea had not been Layla's. "I only learned about this today at my visit with Eden. She was upset when she found out Olivia took the money but refused to drop the custody petition."

He remained silent, and it was frustrating her. He should be asking her questions.

"I found the album around the time Ben told Eden he was leaving her and the baby. She didn't talk much about it to me, but I would listen as she vented sometimes. I never thought—"

Again, she gave him time to put his thoughts together, but again he forced her to respond.

"What didn't you think?"

"I didn't think she wanted him dead then." The words seemed to crack through the room, louder in her ears than seemed possible. Or maybe that was because all the other sounds seemed to fade.

"You think she planned the murder of her husband?"

This was all wrong. He wasn't excited about any of this information—he looked far too skeptical.

"I don't know. I know she was mad at him, maybe even hated him then. She told me he was cheating on her, and she found out he had a baby with another woman."

*C'mon, Detective. You can put two and two together, can't you?*

But instead of making a statement, he thanked her for her time. She felt he was dismissing her.

He led Layla out to the lobby and said goodbye. Her last hope was him finding Jason's number in the back of the album.

As she walked out, Kendrick Morgan, the private investigator who had been following her, passed her into the well-lit lobby, where Detective Turner greeted him with a handshake and a bored smile.

A whisper of warning moved through her like a wildfire. The PI knew something, and now he was visiting with police. She forced herself not to run to her car. She was officially out of luck.

# Chapter 45

Eden

9 days until review hearing

Eden took a deep breath as she listened for anyone outside the stall after hearing the door close softly. She locked the stall door and quietly retrieved the cellphone from its hiding place.

*Did you destroy the information on Ben?*

Kendrick's response was fast.

*All. Even the doctor's invoice.*

Eden shut her eyes and felt the July heat of that day sweep over her.

Kendrick's truck had pulled up next to her Lexus and he got out, joining her in the car. Even with the air conditioner on full blast, the sun had burned against her skin.

"What'd you find?" Eden could tell by Kendrick's somber look, a contrast to his normally easygoing demeanor, that he had found something bad. It couldn't be as bad as last time, could it? The day he told her about Sophie. Since then, she had grieved her failed fertility; she had come to terms with never having a child of her own.

"That bad?" she had said, meaning to encourage him.

"It's pretty bad." He had taken a deep breath. "Your husband is officially the biggest asshole I know."

How could what Kendrick had found be worse than a lovechild? Her fingers had absently clenched the door handle. "Just tell me."

He had handed over a single piece of paper. On it was a doctor's office's letterhead. It had taken her a moment to realize why Kendrick had handed her a bill from a urologist. And when it had finally hit her, a mournful groan escaped her lips. Her heart had rent in two. Ben had gotten fixed four years ago —most likely so he wouldn't get his mistress pregnant again. Two weeks later she had boarded that flight to Miami—something she would never regret, even with the knowledge that killing her husband had been the reason for her to go in the first place.

The soft creak of the outer door brought her back to the present. She dropped onto the toilet, phone clutched in her hands. It had been a long time since she'd recalled that day and all the emotions tied to what she had learned. She didn't want to remember Ben's betrayal—didn't want to think of the utter selfishness that took him to that doctor's office. Had his mistress posed as his wife and signed off? She didn't know. Her secret had almost come out when Olivia officially filed for custody. She would have no upper hand in a battle for a child with no family ties. But she didn't want Finn's father to learn of Finn's birth. The empty space on the birth certificate was enough to create suspicion. She should have put Ben's name. She was never in danger of him filing for custody.

"Nina, are you in here?" Lynsi's voice asked from just beyond her stall.

Eden's heart skipped. "It's Eden." Her voice shook as she stared down at the silent phone.

The door opened and closed again, and the room was filled with silence. She rushed the phone back into the plastic bag and secured it to the tank. When she exited the stall, she was alone again. She had to hold it together for just a bit longer.

* * *

Jenkins was waiting for her. "Day room, Ms. Wyatt?"

"I'd like to go to my room," she said, wanting time to be alone. To process everything going on. She didn't know where the investigation into Olivia's death was at this point, but she expected another visit from Detective Turner.

"Yes, ma'am." They followed the hall down to the bank of elevators and got in. She felt the burden of her past sins pull away from her with each new step. The police wouldn't be able to prove anything. She had never paid anyone to kill anyone. It wasn't a crime to want someone dead. Ben and Olivia both fell into that category.

Jenkins stopped outside her open doorway just as his radio chirped about a missing patient, and he rushed her inside.

"Lockdown," came a voice over the radio.

"Thanks," Eden said as Jenkins secured her door, and his heavy footsteps moved quickly down the hall. When she turned around, she was standing face to face with Jinx. Her red hair was muted in the shadow of the semi-dark room. Her glossy eyes trained on Eden's face as she slowly walked toward her.

"What are you doing in here?" Eden's voice shook, and she told herself to breathe. She must have been waiting for Eden to return.

"The ten-thirty spot was my spot," Jinx snarled, and when

her face met the sunlight streaming through the window, Eden could see rage seizing her features.

"What are you talking about?" Eden began, but Jinx clapped loudly to quiet her.

"Why didn't you tell me?" Jinx's shoulders were rigid, and her teeth snapped shut on the last word.

"I don't know what you're talking about—Doctor Jones had a conflict—"

"Yeah, blame it on someone else." Jinx shifted again, and Eden backed away; her fingers found the edge of the bed and stopped. "I see the way you look at him."

"No—"

"He loved me, and I loved him until you came along." Eden caught sight of something in Jinx's hand—paper twisted and rolled into her clenched fist. Paper just like the paper from Eden's journal. This was why she was here—it was Jinx leaving the notes!

"You—" Eden felt anger rising. All because of some misperception, Jinx would make sure Eden never got out of here. "You're trying to make it look like I'm—I'm a danger to others." She scrambled for the words as Jinx continued to advance. Slow like a predator.

"You're stealing from me." Jinx ground the words out through her teeth and spittle slapped Eden's cheek. "Just like Jamie and Jaybird and all the rest. And that stupid asshole Gilmore helping you—were you screwing him too? Is that why he told them about Doc Lucas and me?"

"I don't want Doc Lucas." The statement roared past her lips, louder than she had intended. As if speaking the words loudly might make Jinx understand. But her angry expression didn't waver.

"I love him, and now he's screwing you." She pulled haphazardly at Eden's jumper and the top two buttons popped open, exposing the top of her breasts. Eden bunched the pale blue material back together with her hand.

With two hands anchored on Eden, Jinx yanked at the fabric again.

"I want to see if it's true. Prove to me you're not screwing him," she demanded.

She was taller than Eden and outweighed her by thirty pounds. Eden recalled Chaz's words: "Jinx, she isn't well sometimes..."

"Prove to me you're not having sex with him," she screamed, her red hair bouncing as she jerked toward her again. Eden tried to dodge her, but Jinx's fist caught her hip bone, and a crack of pain traveled up her side. She groaned but ignored the instinct to double over. She needed to get out of this room, but Jinx pushed her farther into the corner, blocking her avenue to the doorway. Where were the staff? Couldn't they hear Jinx's screams?

"How can I prove it?" Eden's voice was urgent. "What can I do?"

"Strip down. I want to see if he's been inside you."

Horrified, Eden shook her head roughly as Jinx's eyes traveled the length of her body. "Please, Jinx. I didn't take him from you. He's my doctor." She was begging. "I don't love him. He's yours. I'll ask to switch to someone else."

Jinx halted her advance. Her head tipped to the side as if she was listening to an invisible friend whispering into her ear. The moment stretched out, and she thought Jinx's eyes looked like those of a predator watching its prey.

"You're the reason Gilmore will be a vegetable for the rest of his life—you made me do that, you know."

She pictured Gilmore's lifeless form under white sheets—a machine breathing for him. She knew he was on life support, but it was the first time she'd been blamed for it out loud. Eden understood she was the reason for his current condition, and couldn't bring herself to be upset about that fact.

"Please," Eden begged.

The door behind her opened quietly, and Marsha took up the space in the doorway.

"He thinks he can screw me, and I'll just what—go away? Just like my ex. And you know what happened to him, don't you."

Eden ignored Marsha as the nurse moved in soundlessly behind Jinx.

"I killed him—" She lunged at Eden, both fists raised over her head coming down onto Eden at once. Her knuckles pelted Eden's skin like hail from the sky, sending sharp snaps of pain through her chest and shoulders, which bore the brunt of the assault.

Marsha pulled something around Jinx's neck. It looked like a tissue, white and slim, and as the long moments ticked past and her punches grew weaker, she realized it was a towel pulled high up on Jinx's neck, choking her.

Her body slowly slumped to the floor, and Eden heard the gasping intake of breath as Marsha slowly lowered her down.

"It's okay," Marsha whispered into Jinx's ear like a loving mother, stroking Jinx's cheek. "I'm sorry 'bout that, honey, but I had to do it."

The loud squelch of sneakers sounded down the hallway, and soon several orderlies were pouring into the room. Looking down, Eden realized her jumper was still pulled away to reveal her breasts and quickly covered herself.

"Restrain her," Jenkins said softly.

"Tell them what you did, Eden," Jinx said, her voice raspy.

"She's going to the fifth floor," Marsha said, and the other orderlies nodded.

"No!" Jinx kicked her legs out, and before Eden could

guard against it, kicks landed against her head and stomach, and she crumpled to the floor.

Jinx's screams soon faded as she was taken out of her room and down the hall.

"You okay, honey?" Marsha asked. "We're going to get you all checked out, okay?"

"She was waiting for me. I think—I think she was here to leave one of those notes you all have been finding." She looked around, frantic to find the piece of paper Jinx had clutched in her hand, but the floor was empty.

"What notes?" Marsha looked at Eden skeptically.

"My journal," she said wearily. Eden tried to recover it, but Marsha stopped her.

"I got it, dear. Don't you worry." Eden watched as she reached for the journal and leafed through it. Her eyebrows rose as she pulled out a single folded sheet of paper.

Her forehead creased when she looked at Eden.

"What is it? What does it say?"

"It's a suicide note."

"What? From who?" She tried to reach for the note as pain caused her arm to drop to her side.

"From you."

# Chapter 46

Layla

8 days until review hearing

F inn's documents were scattered over her desk as she began to organize them. He now had a passport, and she'd requested a copy of his birth certificate, which had arrived in the mail two days ago.

It had been two days since she'd left the damning evidence with Detective Turner. Since seeing that PI at the police department, she couldn't shake the ominous feeling. He must know something, and he'd no doubt told Drew. But what?

Outside at lunch, the sun was hot, and she took one of the empty tables and watched paddleboats go past. The water sloshed off the old dock next to her. A bologna sandwich sat untouched on the table, wilting in the sun. Her cellphone rang —Detective Turner.

"Ms. Hughs, are you able to stop by the station today?" His voice was indifferent, a good sign, she told herself.

"I'm working now, but maybe afterward. Can you tell me what it's about?"

"I'd like to talk in person."

Fear shivered through her. This wasn't at all what she was expecting.

"Umm—"

"I can come by your work."

"No—" she said. "I can come by. Let me check with my babysitter, and I'll get back to you."

She ended the call and sat staring at the water for a long time. What had changed? He seemed to be eating up everything she was saying the other night, and now he needed to talk to her in person. If he had simple questions about Eden, Ben, or Olivia, he would have just asked over the phone; suspects were questioned in person. He wanted to watch her eyes flit away or shifting body language that revealed lies.

She thought of that private investigator visiting the detective. How could she be so stupid? She knew he was watching her, yet she'd gone to Eden's house anyway. She remembered checking to be sure she wasn't being followed, but what if he was already there? It seemed a long time to wait to come forward with information if he had watched her with Olivia that night. Her mind was swirling with possibilities. She needed an excuse. Something deep down told her that if she went to the police station, she wasn't going home.

She would wait a short time and call him back. But first, she needed to book the first flight out of this place. She'd felt the shift when she spoke with Drew—she would be a suspect, and she couldn't risk meeting him.

She rushed back inside and booked a flight to Canada. She and Finn wouldn't stay there, but she could land and regroup, maybe get over to Europe where they could travel more freely. She had researched a starting point to disappear into a network for domestic violence survivors, and once inside no one would be able to find them. This might be a good thing for them; she wouldn't have to worry about Eden's release. She should have fled with Dalila, but she was scared. Not anymore. She was a mother now, and she couldn't let fear overtake her.

Finn was counting on her now.

* * *

Detective Turner sounded disappointed when she said she couldn't meet with him, but she promised to arrive first thing in the morning. When she got home, she packed only the things they would need into four suitcases. As she set the bags by the door, she peered outside.

The truck was there, sitting in the shade of a tree. It was a good thing her car was parked in the garage where she could load it without scrutiny. She would time it so she and Finn could get through security right before takeoff.

"Ready, baby."

There was a sharp knock at the front door, and she jumped. A giggle erupted from Finn, and she shushed him.

She rushed the bags into the hallway closet before approaching the door. Through the peephole, she could see Detective Turner looking back at her. She considered ignoring him and claiming later that she didn't hear him, but what if he lingered and was still there when she had to drive to the airport? She had to get rid of him.

She slowly opened the door while pinching the bridge of her nose. Playing up the migraine she had faked to leave work early.

"Yes," she said, wincing.

"I'm sorry to bother you, but I have some questions." He

smiled at her. It nearly disarmed her until she realized what he was trying to do.

"Detective, can this not wait until tomorrow? My head is splitting." She fanned her face with a hand. A sheen of sweat coating her skin.

"Ma'am, if I could just ask you a few questions and I'll be out of your hair."

She sighed. "Fine, on the porch. I could use the fresh air."

He backed away, giving her room to join him on the stoop. The heat of the day seemed to radiate off the cement as she hugged Finn tightly.

"Yes, as I was saying, I need to ask you how well you knew Olivia Wyatt."

His blue eyes studied her closely, and she tried not to squirm under his gaze.

"I knew her through Eden." Finn began to fuss on her shoulder. "Not well at all."

"I understand Olivia was asking you to see Finn, is that right?"

This would be over soon, and she would be on her flight to Canada. *Stay calm.*

"Yes. Eden told me I could do what I thought was best for Finn. She's his aunt, after all." She quickly corrected: "Was his aunt."

Detective Turner nodded. "How often did you go to Eden's house after Ben's death?"

She paused to think. "A few times. Eden insisted I take all of Finn's baby things, so there were several trips right there."

"Was Olivia present while you were taking the baby stuff?"

"No. That was before she flew in from California." That was right, wasn't it? She was getting all the details messed up because he made her nervous. Maybe she should have a lawyer here.

"What kind of car do you drive?"

"Toyota." She was purposely vague. Had someone seen her car parked around the block? Drew might have gone door to door asking about anything suspicious the night Olivia died.

"What kind? Passenger car?"

"Why are you asking me this?" She wanted to ask why Eden wasn't the prime suspect. Layla had made sure all the evidence pointed toward her.

"The night Olivia died, did you visit Eden's house?" There it was—the question she was dreading—stupid private investigator. "Because you told me you hadn't seen her in a week, as I recall."

"I think we're done talking, Detective. If you have any other questions for me, my lawyer and I will come to see you."

"Suit yourself, Ms. Hughs. Don't leave town, as they say." She considered for a moment that Drew might know about her plans to leave. Why else say that? But they probably said it to all suspects. She needed to stay calm; she'd been through this before. But it didn't stop the image of her and Finn being stopped at the airport and arrested.

She turned and went into the house, trying to hide her shaking fingers against Finn's little body. Detective Turner knew she was there that night, or at the very least suspected it. She watched as he turned and left the porch only to stop and peer into her garage. Her heart hammered as he finally walked down the driveway to his truck. She had no idea what evidence he might have, and she had called his bluff that it wasn't enough to arrest her on the spot. But now she knew he would be back, and she had to get on that plane in five hours, or she would be arrested.

She rushed to double-check that she had everything she would need for at least a few days in Canada. Then they would get as far away as possible.

## Eva Mackenzie

* * *

When she pulled out of the garage, it was almost dark. The truck was gone from the curb when she drove out of her neighborhood for the last time. On the way to the airport, she stopped at several ATMs and cleared out her bank account. It would be enough to get them by until she could find a job.

As long as she had Finn, nothing else mattered.

# Chapter 47

Eden
6 days until review hearing

wo days had passed since Jinx was dragged away, but she could sometimes hear the echo of Jinx's screams while alone in her room. She hadn't seen Doctor Lucas since then either. She was working with a different doctor while he was on leave. Soon, she settled back into her routine. Her sleep was deteriorating, and the sharp edges of paranoia pushed their way into her everyday routine. When she did rest, she experienced garish nightmares, so horrible that she would wake in the night unable to fall back asleep. With the sleeplessness came the ugly voices.

She pinched her eyes shut and began to hum as the morning light crept up the wall. It felt as though someone was watching her, a dark menacing force lingering. It was not an altogether unfamiliar feeling—like she was coming home, but not to a place she wanted to be.

The sharp click of a key sliding into the lock alerted her,

and she turned to see Gilmore stagger into the room, clutching his head as blood oozed through his short fingers, a grin on his face. But when he spoke, it was Marsha's voice she heard.

"Eden, you all right?"

Eden shook away the grotesque image to see Marsha pushing a cart into her room.

"Got to take your blood today, sweetie." She began rummaging through her cart, locating all the necessary equipment while Eden took the cup and pills offered.

"Will she be coming back?" She. Jinx. Even in Eden's deteriorated mental state, she was sure Jinx had been the one who'd set her up with the fork and the notes.

"I don't think so. It's been a good time since I saw her this bad."

"Did she kill that other resident?"

"I don't know about that." A shadow of suspicion passed over Marsha's face. "You just worry about you now." Marsha patted her leg. "You're looking a bit tired today."

"I feel better." A lie. All night she'd resisted the overwhelming urge to drag her bed to the door to assure no one would get in. And the voice...she couldn't let them find out she was hearing voices again. She just had to get the hell out of here, and everything would be fine.

The pinch of the needle was brief, and she watched Marsha collect her sample and put her supplies away.

"You have a visitor," Marsha said while pushing her cart toward the door.

"A visitor? Who?" She recalled her last meeting with Layla. Before she left, she'd promised Eden that she would bring Finn to see her.

She stood so quickly she felt a moment of dizziness, and she had to steady herself with the wall.

"You okay?" Marsha asked, holding her hands out.

"Yes, I'm fine. I think today is the day I see my son." Eden's voice shook, and Marsha frowned.

"It's a policeman." She reached out a hand to rub Eden's arm. "I'm sorry, dear. Maybe your friend will stop by later."

There was no hiding her disappointment. She wasn't sure why she did this to herself—believe that good things would happen to her.

A shuffle from the hallway and Jenkins appeared.

After the short walk, Jenkins pulled the door open, and she recognized Detective Turner standing across from Lauren.

"Ms. Wyatt. It's nice to see you again," he said in a pleasant voice. Like the other day, his dress was casual and his tone friendly. Eden was trying to figure out if it was an act. She took the seat next to Lauren, who squeezed her arm. When she met Lauren's gaze, she noticed worry—or anger—seated in her features. She couldn't determine which.

"Hello," Eden said, looking between the two as the detective took a seat. "Is this about Olivia?"

"My client will not be answering any questions regarding Olivia Wyatt," Lauren said.

"I'm not here to talk about Olivia; I'm here to talk about Layla Hughs."

Lauren's brow furrowed. "What about her?"

The detective pulled out a photo. Layla's dull brown eyes stared back at Eden. Her cheeks were full of youth, and her chin was dotted with acne.

"What's this?"

"Did you know she was arrested for kidnapping?" he asked. She nodded.

"Which one did she tell you about?"

Fear quickly eclipsed her confusion. "Which one?"

"Dianne Hughs, aka Melody Dickson, aka Trish Smith, were all flagged for kidnapping in Tennessee, West Virginia and Virginia. It's now believed that all three attempted kidnappings were the same woman." He pulled out several more photos from what must have been CCTV footage. In Eden's opinion, they were too grainy to determine who the woman was. "According to local police, the woman would rent a hotel room and stalk families at local parks for weeks at a time."

"Stalk families?" She stopped abruptly, eyes shooting up from the pictures. "Wait. Why are you here?" Nausea swirled in her gut, and for a second she thought she would vomit.

Lauren sat up and took the pictures from Eden's limp hands. "We need to get Finn out of there. Today. Now," Lauren said.

"Wait. What's going on? Tell me now." Panic, large and looming, opened to swallow her.

He took the pictures back. "I have a witness who was able to access Ms. Hughs' location the night your sister-in-law died. Did Layla tell you she was at your house that night?"

"No—but I didn't ask her about it." She stopped; her fingers brushed her lips.

"Drew, she won't discuss that with you," Lauren said.

"I didn't ask her about it." A momentary slip in his careful manner. Eden could see his frustration. But what was he frustrated about? "I'm also aware that she was at your house the night your husband was murdered."

"Where did this information come from?" Lauren asked.

"Information gathered from an independent source."

"You keep saying that, Drew." Lauren half-stood, her arms pressed to the table. "You think she asked Layla to kill Olivia, don't you?"

"No—I don't think that at all. I think your client might want to cooperate with me on this one."

"And why is that?"

"Because Ms. Hughs and Finnigan Wyatt are gone."

\* \* \*

The roar in her ears was so loud that she nearly covered them with her hands. What did he say? Her brain struggled to figure out the meaning of his words—of what the words even were. Her hands were rubbing her cheeks, but she didn't know why they were fretting there. Her brain had given no such command.

"Missing?" Lauren asked.

"Two nights ago, Layla Hughs and a baby boarded an international flight to Canada. We don't know where they went from there or if she's using a different name."

"No. You're lying. She wouldn't do that to me. There's some sort of misunderstanding." Eden looked to Lauren for her quick agreement, but Lauren only frowned. As Eden spoke, she knew she was in denial, but the truth would hurt too much to even consider.

"She loves me. She wouldn't take my son." Her hands began to tremble, and Lauren closed hers over them. She felt so utterly lost.

"Drew, we need a break. Eden's having a hard time." The detective nodded and stood to leave. At this, Eden felt her panic rising. No—he couldn't go. He had to find Finn.

"Where's Finn? Where's my son?" She jumped up, and her voice shrieked through the room like a flock of wild birds scattering in all directions. "Where is he? Find him. Bring him to me, please." She was moving toward the detective now, pleading with outstretched arms. "Do you have children? Please, help me."

Eden felt someone grasp her wrist but didn't turn away from Detective Turner, afraid that he would give up if she broke the connection. He needed to understand her desperation—feel her pain.

"This visit is over, folks," Jenkins said from her side.

"No, wait. I need to know where Finn is. I need him. He's my everything. He's all I have left." She fell to her knees, and Jenkins pulled her back up. Her brain continued to scatter as he guided her out of the room and down the hall.

Her room was silent, and the sound was the sound of loneliness. She melted into a cacophony of sobs. She felt a pinch in her arm as she was lowered to her bed. Sweet Finn. She barely knew him, and now he was gone.

# Chapter 48

Eden
Day of review hearing

"They're going to be here soon, to get you." Doc Jones's voice spoke. Eden's eyes were pinched shut against the harsh light of the blindingly white room. Her body pulled impossibly tight, wrapped in a white coat as she sat on the edge of a bed. They said it was for her own safety.

"You won't be released today." Doc Jones continued to drone on and on. *Why is she here—what does she want from me?* Couldn't she sense with all her degrees and classes that Eden wanted to be left alone? Didn't they teach her that at the fancy conferences where she sipped champagne and rubbed elbows with elites?

"You will need significantly more treatment before you leave." There was a pause, and the screams in her head writhed and bumped against her temples in a constant pattern. She tried to raise her hands to press the tender area, but her arms wouldn't move. Spit slid out of the corner of her mouth, and she wondered where it had come from, as her mouth was so dry.

"Thirsty," she said in a raw whisper. A hollow cough followed.

"Do you understand what I'm saying?" Doc Jones again.

"Why won't you just leave me alone?" she asked. Maybe if she didn't answer the voice would go away—Doc Jones would go away...

"You're staying here. For how long, I don't know. I'm sorry, Eden." A moment later she thought she heard a door close, and she was alone.


Deputies arrived soon after to bring Eden back for her final hearing. She was vaguely aware that this was the day she'd been working toward, but now that it was here, she couldn't bring herself to care what they did with her. She stared at the knot in the large oak table before her. Everything moved in slow motion behind her eyes as if she were drunk—faces and figures undulating.

Finn was gone. How long had it been since that cop came and told her that Layla had taken off with him? She didn't know. Her days were fog-filled and irrelevant. A silent force sucked the life out of her, and she gave in to the darkness—too tired to fight. Layla was a much better mother than Eden ever was. She was willing to go to the ultimate length to get a child. Lie to deceive her best friend. Steal.

"Your honor, my client's struggling with some recent events." Lauren's voice broke through Eden's fog. "She needs a few weeks to get back on track. I'm asking for a continuance so that we can get this in the rearview, and Doctor Jones can reevaluate her decision."

A man's voice: "Your honor, she's more of a danger now

than she's ever been. She's attacked ten staff members. She's attempted to escape on three occasions, and she tried to kill herself multiple times." He sounded disappointed. She had spiraled, and she wasn't so far gone that she didn't remember what she had done. "The doctor is recommending placement in the behavioral health system until Ms. Wyatt can adjust to society and her mental health issues are fully addressed. As you know, the court is required to revisit the placement every two years, and if Ms. Ross is assured that her client is prepared for release, she can always petition the courts to hear the case sooner if things change."

"Your honor—"

A booming voice cut Lauren's argument short. Eden lifted her eyes to the judge behind his bench. "I've made my decision. Ms. Wyatt will remain where she is until I have an evaluation suggesting she's ready for release. I think the state is correct. You can always bring a motion to seek relief sooner if it's justified."

A scream tore from Eden's mouth without warning. She felt steady, muscular arms on her shoulders almost immediately though she couldn't see who they belonged to. She tried to bat them away, but her hands were secured somehow, leaving her immobile.

"Don't touch me," she snarled, but it was too late. They were already pulling her from the courtroom.

# Chapter 49

Eden
After

I t would be months before Eden began putting her short-term memories back together for a second time. Each day was a new struggle, and she would end up in a fit of rage, forcing the staff to subdue her. She wondered if they'd moved her to the fifth floor or another place. It wasn't the room she had been in before, that was all she knew.

Her son was gone. When she could communicate, it was nearly incoherent mumbles begging for Finn. There were gaping holes in her perceived timeline, and she could only assume they were sedating her.

This was the beginning of the end. In the last few weeks, she'd heard many people telling her that what happened to her wasn't her fault. All she knew for certain was things had changed since Finn was stolen. Some chasm opened in her and shifted everything she knew. No amount of psychobabble bull would change that. Who cared about placing blame when she was struggling to function. The looming fact was, she was never getting better here, only worse.

Food had no flavor, colors were dull and monotone, voices were melancholy, and actions were slow and exaggerated. She often found herself staring into her open, empty palms, for what reason she didn't know. Her neck ached from resting on her chest as she slumped into a chair until someone came to get her and her entire body would vibrate as they pushed her in a chair to another spot.

She tried to hang herself the first night after getting the news of Finn. The second night, she tried to slit her wrist on the rough edge of the door frame in an otherwise empty room. This proved much more challenging than she would have believed. She ended up strapped to a bed with scratchy gauze applied to the harmless abrasions she had caused. After that, she attacked the staff and other residents. She had so much rage growing inside of her that she needed to quell, and to let go felt so good—so right. The mania was gone, replaced with an empty sadness she didn't want to recognize. Feeding the anger of how unfair the situation had become seemed her only goal.

There was nothing she could do to take her own life, and that powerlessness was the source of her frustration. She couldn't put into words what she felt—because she chose not to speak, mostly because she could no longer stand the sound of her voice. She was the mother who gave her son away. How could she be so blind? This new rage turned inward, trying to destroy her, burn herself to the ground and leave the shifting shadows behind.

Sometimes, she could hear a voice talking to her inside empty hallways and rooms. His booming tone bounced around, telling her she was a bad mother.

She shook her head—it wasn't true. He wasn't real. It didn't stop the shivers descending over all the nerve endings in her body. It would take days to recover from one episode. She would become so agitated they had to restrain her. Was this what happened when she killed Ben? Did she hear the voice and follow its orders?

They said, "Ms. Wyatt, you suffered a postpartum psychotic break. Nothing you have experienced in the last year can be considered accurate or authentic." What she knew: she was a killer; all other identities dropped away. She wasn't a mother, and this wasn't surviving.

This loss was too significant to bear.

"Your loss." What a casual way to say it. Like Finn had been a set of keys or a favorite jacket she'd left on the bus. He wasn't lost—he was taken, and that fact had left her a very different person than she might have been.

They said, "Ms. Wyatt, you suffered at the hands of an abusive husband. You experienced verbal abuse and emotional alienation. You need to give yourself a break." Had she told them he abused her?

She had snorted then, unable to hold it in. These intelligent people all around her must know what was best for her. She was only living the life they casually discussed. Like she was a walking science project they referred to at dinner parties with associates. Perhaps they even assigned her a number to keep her anonymity.

Her days at the hospital blended into a chaotic haze for a long time. She would take the meds they brought her with the small cup of lukewarm water, washing the little pills down until the memories floated away. Unsure of how much time had passed, she began journaling her thoughts under the constant supervision of doctors—no sharp objects. As words spilled onto paper, her mind began to clear.

Then there were the details of Ben's murder, which she tried in vain to remember. I love you. I love you; she scribbled, sharp black ink piling onto the words until a hole grew in the paper. I love you. The quiet of the airplane ride, the man who contacted her when she landed. The man she was going to pay to kill her husband. I love you.

Slowly, she became aware of regret and a newfound sense of urgency. A plan so new in its infancy, she refused to give it much more than a passing thought and was sure to keep its details far from her journals. They read them, watching her closely.

Group therapy for drama hour. Each person was more emotional than the next. Anger erupted with the fragile mentality of its attendees. Some wanted help, while others instigated the frays, happy to sit back and watch the aftermath. It was as if their pain was weaponized into heat-seeking missiles directed at the biggest target. And once it hit—oh, the chaos. Not like the last ward. She wondered absently if Jinx was here in this new place with her. Did she still want to kill Eden?

Soon she began to eat again and to dream at night. Not the still blackness that welcomed her when she could finally settle into the rhythm of sleep, but vibrant notions of what might have been. She had to do something—balance life again.

The dim shadows of first light grew along her wall. Her journal, her only personal possession in the small space, lay on the nightstand.

A small red light blinked on the camera hanging at the junction of two walls, capturing the best view of the space.

The scratchy sheets were pulled up underneath her chin, making the skin on her neck burn. She was probably allergic to the soap they used, but she said nothing.

She had lost track of how long she had been here. The days blurred into others as her mind slowed from the medication. The voice called to her. Whispering to her from the recesses. *Finn's better off without you—*

She pinched her eyes shut to the familiar echo. "You're not real." Unlike his, her voice was flat and quiet, discerning what was in her head and what was real.

*If I'm not real, then neither are you. I am you, and you are me.*

It had taken weeks to purge this voice from her thoughts. Its raspy quality shrank until one day it was gone. She never felt she was sharing her mind with anything until the voice stopped and her thoughts cleared. Reminding her for a short time of what it had been like before it haunted her.

A knock on the door signaled it was time to prepare for breakfast. Her days were regimented—each hour filled with an activity to keep things organized and productive.

\* \* \*

They moved her back to her old ward again. In the TV room, she pulled up onto one of the battered sofas. A woman sitting adjacent to her calmly mumbled, her eyes skipping around. When she caught Eden's gaze, her cheeks turned pink, and she hid her face. Eden wanted to tell her it was okay, she heard voices too—but didn't.

A commentator's voice from a television show drifted around the room, and the brightly colored screen caught Eden's attention.

"The Eastern bluebird's mating habits are not what scientists once thought. Its social monogamous behavior is now coupled with the belief that female bluebirds can sometimes have two broods with more than one mate."

A small bird with brilliant blue wings and a dusty-colored chest fluttered across the sky. Eden rose and moved toward the television, ignoring Pam's angry babbling as she passed in front of her.

She watched as the mother bird sat among her eggs in her nest, her delicate wings flush with her body.

A seed planted in her quiet mind as she shut out the bright colors and the noise all around her and saw a wild flicker of something in the darkness for the first time in months. Hope.

Time to balance her world again; time to find Mr. Right.

\* \* \*

She walked the gleaming white floors of the five-story hospital every day until lockdown, silently moving around in a world that was beginning to feel real again, passing other patients who had the privilege to be out of confinement. Some were far too violent for that luxury. Those would beat against their doors as she shuffled past. Bang. Bang. Bang.

She turned and continued to walk, a man trailing behind her. Doctor Lucas would meet her in her room and take her to her therapy sessions. He was polite and allowed her the space she needed as they moved. Since she'd been taken off twenty-four-hour suicide watch, she still couldn't move about the facility without a doctor or two orderlies, and Doctor Lucas would sometimes come for her if there was no second orderly available.

She passed the bay window near the rear of the building, which faced the pond. It was winter, and large snowflakes floated lazily to the frozen surface. The bare trees, like swollen knuckles, reached toward a white sky that joined a snow-covered horizon—reminding her of nothingness, if that was a thing.

"Ready, Eden?" Doctor Lucas whispered.

They continued past the windows filled with snow until they came to his office at the end of the corridor.

She let herself in and took a seat on the couch.

Day one. Let's begin.

# Chapter 50

Eden
After

D ay after day, her sessions with Doctor Lucas blossomed. At first, it was slow-moving. It was all whitewashed medical terms to describe what had happened to her. She would smile and nod, parting her lips or exposing some previously unseen flesh. She began styling her hair and wearing her new jumper again. Her once-gaunt features returned to their former feminine curves. Her pale skin glowed as her plan progressed. Sometimes she wondered who was seducing who.

"How are you feeling today?" he asked as she took a seat on the couch across from him, crossing her legs, careful to pull her pants up over her ankle to her calf. It was a gesture most wouldn't notice, but Doctor Lucas did. He saw everything these days, his anticipation infectious. Under the surface, she sensed he was trying to deny his attraction to her. He was avoiding her gaze or staring awkwardly at his notes at inappropriate intervals. When they finally had their sessions, he acted as if none of his other patients mattered, just her. His answers became less scripted, his suggestions more personal, and slowly he moved into the easy relationship they'd had months before.

*Don't think I didn't do this on purpose, Doctor Lucas.*

More and more, her mood was improving. She'd even taken part in the last few group therapy sessions. She kept track of the days, and she was sure that tomorrow would be the day. If only Doctor Lucas knew what would hit him. She smiled and bit her lip gently. His eyes didn't miss the overt gesture. She would have to start from scratch if she was reading him wrong. Find a new doctor.

"I'm quite well," she breathed.

"How about your dreams?"

"I still have them," she said. Good. He remembered. His long, lean body rested in his overstuffed chair, notebook propped in his lap, pen resting against his cheek. He'd been taking fewer notes, talking more...watching her morph into a butterfly.

"And has the man in your dream revealed himself?"

She could see by the slight shake in his hand and his steady gaze that he had been waiting a long time to ask her this. The dream was a topic brought up every session for three weeks. According to their session notes, it was a dream she'd been having nightly for the past two months.

*I need you on board, Doctor Lucas. I can't do this alone.* She thought of Jinx and all her ravings about sleeping with Doc Lucas. Was it true? She dismissed the thought; he was too good for Jinx. He wanted Eden, and she wanted him.

"The man is at the very edge of my vision. I can see his clothes and his hands, but not his face," she said meekly.

It had become a game to her now. A mouse hunting the cat. She even dared to think a trap would work if sprung at this moment, but the optimal time would be tomorrow. She didn't want to get too carried away with her selfish ambitions. For the first time in a long while, she felt a newfound reason to live.

She asked herself, why not? Why shouldn't she be happy?

"You know—he might be..." Her eyes lingered on him as she bit her lip. Hope was written in his features. He wanted to be the man in her dreams.

Did Doctor Lucas know what she was doing? How close she stood to him, claiming him inside of her space? Soon he stopped moving away, finding the comfortable familiarity, just as she had hoped he would. She knew it was wrong to love him —to want him like this.

As she lay there, staring back at the doctor, she wondered if this was her or the monster she had become. She didn't know how to heal her wounds to become who she once was. This plan, this idea put into motion, was only a start, and she wasn't sure now, as she looked over at her prey, if it would even work at all. But she had to try. It was the only thing keeping her going for so long now, even making her smile.

*Look—look how shy I am, Doctor Lucas.*

"Eden." Her name on his tongue was like a caress.

She looked up at him.

"Tell me about the dream one more time."

She left a long pause as she smiled at him.

"I feel heat in my belly at his touch. Like he sparks something in me I haven't felt in a long time. His hand moves up my thigh, and the other grabs my hair and tugs." Eden sighed. Her hand gripped the pillow under her head, her chin tipped toward the ceiling, and her eyes closed.

*Trust me. Love me. Touch me.*

"This is very embarrassing, but he's—" She cleared her throat. "I think it's you," she whispered, and she heard his breath catch. She pictured his eyes devouring her writhing form.

"You kiss me, soft at first, but then deeper, biting my lip, thrusting your tongue..."

She sat up and turned toward him, his eyes focused on each tiny movement of her fingers as she slowly unbuttoned her jumper to reveal naked flesh underneath. Her heartbeat fluttered in her chest as he stood, and she thought he was going to scold her, tell her to put her shirt back on, but instead he walked to her. As he stood in front of her, his fingers hooked under her chin, and she rose next to him. His lips gently kissed hers and her smile was quick, too quick, maybe, but it didn't stop what happened next.

\* \* \*

An hour later, she rested in his arms. The look of contentment on Doctor Lucas's face was evident.

"Do you know how long I've wanted to do that?" he said as his fingers traced her arms, and he kissed her bare shoulder. She closed her eyes, allowing the contentment that came while lying next to him. This had not been the goal. She'd never wanted to fall for him. Blackmail was what she intended, but how could she turn on him now?

"I won't tell if you won't." Eden forced herself not to wink.

A heavy silence fell over the room, and she wondered what he was thinking.

"Do you have someone in your life? A wife?" she found herself asking.

"I have a dog." He laughed into her neck, and she felt desire rising again. She sat up and reached for her clothes. He looked confused as he pulled his khaki pants up over his hips. The sex had been slow and tender despite the buildup of tension between them. She could feel how much he cared for her with each touch, and she hated herself—for what she was going to do to him.

"Eden, I—"

She held up a finger to stop any more explanation. She leaned over and kissed him. It was meant to be a goodbye kiss, but when his tongue pushed past her lips, she opened to him—forgetting her plan again as she let him undress her.

# Chapter 51

Eden
After

Kendrick's large frame leaned over the table at the visitors center as he gathered his papers. Excitement tore through her as she assumed he must have new information for her. She hadn't seen Kendrick since her review hearing.

Kendrick had promised to hire a guy he knew over in Europe to track down Layla and spare no expense. Eden didn't care if she spent every last dime she had on catching her. She would find Finn.

"How are you doing?" Kendrick asked as he rose from his seat to give her a hug. Groups of people sat at ten or so tables, the busiest she'd ever seen the visitors center. They both sat and she took a deep breath while waiting for Kendrick to speak.

"You look great," Kendrick said, and she thought he meant it. She felt great. Her medication had leveled her off and things were going amazing with Doc Lucas since he'd begun discussing what things would be like when she was released. She no longer denied loving Doc Lucas, but they couldn't let anyone know how they both felt. And though Doc Jones was still not confident in Eden's progress, it would only be a matter of time before she was out of this place.

"What did you find out?" Eden asked, watching Kendrick's lip twitch. "Something bad?" The air seemed to suspend in her lungs.

"I've got something, but I'm not really sure what it means yet." Kendrick shifted toward her to close the distance. "I talked to Drew—the detective in charge of your case—after I stumbled across some information he didn't have when he was investigating Ben's murder."

She was prepared to hear new information on Kendrick's efforts to find Finn, and her mind was swimming at this turn of topic. "What, about Ben?" She considered the fact that Kendrick might ask her about her trip to Miami, that he knew what she had done. Would that change anything now?

"I was able to get ahold of the GPS located on Layla's car and determined she was at your house the night Ben was killed."

Eden inhaled sharply. "What?" Her eyes cast down to the table as she tried to remember what Layla had told her about her actions the days leading up to Ben's murder. She said Eden had been acting strange, that she'd begged Layla to take Finn because Eden was sure Ben was going to come and take him away. Was any of that true?

"More to the point, Layla was at your house before and at the time of Ben's death."

"She was there when I killed him?" The words escaped as she tried to make sense of them. Tried to make them fit into the version of events she'd been told happened all that time ago. "Okay. Okay. What the hell does that mean?" she muttered.

"It means either she watched you kill Ben, or she did it." Kendrick frowned at her. "There was evidence at your house that indicated you may have taken sleeping pills. Of course, there's no way to determine that now, but added up it looks...odd."

"What about the bloody shoes and sweatshirt they found on the floor of my room?"

Kendrick shrugged. "I just wanted to let you know what I learned. I don't even know if there's anything they can do with your case at this point. It's finished. But you could ask that fancy lawyer of yours for an appeal."

Eden looked around the room. Was this all a mistake? Her being in this place? "What did the detective say?"

"He said what I'm saying. He's not sure it would change the outcome of what already happened or your situation now, but I wanted to let you know. I'm not convinced you killed him, but that's my two cents."

Eden reached out and grasped his hand. "Thank you. For everything." She considered the short list of things she knew to be true, though the list had expanded in the five months since her review hearing; she was coming back to her normal. She clung to the thought that maybe she wasn't a killer after all. That it could be true.

"That's not the only news I have."

"Finn?" Eden's heart skipped.

Kendrick slid a piece of paper toward her. On it, a woman's name she didn't recognize next to Layla's picture. "She landed in Germany two months ago and met with a man named David."

Eden picked up the picture and stared at it.

"David works with an underground network of folks who help battered women and children escape terrible home situations," Kendrick continued. "Layla and Finn disappeared after they landed and popped up again in Spain about three weeks ago."

"How do you know all this?" Eden interrupted. "Have you found him?" She held her breath as she waited.

"No." Kendrick frowned. "But I have some contacts in this network. A few years ago, I had a client whose husband would have killed her and their two children if she didn't disappear. I helped them accomplish that. Meanwhile I made some contacts like David."

Eden found herself nodding.

"I was able to fly over there and meet with David and he gave me some troubling news." He cleared his throat. "He told me a woman meeting Layla's description told him her name was Renee and her son's name was Titus. That they were on the run from a woman who was trying to steal her son. That they needed to disappear."

Eden shook her head at the lie. Layla was willing to go all the way to get what she wanted. Shame on Eden for being so trusting. She recalled Kendrick's earlier statement that Layla might have killed Ben, setting the whole thing up. Perhaps she was hoping Eden would get life in prison.

"Does he know where they went?"

"He knew one of her stops would be Spain, but not when. I was able to go out there and talk with a woman named Mia who told me the same story about a woman matching Layla's description but using a different set of names."

"And you know for sure she isn't still in Spain?"

"It's very tough for these people to talk to outsiders at all. They were both very reluctant to even talk to me. There's a huge level of trust to maintain so these abused people know their location won't be given out to anyone. In some cases, even the host isn't told—they're just given another contact. And the fact that Layla is being extremely cautious by changing her name each time she moves makes it harder to track her down. I would imagine with her background in IT she's able to make her own paperwork."

"We're so close." Eden felt her heart sink.

"I want you to know I'm still here and I'm talking to anyone that will talk to me," Kendrick said. "David was willing to give me her name and mentioned Spain, and I was able to track that they were in Spain, so we haven't hit a dead end."

"What now?" Eden leaned back in her chair, breathing deeply to release the tension gathering inside of her. They were two needles in a haystack.

"There's one other thing I need you to know. It's not good." Eden watched the creases in his face deepen. "Both David and Mia told me that someone else had come by asking questions about a female with Layla's description traveling with a baby boy."

Eden clutched her chest. "Someone else is tracking them down?"

Kendrick nodded grimly. "In both cases it was a local man, so they were two different people. I think whoever is looking for Layla is paying locals that these two people know, and maybe trust, to find her."

"What does that mean?" Eden was on the edge of her seat now.

"It means this person has a better chance of finding them before we do," Kendrick finished. "And I have no idea what their intentions might be."

# Chapter 52

Eden

After

When Eden had first arrived at Middle State, she was surrounded by a ground covered in bright hues of dying leaves. The trees had been bare, their branches reaching into the gray sky jagged and sharp; now, they were covered in soft green leaves that fluttered and crackled. The warm breeze carried the sweet scent of summer flowers.

Her nerves crackled as her palms felt the hot metal door handle. This would be the first time in six months she'd see Lauren, her last visit to Eden being a month after her review hearing.

Eden's eyes traveled over the tables and benches around the yard, and she saw Lauren's platinum blond hair in its usual perfect style. Eden watched as curiosity turned to some sort of open revulsion as Eden drew closer.

Lauren's fingers shot up to her mouth, and her eyes grew

wide, an expression of momentary panic on her face—as if Eden's condition was irreversible. Well, that was an accurate assessment.

"You're—" Lauren shot up from her seat but made no attempt to come to Eden as she approached. Instead of stopping at the bench seat, Eden continued until she was able to wrap her arms around Lauren, trapping her against her body.

"How?" Lauren murmured, shaking her head.

"It's so good to see you." Eden ignored her shock. She'd been expecting this reaction but hoped for the best.

"You too." But Lauren didn't sound happy to see her. She sounded appalled.

"Sit. Please," Eden said as she took her seat at the table.

A breeze pushed up around them as Lauren finally sat.

"You look amazing," Lauren added, and she seemed to mean it.

"I'm so sorry about last time. It took me a while to get to this place. To get better."

"It's nothing." Lauren waved off her concern. "I just...I'm just so happy to see you doing so well. You're—" Lauren had to clear her throat before she could continue. "You're pregnant."

Eden smiled as she pulled her legs underneath her and rubbed her developing belly.

"Group and one-on-one therapy. Journaling and a recovery group for PTSD survivors." Eden ignored Lauren's declaration.

"That's great. That's fantastic." Lauren seemed to be scrambling for words.

"It's not always easy. I think about losing Finn all the time." Eden's smile faded into a thoughtful glance. "Especially with my delivery coming up."

"When are you due?"

She leaned toward Lauren, their bodies close as she scanned the area. "In November. I'm beyond excited."

Lauren shook out her hands. "But how—"

"Everything will be better; you'll see," Eden assured her. "Please, don't worry about us anymore."

"Us?"

"Lucy. My daughter." She couldn't tell Lauren she was in love with Doc Lucas. He would get in all kinds of trouble, but they were beginning to talk about what life would be like when she left this place. The three of them together.

Eden had been expecting this. She was prepared. She no longer cared if anyone thought she was wrong. This was what she wanted, and she'd learned she had to take what she wanted or make a way. Like Layla had done when she stole Finn. Doctor Lucas loved her, and she loved him. Events, bad and good, had brought her to this place—and opportunities for happiness lay before her. If only she were able to let Layla go.

"It's a perfect baby girl," she proclaimed. "And when I get out of here, where clearly, I don't belong, we will be the perfect little family. Just her and I."

"Who did this to you?" Lauren asked, unable to mask her harshness.

"I don't want to talk about all that." Eden brushed fingers through her hair. "What about the appeal? Anything on Layla?" It was much easier to confront the absence of information knowing she would have a family soon. Now that Doc Lucas had convinced her it was best, after assuring her the baby would be fine, she was continuing her lithium. She was starting to feel like her old self again. She rested on the fact that he wouldn't poison his own daughter.

"Yes, about that." Lauren seemed relieved to move the conversation in a different direction. "I've spoken with Drew, and he told me they've completed their investigation into Olivia's death. They've issued a warrant for Layla's arrest but still haven't been able to locate her."

Eden found herself nodding. But had the mystery person found her yet?

"There is something. When the police analyzed Layla's phone records, they discovered she was in contact with someone from the hospital. She was using Doc Jones."

It was Eden's turn to be shocked. No, it couldn't be; the consummate professional.

"Layla was blackmailing her to plant evidence in your room to make you look unstable. She also admitted after some questioning that she prescribed the wrong medication for you."

"Not her." Eden felt a frown pull on her face. "What are they going to do with her? What about my evaluation?" Eden thought of the mania she'd experienced leading up to her hearing. That was why—they weren't giving her the right medication.

"I'm sorry." Lauren placed her hand on Eden's. "I've petitioned the court to review your evaluation to be completed by Doc Lucas next week. I'm confident he's going to recommend your release." Eden smiled again. Yes—she needed to look forward and not back. She would be out of here soon, and she'd find out who was hunting Layla and her son.

# Chapter 53

Layla
After

Layla rushed down the hallway, a bag in one hand and Finn's fist in the other. He was holding the front of his jeans.

"I know, honey. Mommy's hurrying."

It had been two and a half years since they'd left the United States and settled in a small coastal town in Italy. They had used Eden's money and savings to travel undetected all over Europe. She was waiting to make new paperwork before they settled down for good. She could never seem to shake the paranoia that they were about to get caught. She had decided to call her brother on a whim and ask about her status, and after yelling at her and begging her to turn herself in, he had finally told her she was wanted for Olivia's murder. There was never really any possibility she would go back anyway.

The day before they were at an internet café. While Finn enjoyed a smoothie, she had learned Eden had been released from Middle State just under year ago. Eden would be looking for them. She would need to take extra precautions.

The thought of her old friend sent a pang of guilt through her. She didn't want to hurt her, she loved her, but her own fear of losing Finn was too much to bear. She had to do what she did.

They arrived at the paint-chipped door, and she fumbled for her apartment key as Finn did his potty dance next to her.

"Sorry, honey," she said as she flung the door open, and he shot off like a rocket toward the bathroom.

She closed and locked the door behind her and took the groceries to their small dingy kitchen. This was only temporary, but it depressed her. It reminded her too much of her apartment in Cedar Lake. But she was alone then—and that would never be the case again.

"Make sure you wash your hands," she called over her shoulder as she heard the toilet flush. After she stocked the refrigerator with foodstuff she could hear Finn's quiet voice in the other room.

"Honey, I can't hear you. What did you say?"

Layla walked into the living room and froze. A man, elegantly dressed, with shiny black hair and a charming smile, sat on the chair. Finn sat on his lap as the man held out a light-up ball in his palm, fascinating Finn with its blinking colors. The presence of this stranger didn't register as odd in his young mind. He met strangers every day. But Layla recognized him from the news articles she had looked up.

"Come here!" Layla shouted.

"Shhhhh," the man whispered, not taking his eyes off Finn. "No need to yell. I'm not going to hurt him." There was a sort of sadness in his voice, and Layla rushed over to pull Finn away from him.

"Let's talk, Ms. Hughs," the man said evenly. She didn't

like his calm manner. It was unnerving. Panic shot through her veins.

"What do you want?" She felt Finn squeeze her hand.

He laughed as if he knew something she didn't. Then it dawned on her. If Eden could hire someone to kill her husband, why wouldn't she hire the same man to kill the woman who took her child?

"Go to your room, honey," she told Finn. "Lock the door and don't open it for anyone but me."

He didn't hesitate, shooting across the room and out of sight. Good boy.

"You know me?" he asked.

She nodded. Her mouth was so dry she couldn't force herself to swallow. "I don't know you, but I know who you are and what you do."

"Do you know why I'm here?"

"I have money. Whatever she paid you, I'll pay more. Please don't kill me," Layla begged.

Layla recalled the day she had bought the burner phone Doc Jones would later plant in Eden's room. The man's voice had echoed over the line. "Hello—who is this?"

After she hung up, she'd sent several text messages to Olivia, and left the phone outside Doc Jones's door with the promise that it would be her last request.

It was Layla who'd involved this psychopath. And now Jason Sandoval was here, only feet away from her.

"That's not what I asked." His head tipped to the side as if he were hunting her as she stood, vulnerable before him, locked in his sights; she didn't dare move.

"You're here to kill me and take Finn."

He clapped his hands loudly, and she jumped. "How did you know!"

Dread seized her, and suddenly she was handing over

Dalila to the police again. Felt the fullness of motherhood drain from her to discover she was alone. And she would die alone. At least she would have no time left.

"You won't hurt him, will you?" She choked back a sob.

He took a deep breath as if he were displeased with her question. "I would never hurt a child. You make me sound like a regular monster." His voice filled with passion.

Finally, she was able to swallow.

"I'm here to acquire someone very special to me." He looked down at his long slender hands for a second.

"I have nothing—"

"Oh, that's not true." He smiled, and she thought it a kind smile, loving almost. "You have my son."

# Chapter 54

Eden
After

"Hello again, Eden," Detective Turner said when she opened the door to him. She felt her heartbeat speed up at the sight of him. Something had happened.

"Detective, come in."

He followed her to the kitchen. She had put the house up for sale three weeks earlier, and most of the furniture was being left behind with the sale. She didn't want any of this stuff when they moved to Florida.

"You're doing well?" he asked, taking a seat at the bar as she poured him a lemonade. Lucy was napping in her Pack 'n Play in the living room while Eden packed more boxes.

"Yes. I feel like myself again." She pulled a hand through her hair and stared back at him. She found that she meant it. Her release preceded the birth of her daughter. Doc Jones had been fired; she was embroiled in a legal battle to retain her license and could face criminal charges.

When Eden had announced she was moving back to Florida Lucas decided on his own to follow her as soon as he was able to find work, and they decided to try out living together. If that worked out—who knew.

"See you got a dog." Drew motioned to the old Great Dane lounging on the patio. Lucas's dog. "And you've sold the place?"

She nodded. "I'm moving back home. This place is full of bad memories."

"I can understand that. I'm sorry we were unable to get more answers for you." He didn't have to tell her he was talking about the night Ben was killed. She had permanently moved it off her facts-about-herself list. The truth was, she didn't know if she was a killer—

"I wish you the best. Unfortunately, I have some bad news." Drew frowned at her, and she gripped the countertop. Finn.

"We found Layla." His eyes were trained on her.

"Finn?" Heartbeat racing, she leaned into the counter. "Did you find my son?" She didn't care about Layla—she hadn't in a long time. She wanted to know if she would ever lay eyes on her son again.

"I'm sorry, Finn wasn't with her."

"Can I talk to her? Maybe she'll tell me."

"I'm sorry to tell you, but she's dead. She was murdered, and there's no sign of Finn."

Her breath caught in her throat. Layla had probably relaxed into her life on the run and thought she was safe. Eden recalled what Kendrick had told her about the person hunting Layla. Had they found her? What did that mean for Finn?

"Do they know what happened?"

He looked at her without speaking for a long time, and she felt sweat break out on her neck.

"There's an ongoing investigation."

"And what about my son? Are they trying to find him?"

"Of course," he said, sensing her distress. "I just wanted to tell you in person before you moved." He handed her his contact information, and she nodded absently.

He stayed for another thirty minutes until Lucy woke, and then he said his goodbyes. When she closed the front door to him, her head leaned back, and she felt tears roll down her cheeks. Knowing that Layla was dead didn't make her feel any better because she still didn't have her son. At least when she was alive and had Finn, Eden knew he was taken care of. Layla loved him.

She pulled her phone out and dialed Kendrick's number.

"What happened?" she asked. "Who killed her? Who has Finn?"

"I'm sorry I didn't get back to you sooner—Interpol just let Drew know and I was trying to do some legwork before I spoke to you."

"Do you know where Finn is?" That was all she cared about.

"I'm sorry, Eden." She could hear the defeat in his voice. "I think it was whoever was tracking her across Europe."

There was a pause before Kendrick spoke. "What do you know about Finn's father?"

Eden, momentarily shocked by the question, stumbled with the answer, instead asking, "Why do you ask?"

"This is personal, Eden. Someone you know did this."

"What do we do?" Eden asked breathlessly.

But Kendrick had no reply.

As soon as Eden hung up, she rushed to her computer and typed in his name. She forced herself not to think about the dim lights of the nightclub where they had met. His handsome smile and black hair.

"May I join you?" His voice was deep and warm, and she was overcome with her mania—giddy and free from the terrible thing she had almost done.

They had spent four days together, before she left his apartment in the middle of the night. She had shown up at her mother's house, where Ruby recognized her state and took her to a hospital where she stayed for three weeks to recover.

Now, as Eden read the news articles about her ex-lover, she understood everything. How different it all would have been if she had met Jason Sandoval at the lounge and paid him to kill her husband, rather than at the hotel bar, not knowing who he was. If she had paid the man to kill her husband and not sleep with him and conceive a child. If she only knew...

# Chapter 55

Two years later

He walked into the guidance counselor's office. She smiled warmly at him and asked him to sit down with a wave of her hand. There were two stern-faced men in suits sitting next to Mrs. Winslow. He put his bag on the floor next to his chair.

"These are detectives, Liam. Why don't you tell them what you told me? Don't worry. They won't let anyone hurt you."

He looked over at the two men, unsure if it was the right thing to do. Tell the truth...

Mrs. Winslow smiled and encouraged him with an eager nod.

"Hi, Liam. I'm Detective Brian, and this is Detective Trey." Both officers smiled. "Mrs. Winslow told us about what you said, and we wanted to have a chat with you. You're not in trouble, we just want to hear what you have to say."

He swallowed the lump in his throat and spoke. "I think my dad hurt my mom."

Mrs. Winslow frowned just as she had when Liam first told her about what happened.

"What did he do?"

A deep breath, and he continued. "He took me away from her and I never saw her again..." Tears pinched out of his eyes, and he pushed them away with his sleeve.

"What's his father's name?" Detective Brian asked Mrs. Winslow.

"Jason Sandoval."

# If you enjoyed this book...

Want to be notified when Eva's next book drops?

Visit her on social media:
http://instagram.com/evamackenzie_reads
http://www.facebook.com/eva.mackenzie.3762
http://goodreads.com/evamackenzie

If you would like to contact Eva Mackenzie personally, please e-mail
her at Evamackenzie.thrillers@gmail.com

Lastly, if you enjoyed this book, Eva would greatly appreciate if you left a review on Goodreads or Amazon.

# About the Author

## About the Author

Eva Mackenzie lives on the east coast with her husband and her three littles.

When she isn't writing or spending time with her family, she can be found hiking, training for another marathon or cooking. On top of the aforementioned she writes domestic suspense, psychological thrillers and romantic suspense novels. She enjoys writing about good people who do bad things for complicated reasons.

Please feel free to reach out to her via her social medias or e-mail.

## Also by Eva Mackenzie

Buried in My Past

Safekeeping